THE BIRD OF PARADISE TREE AND OTHER STORIES

IAN AISCH

ZYGOL BOOKS

CONTENTS

Zygol Books

21 Barbara Street,

Woodend, Victoria

Australia 3442

(03) 5427 2182

ISBN: 978-0-6487008-5-2

INTRODUCTION

This book consists of five stories; three of which are science fiction and two are straight fiction. A recurring theme is men who wield power behaving badly.

The first significant draft (FSD) of *The Bird of Paradise Tree* dates back to 2013. Over the subsequent years, I have written innumerable drafts of the story, in between the innumerable disruptions of daily life and the writing of other stories (notably my sci-fi novel, *Lost and Plooglitless* {FSD 2012}!). *TBOPT* represents by far my most challenging piece of writing. Apart from the huge number of redrafts, I lost count of the number of times I put the story temporarily aside believing it only required a quick run through. Over and over, I came to realise how utterly wrong I had been. *TBOPT* became such a long, hard grind that I often couldn't bear to look at it for days at a time. I hope my efforts have proven worthwhile.

My escape from the tedium of writing the latter drafts of *TBOPT* was to write *Popsicle* (FSD 2021). The dark humour of *Popsicle* flowed easily. I actually enjoyed writing it. I hope the reader also finds it as enjoyable.

From Little Acorns Grow (FSD 2015) was also put

aside on several occasions over the years. While I had no person in mind when devising the story (honest!), the major theme of the work has become ever more relevant with the advent of mass disinformation, devised to spread uncertainty, intolerance, attack science, and to basically seek to brainwash many people.

The reader is prompted to consider what is important in life (or should be) in *A Return to a Peaceful Place* (FSD 2021). As my Welsh uncle told me years ago, "learn to count your days". *There's a Light that Shines* (FSD 2017) sheds light on commercialisation and the risk of creative uniformity. It also stresses the importance of finding those who have faith in you.

In finalising TALTS I became aware that I was describing the uneasy feeling that comes with being subjected to the scrutiny of editors. As vital as their inputs are (truly), I cannot help but reflect that it is odd why there aren't any conferences held for editors, as happens for authors. In such conferences, editors could surely benefit from being instructed in the use of a more comprehensive variety of instruments of torture. Only kidding. Well…

So here I present this book of five stories. There have been (and still are) many authors whose ability dwarfs mine to a degree that causes me embarrassment, but the stories in this book are proudly and uniquely mine. And mine alone. I approach my writing with three aims, with each story having a different mix. I desire to: entertain; inform; and to encourage debate. If the stories achieve these aims in some way, my wish will be fulfilled.

Ian Aisch
February 2023

THE BIRD OF PARADISE
TREE

PROLOGUE: COLOURS

The pre-dawn darkness is illuminated by starlight breaking through a patchwork of wispy clouds. There are many more stars in this alien sky than on Earth's. Both of the planet's moons have sunk below the horizon. The morning air is still and balmy.

A spearing blade of light streaks out near the base of a rocky hill. A second spear follows, close behind. Then a third. The tightly intertwining blades wind slowly but steadily up the steep hill, dwelling on boulders, loose rocks or precipitous drops. Those carrying the torches know the route well. Four others—three men and a woman—are making their first ascent.

The newcomers belong to a six-person construction crew that had been deposited by the Chute during twilight the previous day. Two of them puff, grunt, and protest with the exertion. All four are still queasy from the Chute, darkening their mood.

'I got out of my bunk for this,' growls a man, who bends over to suck gulps of air.

'Please! Be a little patient,' comes the voice of a woman with a broad Scottish accent, who holds one of the torches. She wears the uniform of the mineral exploration team. 'You are about to see a spectacle the likes of which you have never seen before. Believe me. And what a perfect morning it is.'

Her words evoke grunts from two of the construction crew.

'Well… it better be worth it,' snaps a thick-set man with a gravelly voice. He pauses to lean against a boulder, breathing hard. The newcomers progress slowly. Two of them sip black coffee from a shared thermos. They snort at the waiting guides but press on.

'Almost there,' says a man with a torch. The comment arouses jeers.

The three beams of light converge on a large, bulbous slab of rock: the lower of the hill's twin summits.

The newcomers stagger to the top, grumbling.

'We're here,' announces one of the hosts.

'Thank God!' Two visitors suck air, hands on their knees. Two torches reveal a ledge to their left—a warning. The third illuminates five flat rocks arranged in a low row, two steps back from the ledge.

'Take a seat. Please,' says the female guide.

The visitors do so. The three guides sit on bare rock beside their visitors. Two torchlights extend downwards, revealing a steep slope.

Far in the distant, jagged and dark horizon, a deep-red glow signifies the rising of the sun. This sun is larger than the one seen from Earth and rises quicker. When it is high in the sky, it will shine orange.

'The display takes place directly below.'

The visitors lean over. Their pursed lips reveal disappointment. 'It starts soon,' comes the reassurance. What the newcomers see in the gloom is a faintly pulsating and shimmering dark-purple phosphorescence. It could be the gentle ebbing of a soundless inlet.

The downward beams of torchlight extend further to reveal a tangle of wide fronds of vegetation that somewhat resembles palm trees. The coppice of trees covers an area the size of an elongated, undulating sports ground. The fronds are still; the gentle shimmering comes not from any breeze. Here and there, small segments of a dark ribbon can be made out, signifying a creek and two narrow water holes.

The light from a torch dwells upon a frond, eliciting a patch of pulsating, bright purple.

The torches are switched off; only the dark-purple phosphorescence remains. The dark-red glow above the jagged horizon rises and expands. Extending from it are expanding halos of purple, red, orange, yellow. 'Nice sunrise,' one visitor remarks.

'You haven't seen anything yet,' replies a male guide.

'When does this thing start?' comes a man's impatient voice.

'Soon,' is the hissed reply. 'The build-up is part of the experience.'

The man snorts. Another visitor mumbles.

The fronds of the trees below transform into shades of shimmering purple and mauve.

A ray of faint orange sunlight streaks across the sky to gently kiss the frond of a taller tree on the perimeter of the coppice. The frond shudders pink. Almost immediately, two adjacent fronds transform into a dark blue. A patch nearby shines, at first dark green, then pea green. The visitors now lean over further as the coppice quickly transforms into pulsating blues, greens, mauves and pinks that brighten, then dim, and brighten once more. Explosions of bright reds, orange and yellow follow. Some fronds sparkle silver or gold, as if set on fire. The observers gasp.

A gentle breeze springs up; the colours ripple, passing across multiple fronds in seamless harmony. Iridescent light streams out like an erupting volcano in the midst of the coppice, flowing outwards as waves. The exclamations of wonder come not only from those viewing the spectacle for the first time.

Another burst of volcanic colour erupts. Then another. Each is beguiling, ever more mesmerising. Colours and patterns swirl, merging or flowing through one another. Some patches brighten as others dim, as if to draw attention to the more colourful display. A sphere of bright silver light shoots across one frond and along the tops of neighbouring trees until it explodes into hundreds of star-shaped fragments. Many of those watching gasp or cry out; one swears in admiration. Then another sphere shoots out, this time golden. Colours swirl, pulsate, flow, explode.

The sun continues to rise, and the displays of colour below gradually tone down, softening to bursts of orange and red, then greens and blues. They fade until the morning light reveals only a tight patchwork of bland blue-green fronds, swaying gently in the breeze like the wings of a giant dragon in repose.

The entire colour-and-light show lasted little more than twenty-five breathless minutes. The most intense display lasted half that time. Five minutes after the light show ends, those atop the hill are unmoving, captivated.

'Should have brought a camera.'

'Cameras never do it justice. We have a collection of videos to download if you wish. Each day the display is different. It changes with the seasons, the wind or cloud cover. Or with misty rain. At times it is different for no reason at all.'

On the far side of the coppice, the undulating hills are covered by low-lying, lush blue-brown or green-blue vegetation. Beyond, the hills become more rugged, grey, and almost bare. The horizon is defined by jagged, dark mountains. There are a few trees with fronds at the base of some of the rounded hills, in clumps of threes and fours, but they are not tightly interwoven. None of the spectators gathered on the bulbous rock had given those trees anything more than the very briefest glance.

THE TASK

The works engineer groaned as he rose stiffly to his feet. The man, in his early-fifties, was tanned and thick-set with prominent jowls and bushy, black hair. He wore heavy denim shorts, black T-shirt and a worn, blue cap. When he stood, his crew followed suit. 'Really glad I came.'

His fellow workers smiled and nodded to their guides. 'Yeah. Absolutely amazing,' said a young man. 'Wish it went for longer.'

'Glad it didn't,' said a colleague. 'If it had've gone on longer, I think I would have fainted.'

'You were impressed, Mr Longley?' volunteered the commander of the mineral exploration team as he tucked his torch in his deep pocket and drew up beside the works engineer. He was a thin man of medium height, with well-groomed, thinning brown hair. The man wore a spotless and neatly pressed light-grey uniform with a triangular bright-blue company emblem on the chest.

'Never seen anything like it,' said Longley, shaking his head. 'Craps all over all the New Year's fireworks.

And, jeez... it was trees that did that!' His workmates, walking behind him, grunted their agreement.

'I told you you'd be impressed.'

'Yeah. Just as well. I would have slung your hide on my cabin door if I'd come up here and it had've been crap. Got to see it again.'

The group made their way steadily down the hillside muttering. *Did you see when...?* The commander smiled, relieved. Dispatches had described the contract-works engineer as surly. The man had a reputation of letting loose with a stream of expletives when asked to do extra, or ill-conceived work. 'Believe me, what we witnessed never loses its appeal.'

'Yeah, amazing.' The thick-set man grasped a boulder to steady himself as he stepped gingerly down a steep, uneven slope. 'For Christ's sake, get a chopper. It would've made it damned easier to get up here.'

The commander grinned. 'We get one when our project is operational. Until then, we must make do with hovercraft. But what intrigues me most is that there were no eyes on this planet to see what we just witnessed before we humans arrived. There's only plant life here. To my way of thinking, the spectacle convinces me of the existence of some grand universal master plan. A sign that mankind was destined to explore outer space.'

Longley grunted. 'Dunno,' he said, shrugging. 'That stuff is too deep for me. Anyway, sun's up. Time to get to work.' He broke into a grin. 'One more job after this one and my twelve-month stint off-world is done. Then it's back to good-old planet Earth. No more putting up with the heat. Or the freezing cold. Nearly suffocating in oxygen suits. Trying my damnedest not to puke each time I step out of the Chute.' He chuckled. 'Me and the wife and kids are getting ourselves a beach house. Then we can enjoy... some of the finer things in life. I do one more stint off-planet in a few months' time, then I'm done. Bugger living like this any longer than I need to.'

'You're being a little bit ingenious aren't you, commander?'

The two men spun around to face the woman with a broad Scottish accent. Short, with wavy red hair that hung to her shoulder blades, she flashed her blue eyes as she came up beside them. She was in her early thirties and wore her light-grey uniform loose. Her easy movements showed her to be someone who kept fit. 'Mr... Longley? You should know a couple of things about what we just witnessed—'

'I did say experience *with eyes*, Karen,' growled the commander. 'What I'm sure Ms McGowan wishes to say, Mr Longley, is that the trees you saw down there differ considerably from the trees on Earth. Their structure is far more complex.'

'That surely must be obvious,' McGowan said firmly, her eyes fixed on the commander. 'Indeed, while the trees do not see their light show as we do, they are, nonetheless, able to experience and communicate the display in their own, highly sensory, way. They gain a great deal of pleasure from the light they receive and transmit. The show you witnessed is best described as a dance to welcome the rising sun. And what a joyful dance it is.'

The engineer stared at her, bewildered. 'What? How the hell do you figure that?'

'Because one of the trees told our resident botanist and geographer.' After flashing a self-satisfied smile, she slipped past to stroll away without glancing at her stony-faced commander.

'What!?' Longley's nonplussed gaze shifted from the retreating McGowan to the contrite-looking commander.

The commander watched his generalist officer disappear behind a tongue of rock. 'You need not concern yourself with issues we are still investigating, Mr Longley. Her claim is yet to be fully verified. Which explains why we have delayed publicising our observations. Regardless, what she said and what I said are not contradictory.'

The works engineer squinted, confused. 'Huh' The commander beckoned the two men to move on. They followed McGowan down the hill, at a distance.

The works engineer shook his head. 'Well...? Was she was bullshitting? Or what?'

'Best we talk about it later. Follow me. There's a vantage point along to the side that shows the lay of the base camp and the land. You should find the view useful.' The commander stepped off the rough path and leapt easily across weathered rocks to a flat outcropping that jutted over a fairly square, flat valley. Grunting, and stepping awkwardly, the works engineer followed, at times steadying himself with his hands.

'The cave where our headquarters are located is beneath there,' the commander said, indicating a distinct grey rock face below and to their right. Longley nodded.

They moved a little further. The two men stopped at a level vantage point to look upon the valley. The base camp was built on two wide, gently rounded mounds. A narrow river followed a line of hills on the left before turning sharply to pass out of sight. A meandering creek, in places visible as a series of gritty, narrow ponds, came in from the right, to pass between the two mounds to then bend and join the river.

A shallow wave of stone debris extended fan-like across the middle of the valley. Beyond, the valley was pristine, and retained much of its speckled orange and green-brown grass, and green-blue, gnarly bushes. The valley ended at a long ridge, interspersed by hillocks. The ridge bore a deep gash, through which a narrow stream, flanked by a rough vehicle track, emerged to flow into the river a short way beyond its sharp bend. A small brown lake could be made out on the other side of the ridge. Extending in three directions from the lake was an expanse of rocky desert and hillocks. It was there where the mining of minerals would take place.

'This is how the base camp looks now,' said the commander. 'The destruction caused by the massive wave that slammed into us is still very visible. Our half of the valley was practically ripped to shreds. You can see gouges, piles of rock and debris all around. We cleared up around the base camp buildings. The piles near the buildings are material we collected. You should find that material useful for your work.'

Longley nodded, 'Yep. Very useful. Thanks. And the loose stuff further away too.' He stroked his chin. 'The video you sent me came from here, huh. We've blown up some images and marked them up.'

Four buildings stood huddled together on the rounded mound to the left, beside the river. Three mid-sized food domes with clear, thick plastic walls and roofs dominated the space. The dark-green vegetation inside provided a splash of colour that offset the fractured greyness of the surrounding land. Behind the three domes was a pumping and filtration station where some scientific equipment and tools were stored, as well as a toilet and a sink. Two long, light-grey hovercraft lay under an attached lean-to with no sides. Beside the pumping station were two large, green water tanks. Snaking pipes, partly exposed in the fractured earth, extended from the cave headquarters to cross a shallow, wide gully and reach the buildings, to then join the river. A black outlet pipe led out from the pumping station to the rubble-filled creek.

Longley frowned. 'Whose stupid idea was it to build the base camp in a bloody flood plain?' He stood with his hands on his hips.

'It's not a flood plain,' the commander answered grim-faced, indignant. 'It might look like that now, but the giant wave that smashed into us tore away a massive chunk of the protective riverbank and flung it everywhere. If you'd been here before the wave hit, you'd have seen a pleasant creek, colourful vegetation, a couple of small ponds and some trees like the ones we just saw.'

The works engineer grunted. 'A freak event you think, eh? Maybe... The new research station goes behind those buildings, yes?'

'Yes. The previous research centre was located where that ugly gouge is beside the river. The wave came thundering down the ravine around to our left.' He made a wide sweep with his arm, his eyes misty. 'It was late afternoon. Most of us, thankfully, were in the cave. There was no warning. We'd had a lot of rain, certainly, and the river had been rising for a few days. Even so... We heard this almighty crash, followed by a long, massive roar. We came running outside to see the tidal wave and debris careening through the camp.'

'Scary.'

The commander became solemn. 'Yes, it was terrible. Our generalist, Ms McGowan, who you met earlier, told us how the huge grey wave flowed high up the steep hill opposite the camp and hovered there, before it came hurtling down. Fortunately, she made it to a far window as the building was being torn apart. She grabbed hold of one of the dome supports and clambered onto the dome's roof. Her companion, a delightful young lady from Chennai, was drowned.' He sighed.

'I was told about that,' Longley said gravely.

'It was horrible. Just horrible.' The commander gazed at the valley. 'We watched, helpless. Even above the din of the surging water, the land being ripped apart, and the splintering of the building, we could hear her scream. She was our head geologist. Standing here, I can still see the surging floodwaters. And I can still hear her screaming. One of our men tried to rush down and help. But it was no use. He couldn't get anywhere near the base camp.'

'A tragedy for sure,' said Longley. 'I'll do everything I can to make sure it won't happen again. Can't guarantee one hundred per cent. Our time here is limited. But—'

'It *can't* happen again,' the commander pressed. 'The rest of us were fortunate that the cave is higher than the base camp, and that the food domes held. They must have protected the pumping station, which only lost its doors and windows. The water tanks were swept off their supports. The hovercraft were covered in muck.'

'Right. The Chute was undamaged, though.'

Their eyes drifted to the other, slightly higher and larger mound, further to the right. 'Yes. It copped some debris. Much less than the buildings. But the structures were, thankfully, undamaged.'

Two sides of this mound were covered by a semi-circular array of solar panels, while three small wind turbines spun listlessly in the gentle breeze. A solid concrete building, housing a bank of storage batteries and the control room, stood to the leeward side. On the mound's flattened apex lay wide, waist-high concave slabs of concrete, arranged as a mostly complete circle. This was the Chute. Three sturdy seven-metre tall, blue metal towers topped by shielded, segmented flanges, hung over the concrete ring like lotus flowers. Close to the Chute were three earth-moving vehicles, a large-wheeled dumpster, two large trailers and a number of sizable crates, all brought across by the construction crew.

'First job is to set up paths so we can move our machinery about,' Longley said, with a sweep of his arm.

'That's what the brief states.'

The commander watched as Longley contemplated the valley. The river glistened in the early morning sun. To the right of the Chute was a spread of undulating, dry hills.

'Mr Longley; understand that your work here is vital to the success of our venture. Another disaster and we pack up and go home. Our financiers have already incurred considerable debts.'

The works engineer nodded absently. 'When we're done, pretty well any flood should be contained. Trust me. Good news; the buildings are okay where they are. We'll build a reinforced levee between the buildings and the river. Won't be pretty, but it'll be strong—and we'll improve the drainage. We need to raise the buildings... big job, even though they're kit buildings... put in deeper stays with wider flanges at the bottom. We add stone to reinforce the stays, and glue-cement the whole thing. You can pretty it all up later and bolster the foundations more. One thing; you guys are putting together the new research building. The plumbing. Electrical. Everything. We only do the foundations.'

The commander nodded. 'That's right. Our Mr Rafferty was in charge of setting up the base camp. He's a wizard with these light-weight kits. Your main contact with us here, though, will be Frida Stenson, who was sent here to prepare the brief. She'll coordinate our people. We'll do any grunt work you require.'

Longley nodded, satisfied. 'Good. We'll gouge out a couple of deep ponds along the creek to slow down the water run-off. Also gives us another supply of material for the foundations and the levee. We'll firm up the banks of the river and creek near the buildings.'

The works engineer stepped carefully from a boulder to a rocky outcropping. There, he further examined the lie of the land.

The commander sidled next to him. 'The final part of the brief, Mr Longley, is to ensure we can bring our equipment, hovercraft, and people from the base camp up to our headquarters. We need a path that will pass by the front of the Chute, to hook around and climb to the cave. It's needed both for our safety and our convenience.' His arm traced the lie of the concave hill.

Longley pursed his lips. 'Been thinking about that path. Real big job. Even doing something rough. Look at that pile of light-coloured rubble over that way. That came from a landslide. Yet you're expecting us to make a gradient with barriers to protect the path from landslides and put in drainage for the water run-off.' He stroked his chin, displeased. 'Don't see how we can finish it in time.'

The commander sucked in a breath. 'My understanding is that the project was scoped to take those matters into consideration.'

'Maybe,' Longley added testily. 'Okay, our machinery is the best there is. Laser cutters can do amazing things real quick these days. Our mechanical shovels shift material as fast as a man can run. Well… me anyway.' He grinned. 'But there's lots of preparatory work to do first.'

'Our Frida Stenson has made recommendations.'

'That's a good start, sure. But your people need to be trained on how to handle our equipment.' He pursed his lips.

'I'm sure we'll manage.'

'Look; I don't do half-baked, jobs. And I won't have people getting hurt. The way I see it, we might only get your path three-quarters of the way. Can't tell.'

The commander sucked a breath. 'Mr Longley, if the path only comes part of the way, we'll barely be better off than we are now.'

Longley shrugged. 'Look; we can't stay longer than the contract says. Maybe I can report that one of the small and older laser cutters broke down and I left it behind. It'd be slow work for you. Done at your risk. But I can't offer you any more than that.'

'But that path is vital.'

Longley stared hard at the commander. 'We're a good team. We'll do our best. But understand, every job we do we get pushed to do more. But we can't. We work to set times and regulations.' The commander was not pleased. 'You said you bring your hovercraft part way, coming from our left,' Longley said. 'How do you do that? Is that a ramp I can see?'

The commander sighed. 'Yes. It's a make-shift ramp. We made it from the double doors from the research building. The damage done to the riverbank means we now need to drive our hovercraft from the back of the base camp, then manoeuvre our way beside the river to a smooth rock face, then, using the doors as a ramp, we cross onto the bank of the muddy gully below us. The manoeuvre is tricky in strong winds or when the river is swirling. From the smooth area, we can only progress a short distance further by craft. The terrain is too uneven. It's worse now after the tidal wave hit. Our intrepid gardeners, Bob and Karen, bring produce the rest of the way using rucksacks.'

The works engineer broke into a wide grin. 'Got great news for ya. Got a better solution. It's right there before our eyes.' The thick-set man was triumphant. 'Can't believe no one figured it out. We don't bring your path from the right. We bring it in from the left! Much easier job. Less distance. The terrain that needs to be smoothed out looks much more straight-forward. Less risk of a landslide. Water run-off looks easy to sort out.'

'Sorry, Mr Longley. We can't come from that way.'

Longley wasn't listening. 'Look; the gully below us gets narrow where you bring your hovercraft. We ditch your doors, throw in drainage pipes and build a proper ramp. Connect it straight from the base camp. Easy as.' He spread his arms wide, smiling.

The commander sighed and looked at his feet. 'We can't do it that way, Mr Longley. I'm sorry.'

The works engineer spread his arms again, his face contorted in confusion. 'Hell, why not? The path coming from the right is a stupid idea.' He stared at the commander, narrowing his eyes.

The commander drew a breath. 'We need you to build a path coming from the right. Even if you don't finish it by the time you leave.' He cringed, anticipating the reply.

Longley spun around to re-examine the lay of the land below, then he looked the commander in the eye. 'The hell, why not?'

'My team have had some robust discussions on this matter. It's because...' He looked at his feet, sheepish. 'You can't see it from here, Mr Longley, but there's a permanent water hole below us. Beside the water hole, there's—'

'No problem,' Longley shrugged. 'We build around your water hole. Put in a retaining wall with an overflow outlet. We'll even make it all pretty for you. Great place for a picnic. Simple.'

The commander shook his head slowly. 'I'm sorry, Mr Longley. You see, around that water hole are four trees of the type you saw this morning.'

Longley blinked. 'What's trees got to do with it?' He stared at the commander, puzzled.

The commander gritted his teeth. 'As Ms McGowan emphasised, these are no ordinary trees.' He cleared his throat. 'Building the path so close to the trees would cause a great deal of noise and vibration from your equipment. Unfortunately, the trees are highly sensitive to loud, foreign noise. Highly sensitive. They apparently came very close to outright panic when the base camp was set up initially. They dropped branches and took a long time to recover afterwards. In fact, the trees are still recovering.'

Longley was incredulous. 'Are you telling me that upsetting four trees... four dumb trees... is stopping us from building the easiest path to your cave? Guaranteed to be finished on time. Hello!' He swore.

'Yes. That's exactly what I'm saying, Mr Longley.' The commander momentarily shut his eyes. 'We can't risk harming those trees. One of the trees in particular is vitally important to our scientific work.'

Longley looked away, exasperated. 'What? How?'

'That tree is the one that communicates with our botanist, Mr Starkey. Because of that—'

'What? This talking tree crap again. Okay. Let's go and tell the trees what we're going to do. Tell them we'll be quick with the work we need to do.'

'We can't communicate with them. Only Mr Starkey can do that. With the one special tree.'

The works engineer puffed his cheeks. His face began to redden. 'Oh, come on! Ain't it clear? That guy is bullshitting you! If he isn't bullshitting, he's been away from home for way too long. I've seen it happen before.'

'Mr Longley, we are required by law to recognise the trees as sentient, unless we can prove otherwise. Think about what we witnessed earlier. And tell me there isn't a likelihood that the trees are sentient.'

Longley scowled. 'Okay. So, what is this oh-so precious tree saying?'

The commander sighed. 'The tree communicates by some form of telepathy, according to Mr Starkey.' The engineer stared at the commander blankly. 'It places thoughts in Mr Starkey's mind.'

'What?' The works engineer became more incredulous. 'And you believe him? Well, where I come from, people who hear voices coming from trees get locked away.'

The commander shrugged. 'Our geographer and botanist, Dr Ben Starkey has been examined and tested thoroughly and been adjudged to be sane and truthful.'

Longley rolled his eyes and grimaced. 'Okay... Enough of this crap. Tell me; who is going to give a shit about a couple of damned trees pissing themselves for maybe one day? For the good of the base camp. What about this higher purpose you yabbered on about?'

The commander winced and pursed his lips. 'The Laws of Space Exploration concerning sentient life states that—'

'I know the damned law!' snapped the engineer. 'Don't preach to me. Every job I get sent to I have to put up with idiots who have no idea what the hell needs to be done. And I get here to find I've got to deal with a bunch of crackpots.'

The commander sighed. 'Regardless of what you think, our hands are tied, Mr Longley. It's not just Mr Starkey's opinion. All of us on the base camp would testify that the trees are highly likely to be sentient. My fellow workers have made it clear to me that we must respect the welfare of the trees. So, please, go ahead with whatever you can finish, even part of the way, coming from our right. It is stated in your con-tract.' The commander gazed at Longley intently. Should the works engineer become annoyed and decide to go slow...

'Okay then. Your problem,' Longley growled. He shrugged. 'I'll do my job for the time given to me and then I'm out of here. I'm not losing any sleep over this. You're the one who'll have to wear it.'

'I'm sorry,' said the commander. 'There's no other option. I'd be risking my post. And it would be a dereliction of my duty.'

'Think so? My bet is that your superiors would be mighty pleased if we finished the brief ahead of time and under budget. Who is the tree going to complain to? If the guy who talks to trees complains, who will give a shit? No one.'

'The path gets built from the right,' said the commander. 'No more needs to be said.'

'Fine with me,' Longley grunted. 'Let's get started. Like I said, it's your problem. It's just another job for me. I got a communication to send to my boss before I start. I'm going to explain why I most likely can't finish the contract. And I won't pull any punches. Just hope your superiors will back you up.' The engineer brushed past the commander to re-join the path to the base camp headquarters.

The commander followed him in brooding silence.

ZALLY

B en Starkey rolled up his sleeves and doused a bucket into a tear-shaped pond. The pond sat in a cleft of the stony hill, below and to the right of cave headquarters. A gentle spring gurgled into the pond from a narrow fissure. The overflow trickled soundlessly, glistening, into a wide, muddy gully, where water passed through a deep slit between large, rounded boulders to descend into the river. The base camp stood on the opposite side of the gully.

Starkey was a nondescript, middle-aged man of average height. He had short, black hair that was greying, a thin and suntanned face, and brown eyes. Starkey lifted the filled bucket and carted it to one of the four palm-tree-like forms that flanked the gritty banks of the pond. After emptying this fourth bucketful—one for each tree—near the trunk, he set down the bucket and flopped onto a smooth rock in the tree's shade. Its broad, single trunk was greener than the others, marking it as the youngest of the group. Yet, at four metres it was the tallest, being best positioned to absorb the sun's precious rays. The tree had eight wide, velvety fronds that drooped slightly like the stationary rotors of a helicopter. Five fronds extended out nearly three metres, arranged in a regular pattern: one higher, one lower, and so forth, around the bulbous top of the trunk. Three other fronds were shorter, greener, and so newer —one especially so—than the other five. The other three trees around the pond sported six or seven fronds, almost half of which were short. The outer reaches of their longer fronds overlapped with the fronds of their fellows.

'Good morning, Zally,' Starkey said cheerfully. That he could converse in his own language, with a being that was unable to hear, never ceased to astound him. Only strong wind or solid rain blocked their conversation. 'Hearing, to us humans, is like feeling the wind,' he had once explained to the tree, 'with that wind carrying to us words. Which have meaning.'

'Good morning, Key to the Stars,' came the tingling thought. 'Thank you for your gift of water.' The words were formed, distinct, inside Starkey's head, as if the tree was playing a verbal tune within his mind. The notion was somewhat unnerving but, to the scientist he was, the botanist's overwhelming reaction was exhilaration. Starkey communicated by speaking; Zally did not respond to his thoughts, even when directed at it by name. He found comfort from that privacy.

'Thank you, Zally, for your gift of shade. I'll be glad when the rains come again. It has barely rained since the big flood. The grass and plants need to grow again to protect the land from being washed or blown away.'

Zally understood. What the tree struggled to comprehend was that Starkey avoided basking in the sheer joy of the energy-giving sun. And, inexplicably, he had no roots. He was able to move. 'The rains will also raise many of my kind from the dormant state they have reverted to. I hope most of them survived the flood.'

'I can see many new shoots springing up along the riverbank. A couple by the creek as well. I expect that the valley will soon be joyful once more.'

His mind became infused with warmth; Zally's equivalent of a smile. 'As for me, Key to the Stars, I tell you again, even if the water in the pond becomes far less than it is now, it will only cause us to drop a frond, maybe two. And, if the dryness is prolonged, we can… hibernate, because we can store water and nutrition within our roots for a long time. But your offer of water is welcome.'

Starkey chuckled.

'Why do you laugh, Key to the Stars?'

The botanist stroked his chin. 'I can't help it. I'll never get used to the name you've given me, no matter how many times I hear it.'

'Yes; I understand that I call you a name you inherited from those who gave you life. It is not supposed to have any meaning. Yet, to me, it has great meaning.'

'But you don't really know what a key is. And you know the stars only by the starlight that touches your fronds.'

'A key reveals something that is hidden, isn't that right? That makes you a key. You tell me about what you call a universe that I could never discover. The knowledge you give me is interesting, enjoyable, although not entirely necessary. As for the stars, you experience them with your greatly limited senses. You do not experience the pleasure they bring as their soft energy sweeps slowly and gently across us. I feel sorry for your kind, not being able to feel what I do. Of course, experiencing the starlight is nowhere near as pleasurable as basking in the sun. Also, the moons, rain and wind provide me with wonderful experiences to savour.'

'Oh, how I wish I could feel what you do, Zally.'

'I, too, wish you could. I would find having senses as limited as yours to be unbearable.'

Starkey smiled.

Their first contact had happened the morning after the debris-filled torrent smashed through the base camp. Standing at the cave entrance, Starkey looked across the valley. None of the bird of paradise trees that grew along the riverbank remained. He clambered down to check on the six trees that tightly surrounded the pond in the cleft. It was in this place he often sat in the shade, composing his notes and making recordings of his observations. What confronted him that morning made him flinch. The two largest, outer trees were gone, swept away by the torrent. An ugly dump of rubble, gravel and mud lay in their place, spanning the width of the cleft. The rubble barrier was causing the water level in the pond to rise; the lower trunks of the four remaining trees were immersed in water.

As Starkey lamented the loss of the two trees, he felt... peculiar. That uncomfortable feeling transformed into... alarm. Unthinking, he waded into the pond and began clawing feverishly at the debris wall with his bare hands. Starkey paused only when water began spilling into the gully. With his hands red-raw and bloodied, and him gasping for breath, he clawed at the barrier once more, stopping only when the trees stood on dry land. Relieved, he doubled over in exhaustion as blood dripped from his torn hands. Yet he felt an odd ecstasy. Suddenly, his head ached. He feared he was having a stroke. The discomfort subsided. Distinct words formed... in his head.

'What are you?'

Starkey had spun around, expecting to see... he had no idea who... or what?

'What are you?' the words formed again.

'I call myself a human,' Starkey blurted, looking wildly about him. It dawned on him that the words had been implanted in his mind, not spoken. 'I am from a planet called Earth. What are you? Show yourself.' He backed away, anxious, tripping in the pond.

'I am beside the water that we feared might engulf us,' came the hesitant reply. 'Thank you for helping us.'

Wide-eyed, Starkey kept looking for... what? He was dumbfounded. The only life forms he could see were the four trees. Only an insane man would contemplate the remote possibility that he came to suspect. And he had found Zalltextrophene. Zally.

'What unusual beings you are,' Zally reflected, as Starkey sat in the tree's shade eight weeks later. 'You live, isolated, from your fellow humans and from all that surrounds you. That emptiness must be unbearable. It is because of your isolation, I believe, that causes you to explore what exists about you as best as you can with your highly limited senses. It is your act of desperation to compensate for the desolation you must feel, being so removed from everything. This feeling of dissatisfaction must bring out a restlessness within you. It engages you with sad longings that can never be satisfied. Yet, by applying yourself to learning, you seem to find some manner of solace. Yes, I can anticipate your reply, Key to the Stars. I know that learning is a wonderful thing.'

'If what you say is true, can you explain why you are so curious, Zally? For you are the most curious being that I have ever encountered, human or otherwise.'

Starkey felt a tingling—something akin to laughter—

in his head. 'Yes, I have some form of longing too, it seems. You provide me with a new dimension to my existence. It infuses me with a sense of wonder. But be aware, I do not seek this knowledge to compensate for wanting to strive for ever-impossible, lonely goals.'

Zally. Zally, Starkey contemplated. *If I were to tell you about war, or what acts humans inflict on one another, what would you make of our dissatisfaction then? You must never know about such barbarity.* 'Zally. Your observations never cease to amaze me. But we humans are not as dissatisfied as you believe we are. Perhaps we bask in our ignorance. And do not know any better. I detect that you have been thinking a great deal since we last talked. Is it because you are worried about the new machines that have arrived?'

There was a pause. 'Yes, I am concerned, Key to the Stars. As each of us are. The machines can wield immense power, like an avalanche. But they are far less predictable. It is unnatural. They have movement, as you do. Worst of all, the alien noise they make is horrific and goes on and on. Their horrible vibrations also evoke in us a terrible... agony. Key to the Stars, I cannot describe the pain. Each of us shed branches when the machines were here last. And didn't you tell me that some machines this time are bigger than before?'

Starkey winced. 'Yes. One is. But this time we are aware of how the noise affects you. We are committed to showing more sympathy for your well-being. Even so, there will be pain for you to endure for some days. We cannot eliminate that. But we will have pauses to prevent the pain from becoming too much to bear. Remember how you have learned to live with the humming of our farm machinery and the hovercraft?'

Zally seemed poised to reply when the pager on

Starkey's shirt buzzed. The commander's code lit up. The botanist tapped the receiver. 'Starkey.'

'Ben. Get up to headquarters right away. The contractors are ready to start. You need to advise them on how they should proceed.'

'Sure. On my way. They're starting work near the Chute, yes?'

'Yes. Nowhere near the trees.'

'Good. That gives me a chance to assess the situation.' He tapped off the pager and turned to the tree. 'Zally, I must go. I will look after your needs as best as I can. But regrettably, like I said, you must expect some degree of pain.'

There was an awkward pause. 'I understand, Key to the Stars.'

'The machines will start moving earth and rocks close to where the machines are already located. The biggest machine will work further away. We will have pauses from the work. I'll keep in regular contact with you. You only need to tell me whenever you find the noise and vibrations unbearable. If that happens, we will have longer pauses or seek better ways to do our work.'

Starkey felt Zally's reluctance to speak. Then the words formed. 'I hope we can find a suitable compromise. And…'

Starkey waited. 'What is it, Zally?'

'Forgive me, Key to the Stars. But your species instils fear in us. Not just your machines. We cannot predict how you will behave.'

Starkey cringed. 'I understand your concern, Zally. But we only desire to make our lives on your planet easier. The work we do will repair much of the damage done to the valley. That work will benefit us and also enhance the regeneration of those of your species that are waking from hibernation. We will not damage the shoots of dormant trees. That is a promise. Only the noise will cause you hurt.'

There was an awkward pause. 'I will keep you informed, Key to the Stars.'

'Thank you, Zally.' Starkey stood up, uneasy. 'I will come back soon.' Stepping around the edge of the pond, he made his way haphazardly through the junk-field of scattered and jagged rocks, rubble, outcroppings and fissures, to the cave headquarters.

PLAN OF ACTION

The cave housing the base camp headquarters was wide at its entrance but was habitable only for the first seventy metres. Double doors kept out the elements. Simple wooden partitions separated four small rooms: a toilet and bathroom; a basic kitchen; the captain's quarters; and, towards its end, a tapering bedroom.

The loss of the research station was deeply felt, not merely for the tragic death of a bubbly colleague and the abrupt halt to the team's research. The building had also housed cramped living quarters. A democratic vote was called upon to decide who would be housed there; the women won—their two votes against the males' four, with a feisty McGowan strongly advocating the case for the women. The loss of the building forced the entire team into the cramped cave. The arrival of Frida Stenson further crammed the space. The kitchen was modified to contain a double bunk as was the commander's quarters, although Bob Chase, the head gardener, often chose to sleep on a hammock in one of the food domes. The women shared the bedroom at the back of the cave.

Starkey walked briskly inside the captain's quarters. Its bare, grey walls, as were all rooms, was lit only by a single light that dangled limply from the ceiling. The commander and Longley had commandeered the only two chairs, behind a small work bench. The works engineer greeted Starkey with a grimace. Stenson, who had prepared the works brief, sat on the gardener, Bob Chase's bunk bed. Starkey sat down beside her. As he settled, McGowan slipped into the room, cradling a mug of coffee, to squeeze in beside the botanist.

'You don't need to be here, Karen,' the commander said.

McGowan smiled. 'I was told to report to Frida first thing after breakfast. Might as well wait here rather than twiddle my thumbs.' Her smile broadened. 'Besides, if I'm here I can answer any questions regarding my expertise.'

'Your reports are not disputed in any way,' replied the commander, looking at her intently.

'Good. But, like I said, I'm not doing anything at the moment.'

'Fine. Let's begin,' the commander growled. 'We'll keep the meeting brief. There's much to do. Ms Stenson, outline our plan of action.'

Stenson, aged in her forties, tall, with cropped, blonde hair, cleared her throat. 'Our Earth colleagues have, unfortunately, short-changed the time allocated for the works,' she said, grim-faced. 'Obviously their skills are far more attuned to imposing arbitrary cuts to budgets than recognising how long construction tasks take to complete. Their bloody-mindedness means that we must work at maximum efficiency. Basically, most of the construction team will begin by re-establishing the main transportation routes and clearing the creek near the base camp. They'll build a sturdy, wide ramp to connect the Chute to the buildings. Then we'll use powerful hydraulic jacks to raise the base camp buildings, one building at a time. We of the exploration team will be required to do mostly grunt work, moving stone and gravel about by hovercraft, or by mechanical shovels. We also have at our disposal top-of-the-range laser cutters, brought here by Mr Longley. All major earthworks will be done by the construction crew.'

The works engineer beside her nodded. His gaze remained uncomfortably focussed on Starkey.

'Excellent,' the commander enthused. 'You've informed the tree about this activity, Ben?' He shifted in his seat.

Starkey nodded; his gaze focused on Longley. 'Yes. It's great that the main heavy-duty works will begin near the Chute or further away. Hopefully, this gesture will acknowledge the sensitivities of the situation. Be aware, any foreign mechanical noise for prolonged periods will nonetheless cause the trees severe pain. Zally is deeply concerned but—'

'Sally!' exclaimed Longley, leaning back in his seat. 'She's called Sally, is she? Right.' He guffawed.

When the commander didn't intervene, Starkey took a deep breath. 'Mr Longley, Zally is my best interpretation of the sounds the tree communicated to me. The bird of paradise trees have no gender. Any tree can pollinate a seed generated by another through their roots. A dying tree directs its remaining energy to create a seed and lets its fellows know the seed has been created.'

'Sally,' guffawed the engineer.

McGowan leaned over. 'Mr Longley. We are discussing serious matters here.'

The engineer straightened in his seat to glare at her.

The commander intervened. 'Let us stay firmly on-topic, Karen. Mr Longley, please accept that the tree's name is a useful derivative of what it calls itself.' McGowan gave the commander a thumbs up. She and the thick-set engineer continued to exchange glares. 'Continue, Mr Starkey.'

'Thank you. The… er… tree understands that the works are vital to our mission. And that we are organising our schedule to limit the mechanical noises. Frida is on top of this.' Stenson nodded. 'Even so, any large machinery used around the base camp will need to be used as sparingly as possible. At times, we will need to have short pauses from every generated noise. During the works, I will touch base with the trees regularly. We are guests here after all. Of course, I will do whatever I can to keep the works progressing.' Starkey looked from face to face. 'The pauses will help the trees recuperate, but only briefly.'

'But the trees did survive the initial works to set up the base camp,' said the commander, looking intently at Starkey.

'That earlier work mostly involved erecting buildings that came in kits. It did not involve as much use of heavy machinery. Nonetheless, the work caused the bird of paradise trees to drop fronds, particularly those trees that used to line the riverbank. The trees by the pond also dropped fronds when the torrent smashed into us. It delayed their recovery.' He looked at Longley. 'Understand that dropping fronds is the second stage of preparing the trees for hibernation. Each dropped frond represents a significant loss of energy. Before a frond is discarded, the trees lose… feeling… in the outer areas of that frond. This loss of feeling shows up as brown patches. Seeing brown patches will be our warning signs. If we spot them, we must then re-assess our work practices.'

'But the trees are able to survive nonetheless,' insisted the commander. 'And they have endured storms and landslides and the like.'

'Commander, the bird of paradise trees accept, and bask in, being part of the natural world, and the noises their surrounds generate, though it too can cause them anxiety. But the continuous loud noise and vibrations from our alien metallic machines is much more damaging than any natural phenomena. If we pay no regard to the trees... we risk the trees incurring untold suffering.'

'Not to mention compromising our obligation to protect sentient beings,' McGowan added.

'Of course,' said the commander, lifting a restraining hand to Longley, who appeared poised to speak. 'That is understood, Karen.'

'Also, Ben, explain to Mr Longley the situation regarding the newly spawning trees in the valley,' she said.

'Thanks, Karen.' Starkey looked at Longley to ensure the engineer was paying attention. 'Alongside the riverbanks are six green stalks that look like leek stems. There are two others beside the creek, near the river. These, too, are bird of paradise trees that are emerging from hibernation or are newly spawned. These plants are not to be damaged because they are also sentient. I've marked the two by the creek with red ribbons. The good news is that these trees are dormant. They gain consciousness only when they sprout fronds, and so can draw energy from the sun. That means we can conduct earthworks quite close to the stalks. No problem. As long as the stems and their seeds are not damaged. The seeds look like leathery grapefruit. If they are disturbed, replant them immediately.'

'Okay,' said Longley. 'So, the only trees we worry about are the ones with branches?'

'With fronds, yes. That's basically it. The only four conscious trees remaining in our valley are all located around the pond just down from the cave.' Longley seemed lost in his thoughts.

'How high will you be lifting the base camp buildings, Mr Longley?' the commander asked.

'In the time we've got, about one metre higher than now. The new stays will be driven half a metre lower than those there already. The foundations for the new research building get done last.'

The commander spoke before Starkey could interrupt. 'You're raising the buildings further by only a metre?'

'Yep. That'll be enough, what with the levee, better grounding and better drainage, the buildings will have protection from all but the most massive flood,' the thick-set works engineer answered with emphasis. 'Take my word for it. The higher we take the buildings, the more time it takes. We'd need to gouge out lots more stone to strengthen the foundations. Lots more noise. Your precious trees won't like that.' He grimaced at Starkey.

'I see. A metre will do then.'

'Shouldn't the foundations for the new research building be done first?' Starkey asked. 'It's our main purpose here after all. Not having it until later limits our ability to get on with our mission.'

'I understand your preference, Ben,' replied the commander sternly, 'but our safety and food-security needs must come first.'

Starkey recoiled. 'But should the trees call for longer pauses to the earthworks, we risk not getting the foundations for the research building finalised in time. What then?' He stared hard at the commander.

'Rest assured; we will get everything done. The schedule for the construction works won't be revised, Ben.' His frown made it clear that there would be no further discussion.

'Mr Rafferty is busy disconnecting the electricity and water from one of the food domes,' said Stenson. 'He'll do the same preparatory work each day. Mr Chase is removing all anchoring bolts. So, we can get straight to work.'

'Excellent.'

'There's something I need to add,' said Stenson. 'Mr Longley has delivered a simple bucket and pulley system that will link the base camp to the cave. This also needs to be set up in the time available. A small laser cutter will cut the post holes near the cave entrance. This task will involve minimal noise, Mr Starkey.'

Starkey nodded assent.

The commander stroked his chin. 'Can the bucket carry a person if required?'

'Two if they sit on the sides,' Longley answered.

The commander sighed. 'That's little comfort if there has to be an urgent evacuation.'

'The pulley system is for transporting food,' Stenson replied, gazing at the commander. 'Other measures will make the base camp safer. In an emergency, people should run into the nearest food dome.'

'But we surely need other measures should an emergency evacuation be required.'

'We can talk about that later,' Stenson said, her eyes narrowing, looking a little irritated. 'Right now, we need to get to work.'

'Okay, then, enough talk. There's much to do. Let's get going.' The commander rose from his seat.

'I'll need to be excused for maybe half a day, sometime,' Starkey said. 'You'll recall I raised with you the need to check how the river is recovering upstream. That task is important, not just to check how the trees there and the water catchment are regenerating. We need to make sure there aren't any dangerous blockages forming. The equipment Mr Longley has brought here can be used should any preventative work be required.'

'This may not be the right time, Ben. We have a very tight time frame.'

'But commander, we agreed—'

The commander puffed his chest, annoyed. 'Ben, the works here require more manpower than we estimated.'

Starkey was poised to speak but Longley got in first. 'Ah, let him do his thing. Anyways, some basic earthworks can be done after my people have checked out from here.' He smiled at Starkey.

'Maybe after finishing all the foundations, Mr Starkey,' said Stenson.

'Clear it with me, Ben,' said the commander. 'I'll assess the situation day-by-day. Okay, everyone, let's get to it.' He wrung his hands.

Longley barked instructions into his pager. By the time the group stepped into the open air, the works machinery near the Chute had sparked to life. Starkey sucked in a breath. The difficult days for the bird of paradise trees had begun. As the appointed mediator, the coming days threatened to become deeply problematic for him, as well. When the others headed briskly towards the base camp buildings, Starkey diverted to the pond.

FOUNDATIONS

Starkey huddled, anxious, beneath Zally's fronds.
Each time a throttle was pushed, whenever a clang
of metal rang out, or the grinding of metal against rock,
he quivered, and a wave of dull 'heaviness' swept
through his mind. Zally was stoic and uncomplaining,
but the trees had to be suffering. Starkey ran a commentary on what was taking place across the other side of
the gully in the hope the trees could brace themselves
for the next bout of pain.

The bulldozer cleared the pathway between the
Chute and the junction of the creek and the river. The
small excavator removed debris from the segment of
clogged creek that separated the base camp from the
Chute. Two concrete pipes were hastily laid down on
gravel, then glue-cemented and covered by a basic but
secure ramp. Closer to the sharp bend of the river, the
large excavator, with Longley at the controls, scooped
up material dumped by the torrent or cleared by the
bulldozer and loaded it onto the dumpster or a hovercraft, with a rumbling thud. Each machine operator
wore earmuffs.

When the small excavator and laden dumpster drove

across the ramp, Stenson paged the botanist. 'Mr Starkey, come and help run the hydraulic jacks.'

Starkey cringed. 'I'll be there soon. Promise.'

'Mr Starkey, we need you here. Now!' Stenson hissed.

Starkey rose slowly. 'I'm sorry, Zally, but I need to go. I'll come back as soon I can. I hope your suffering won't be too great.' He hesitated, waiting for a reply. None was forthcoming.

With Stenson and one of the construction crew barking orders and profundities, the huge mobile jacks carefully and, often haphazardly, raised a food dome, creaking and groaning, until it hovered, flexing, some two metres above the ground. The old stays were gouged out by laser cutters and replaced by longer stays. The laser cutters elicited sharp, whip-like cracking sounds when solid rock was splintered. The new stays were secured by gravel and stone, glue-cemented and compressed, amidst billowing dust.

The trees got no let up from the noise. When the dome was being raised and, later, lowered, the small excavator and two mechanical shovels were diverted to dig a knee-deep trench between the river and the base camp, for a protective retention wall. As the dome was about to be lowered, the commander pulled up at the site in a hovercraft with stone material at the rear. When the stone was being emptied by mechanical shovel, Starkey ran over to his boss. 'There hasn't been any break in the noise yet, commander. This has to be the perfect time to switch off the machinery. Thirty minutes would be good. The trees are expecting it.'

The commander glowered at him. 'We can't right now, Ben. We're working way too slowly.'

Starkey recoiled. 'Only the earthmoving machines

need to be switched off. Okay, make it twenty minutes then.' The commander grimaced. Starkey pressed on. 'Operating the jacks, the laser cutters and the mechanical shovels can go ahead. The issue is; when one earth-moving machine operator takes a break, someone else climbs straight into the cabin. The noise continues unabated. That work practice needs to change for the trees to be given breaks.'

The commander sucked a breath. 'Show some patience, Ben. Go talk to the trees after we've done here. Assure them that we care deeply for their welfare. And will act accordingly.'

Starkey was taken aback. 'If that's so, then when—?'

'Later!'

To Starkey's consternation, the commander drove off in the emptied hovercraft.

Starkey was left gaping. Stenson turned to those gathered. 'Glue-cement sets in about three hours so let us set the dome down.'

'Frida; tell me,' Starkey demanded, arms crossed, as he fronted her. 'What's your understanding of the scheduling of regular breaks from the machine noise?'

Stenson winced. 'If we don't lower the dome properly, now, we'll have to do the whole thing again. Do you want to risk that, Mr Starkey? Come. Let's get started.'

Displeased, the botanist returned to the hydraulic jack he was operating. The promise made to the trees had been ignored without discussion. The dome was duly lowered. Not carefully enough if Stenson's curses were anything to go by.

No pauses were called as the day drew on. A short, first segment of the rough retention wall was erected, glue-cemented and compacted. The jacks were set up beside the next food dome along with piles of stays, stone and grit. Starkey gazed towards the pond. As he did, a dark shadow drifted overhead. Black clouds were setting in.

With dusk descending, the heavy machinery was driven to their parking area beside the construction team's trailer camp. The moment the food dome came to rest on its new foundations, the commander set off by hovercraft to join Longley at his camp, leaving a disgruntled Starkey to approach Stenson to demand an explanation.

Bob Chase, who was chatting to Stenson as he busied himself with the connections to the raised food dome, noticed the approaching botanist, and the clouds. 'Looks like rain, Ben.'

'Fingers crossed only enough to settle the dust,' said Stenson. 'If the rain is heavy, work stops. The ground is already not as stable as I would like it to be.'

'Frida,' demanded Starkey. 'What happened to the breaks we were supposed to take?'

Stenson examined Starkey's face. 'We will do so from tomorrow, Mr Starkey. Understand that today we had to finish the dome and start the retention wall. Unfortunately, our people worked far less efficiently than I anticipated.'

'But we made an agreement with the trees, Frida. For regular breaks. The trees had to endure far more sustained pain than they were led to expect.'

'I sympathise, Mr Starkey. We humans also need breaks. The commander fully understands how vital your involvement is. But understand, we have a hectic schedule to maintain. Rest assured; I will let him know of your concerns.'

'Yes, you do that. I'll raise my objections as well. He

must accept that what happened today was... inexcusable. Tomorrow then, we deliver on our promise. Okay? No excuses.' He gazed hard at Stenson, who looked blankly back at him. 'Right now, I have a deep apology to make to Zally.' He hesitated, allowing his words to sink in, before walking off.

Bristling, Starkey slunk to the pond and sat beneath Zally's fronds. 'The loud machinery will not be used again today, Zally. I hope the day has not been too traumatic. The noise was more prolonged than I was promised... it would be. I have protested the insensitivity displayed by my people today. It was unacceptable.' He cringed. Zally had every right to be furious.

There followed an awkward silence. Then the words formed, slow but distinct. 'It has been a horrible day, Key to the Stars. The noise and vibrations never paused. We greatly fear the prospect of the terrible noise continuing for many days. You need to understand how unbearable that prospect is for us. We risk dropping fronds. With your limited senses, I fear that your kind does not appreciate how agonising this day has been for us.'

Starkey sucked in a breath. 'I'm very angry about what you were subjected to today. I've been promised that there will be pauses from the noise beginning tomorrow. Also know that the machines won't come any closer to you. Keep in mind; we are making the valley healthy again, ready for when it rains.' Zally did not reply. Starkey sighed. 'If the noise and vibrations become too difficult to bear, Zally, we will take longer pauses than we planned.' If Longley and the commander got wind of his pledge, he would be verbally flogged.

'We will *try* and bear the pain for a while longer, Key to the Stars. But it is vital that we be given opportunities to ease our stress. We acknowledge that relief will only be granted in a limited capacity.'

'I fully understand, Zally.'

The botanist wandered about the pond, checking the fronds of the trees with a small torch. A few small, brown patches were forming on Zally's fronds. The brown patches on the neighbouring trees were larger. He described and documented the deterioration using his body camera.

To Starkey's frustration, the commander chose to eat and drink with the construction crew and Stenson. His pager was switched off; a 'Don't Disturb' red light showing. Each member of the exploration team had ended the day dusty, stiff and sore, and sported blisters. After dinner, McGowan and Bob Chase took a hover-craft to the river bend for a quick bath. The Irish fix-it man, Rafferty, finalised the fittings to the dome. Stenson returned to clean the compressors and check how the building had settled. Starkey sat, simmering, in front of the double doors of the cave, impatient for the commander's return.

Later, Stenson paged the team. 'Look outside and see what I've brought you.' Standing in front of the base camp buildings, she held a torch to reveal a large canvas bag. 'It's a three-person tent, with two sleeping bags and inflatable mattresses. Anyone interested?'

Eyes opened wide. With the commander absent, and Stenson not asked, the other three members drew straws. With a whoop of joy, McGowan drew the correct straw, drawing howls of outrage.

'You're not going to camp out by yourself, are you Karen?' Bob Chase pressed. 'Or are you going to ask Frida to join you?'

'No,' she said grinning. 'I'm going to offer a place to

someone in the construction crew. A countrywoman of mine who can't bear Longley's snoring. She's from Glasgow. Supports Celtic. But everyone has their flaws, don't they? Aren't I lucky? I tell you now; I will savour every moment of sleeping in the tent, away from you lot. And out of this musty, depressing cave with its crappy chipboard walls.'

There were mock protests.

McGowan was never one to shy away from some playful deriding. 'Suffer,' she sneered. 'The lot of you. Oh, come on. Show me just how annoyed you are. Please. The more you do, the happier you'll make me. Suckers.'

Her comment was met with mock derision. 'Do the right thing, Kaz,' the lanky and dimpled Rafferty spoke up. 'Sleep in the food dome on a hammock like Bob does sometimes. Let the rest of us draw straws again.'

'There's too much shit in those domes.' A wry smile broke across McGowan's freckled face. 'Just like there is inside you Pat.' There were peals of laughter. Even Starkey managed a smile.

After paging her countrywoman, McGowan punched the air, poked her tongue at her fellow workers, then set off with a torch and day pack. With the others looking on with envious eyes beside the cave entrance, the two women met up and set up the tent beside the raised food dome, with a view up the narrow, steep ravine. 'Karen is going to be unsufferable tomorrow,' said Bob Chase. But he was grinning.

'They shouldn't camp there,' the commander said, grimacing, when he returned at last to the cave. 'There has to be a risk of flooding. No matter how small.' To the approaching botanist he put out a restraining hand. 'I know what you want to say, Ben. Ms Stenson warned me. Rest assured; I'll be more sympathetic to the trees' well-being tomorrow.' He began to stalk away.

Starkey grasped the commander by the shoulder. 'After today, you need to be. We acted with incredible cruelty today. I hope you appreciate that. But… I'll take you on your word. *This* time.' The commander bristled at Starkey's words. Angrily, he brushed the botanist's hand away.

Sitting on the floor beside his bunk bed inside the kitchen, Starkey stripped off his filthy uniform and flopped onto the thin mattress. He was uneasy. The commander had already broken a promise. Would he do so again? Worse, what if Zally demanded that the earthworks pause for far longer than the commander desired? The commander would expect him to convince Zally that such a request was unreasonable. Starkey tossed and turned during the night. It was fortunate that Rafferty, who slept in the bunk above him, was a sound sleeper.

At dawn, Starkey heard the unmistakable sound of gushing water. Rushing to the cave entrance in his bare feet, he found Stenson staring grimly out of the open doorway. It was raining hard. Water flowed freely down fissures in the hill and into the wide gully below, to then cascade into the river.

Stenson turned to Starkey. 'We can't work in that rain, Mr Starkey.' She managed a brief smirk. 'Too risky. Don't be alarmed. With the pulley system installed, the pathway to the headquarters the commander insists be built becomes essentially redundant. He will disagree, no doubt. There simply was never time allocated for that path anyway. We only need to finish the major tasks. He will come to accept the inevitable.'

A relieved Starkey smiled. 'The pause this morning will allow the trees to regain some strength. To them, the rain is a truly wonderful thing. The two Scots women in their tent might disagree, though.'

'Ms McGowan chose to leave the cave. Accordingly, she must endure whatever the outside world throws at her,' she replied with a grin.

McGowan returned to the cave for breakfast. She was beaming, despite her damp clothes. 'We had a lovely night. It reminded me so much of camping in Scotland on a typical summer's day. Patrick Rafferty, did you poke your tongue at me?'

Rafferty and Bob Chase set off to complete their preparatory work for the next-selected food dome. The commander brooded, alone, in his quarters. Starkey and Stenson took turns to wash some clothes in the small bathroom.

The rain eased to a gentle drizzle shortly before noon. Stenson gazed at the sky before striding off to inspect the work sites with Longley. The commander followed at a distance, pacing. He fumbled with his pager when it buzzed. It was Stenson. 'Good news, commander; work can resume. But we must take precautions.'

The commander heaved a sigh. He turned to his team, gathered behind him. 'We will have to work right up until dark the next few days to make up for lost time. Right, let's get to it.'

'But we'll still have rest breaks, won't we?' Starkey said. 'For the wellbeing of the trees. You agreed.'

The commander snorted. 'We'll assess the situation as the day progresses, Ben. The trees have already had a major break. And there is no guarantee it won't rain later.'

'If it doesn't rain, there will still need to be pauses. Even brief ones,' Starkey said. 'The trees must be allowed to re-gather some of their composure.'

'I'll let you know,' the commander said firmly. 'Realise that this work is placing me under a great deal of stress.' He strode away.

There was no further rain. To Starkey's chagrin, the machine noise did not ease up all afternoon. The dome was raised. Holes for the new stays were dug, at times eliciting the loud, sharp echo of fracturing rock. The small excavator gouged a further length of trench for the rough, metre-high retention wall. Starkey slunk about his tasks. Stenson kept her distance. She cringed when he stood before her after the new stays had been set in place. She anticipated his question. 'No! I will not request a pause, Mr Starkey. The building of the retention wall will continue as we lower the dome. We cannot afford to lose any more time.' Starkey swore.

Half an hour before the commander called a halt to the days' toil, the construction crew retired to their living quarters after unloading stone and gravel from both the dumpster and a hovercraft, beside the third dome.

When Longley's crew were packing up, the commander had paged the works engineer. 'Can you keep going a little longer? Hello—' Longley's pager had cut out.

Stenson drew the commander aside. 'Commander, please realise that everyone expects these guys to work twenty-five hours each day. They have designated work hours. The crew had every right to finish half an hour earlier today. And they only took short breaks. You should be thanking them.' To Starkey's annoyance, once again, the construction crew had not taken their breaks at the same time; the machine noise had continued unabated. If Stenson had raised that work practice with Longley, her request had been ignored.

The frowning commander spread his arms. 'But we're way behind schedule!'

Stenson didn't flinch. 'Everyone is now working admirably.'

The commander huffed. He made his way, sullen, to the cave. Stenson looked on with clenched teeth. The commander ignored Starkey, who had beckoned his boss engage with him, leaving the botanist fuming.

The exploration team trudged towards the cave, damp, weary and caked in mud. They examined one another's new blisters, cuts and bruises. Yet they consoled themselves for getting a second food dome to rest on new foundations, while a new portion of the retaining wall, glistening with glue-cement, stood alongside. Separating the river from the first food dome was a rounded heap of compacted dirt and gravel—a segment of the levee, laid against a finished portion of the retention wall. The levee was a little shorter than McGowan, who stood at 1.6 metres. 'That is what the levee will look like,' Stenson had explained. 'We'll add to it after the construction crew have departed.' The jacks stood, ready, beside the third food dome.

Perhaps sensing friction, Bob Chase stepped between an angry Starkey and Stenson, who was blatantly keeping her distance from the botanist. 'Hey, Frida,' he moaned. 'He's driving us too hard. It's relentless, heavy-duty work we're doing. In choking dust yesterday, and today in mud that sticks like concrete to our hands, clothes and boots.'

McGowan, standing beside Stenson, chimed in. 'Yes. Look at us Frida.' She spread her arms; her uniform spattered with mud. She took off a thick glove. A sleave and one of her hands revealed dried blood. She sported a large, purple bruise on her wrist.

'I've tried talking to him a couple of times,' said a sighing Stenson. She shook her head. Stenson worked longer hours than anyone. 'The commander refuses to accept the possibility the brief will not be completed. Even that'—she sucked a breath—'damned path to the cave. He just doesn't get it.'

'I believe he blames himself for the drowning,' McGowan said.

'Why? No one could have predicted what happened that day,' added Rafferty.

'Nevertheless, I think that's what his problem is.'

Starkey pushed in front of Bob Chase. 'How far behind schedule are we Frida?' he growled. 'The commander can't keep refusing to have breaks. The trees cannot be expected to put up with this level of callousness! And, please, no more bullshit excuses! We did a full day's work in half a day today.' When he had a rare, free moment, Starkey had taken up a vantage point on the top step of a raised dome to gaze towards the trees. Expanded patches of brown were visible on their fronds.

'Unfortunately, we are getting further behind,' Stenson said gravely. 'The rain and the muddy ground slowed us down. We had planned to have the next food dome at least raised today.'

'I realise you're in a bind, Ben,' Bob Chase said, placing his hands on Starkey's shoulders. 'But he won't budge. I've tried appealing to him as well.' He shook his head. 'I'm buggered. We all are. Tell you what; how about we speak to him collectively in the morning? For now, let's wash our clothes and have a good soak. And don't we need it? Anyone for the river bend after supper?' There was a chorus of agreement.

In no mood to join the others, Starkey made his way to the pond. To his relief, Zally did not greet him with a burst of vitriol, as he had anticipated. 'The noise was horrible, yes, Key to the Stars. We are not pleased that there were no breaks from the machines from the time they started. As we had been promised.' Zally paused, perhaps to let the words sink in. 'But feeling the rain and sensing so much flowing water during the day, all around us, brought us much pleasure. It helped us cope... to some extent... with the dreadful machines. Also, we are joyful knowing the rain will hasten the day when more of my kind will awaken from hibernation. But Key to the Stars, do not think that we are compliant. I say this; the rain only counteracted the horrible noise a little.'

'I hear what you are saying.' Then he smiled. 'I share your anticipation of your fellows regenerating. It will make the valley beautiful again.'

'But Key to the Stars, answer me truthfully; do your fellow humans comprehend how much agony we suffered again today? It is a pain that I am certain is well beyond your limited senses. Otherwise, you would not have acted as you have done. We dread being subjected to the same agony tomorrow. We anticipate it will not rain.'

'Zally; I will do everything I can to demand that we take regular pauses from the noise tomorrow. My commander insists he understands that your welfare is important.' Starkey cringed; he had spoken out of hope than certainty. He needed his colleagues to jointly make their concerns clear the next morning, with Stenson perhaps conflicted.

S tarkey spent much of the night curled up against the front doors of the cave with a thick blanket wrapped around him. He periodically opened a door to gaze outside. Each time he did, a cold wind blew on to his face. Wispy clouds formed and drifted away. One time, the sound of a misty drizzle stirred him from his uneasy slumber. The drizzle was fleeting. As dawn neared, the sky was a vision of stars, lit up by the planet's smallest moon. There would be no rain to halt the earthworks this day. He'd need to rely on his fellow humans. Weary, Starkey trudged to his bunk. He was nudged awake all too soon by the Irish fix-it man. 'Breakfast time, sleepy head. No lying in. Bob and the commander have already headed off.'

The early-morning sun shone brightly. Stepping outside the cave, Starkey caught sight of the commander inspecting the base camp with a spring in his step before he, along with Bob Chase, commandeered a hovercraft, threw a laser cutter and a mechanical shovel in the back, and headed to the heaped scree that lay on the route of the planned pathway to the cave. Both men had their pagers switched off. The day would not begin with the raising of the team's grievances.

Starkey paused to take in the final stage of the colourful dance to the new day performed by Zally and the other trees. The seemingly subdued display featured converging swirls of colour. His mood dark, Starkey did not dwell. He would talk to Zally later; fingers crossed, with much overdue good news.

His assignment was to help raise the third dome. Nearby, the small excavator began gouging out a shallow, rectangular furrow. As Stenson explained, two pylons for the pulley system would be set within the furrow, reinforced by a metre-high, stepped platform. Once again, the large excavator began extracting gravel and dirt near where the creek flowed into the river, loading the material with a familiar rumbling thud on to the dumpster. Starkey sighed. It meant more suffering for the trees.

After the food dome had been raised, around mid-morning, Starkey checked the time. 'Frida,' he called out. 'Time for the machines to be switched off. Twenty minutes minimum. Best do it now. Inform Longley.'

Stenson stared at Starkey. 'I haven't been notified that a pause is to be declared.'

Her jarring words came as no surprise. 'No, Frida,' he snarled, his arm making a slashing motion. 'Declare a pause right away. If the commander objects, leave me to deal with him.'

Stenson, clearly affronted, pursed her lips and drew a breath. Starkey glowered at her, hands on hips. She pointed to Bob Chase who was driving a loaded hovercraft towards them. 'What I'll do, Mr Starkey, is get Mr Chase to pass on an urgent request to the commander. He'll then notify Mr Longley.' Behind her, holes for the new stays for the dome were being gouged out.

'I need a firmer commitment than that!'

Stenson took a step back, flinching at the look on Starkey's face.

Bob Chase set the hovercraft down to be unloaded. Starkey reached over and grasped the gardener roughly by the shoulder. 'The trees are overdue for a respite,

Bob. Go back and tell the commander he must call a pause. No delay. Or I'll come over—'

'Don't think he'll agree, Ben.' Bob Chase stepped out of the craft, looking nervously at Stenson.

'Excuse me, Mr Starkey,' said Stenson. 'It is my role to deal with the commander.'

'Declare a pause, Frida,' snapped Starkey, his eyes fixed on Bob Chase. 'No Bob! He has to stop breaking his promises. Bob Chase averted his face. 'That's it. I'm coming with you.'

Bob Chase shook his head. 'I won't take you Ben. You're too worked up.'

'Of course, I'm angry. I am sick of being lied to.'

Stenson grasped Starkey by the arm and spun him around. 'I understand your frustration, Mr Starkey. But let me talk to the commander. Please. It's time I set him straight; his path to the cave will not be built. For now, go help set up the pylons.' She half-smiled. 'Remember; with that system set up, the path becomes redundant. It will free us up and we will no longer need to work with undue urgency.'

Exasperated, Starkey slammed his fist onto his thigh. 'So, I get brushed aside again.'

'Listen to me; confront him and he'll only dig his heels in, Mr Starkey. It will defeat your purpose.'

The botanist looked at the bright-blue sky but shrugged his reluctant agreement. 'Last chance, Frida. Bring me back good news,' he insisted, staring hard into Stenson's face. 'If you don't, I *will* confront him. And no one will stop me. Bugger the consequences.'

Stenson nodded gravely. She stepped inside the now-emptied hovercraft with Bob Chase. 'Go chat briefly to the trees, Mr Starkey,' she said. 'Tell them that relief is near at hand.'

'No! I'll talk to Zally when the noise stops. And only then. I need to be sure that I'm not just a fall guy, set up to appease the trees, while the commander has no intention of bowing to their wishes.'

'Don't be so pessimistic, Mr Starkey.'

'Then stop lying!'

The hovercraft drove off, with Stenson biting her lip as she gazed back.

Starkey blinked. Surprising him, the small excavator was switched off. From its cabin floated the unmistakable sound of Mozart. A beaming McGowan approached him. 'Ben, apparently, the brakes are a bit loose on the excavator my tent-buddy is operating. Apparently... Well, she's taken off her earmuffs and turned on some music while she checks out the... err... problem.' She smirked, raising an eyebrow. 'The bulldozer driver is on foot helping to set up the pylons and lay down stays for the dome. That's the best we can do to help out. But it won't be for long. Sorry.'

Starkey glanced to where Longley's excavator continued to gouge and rumble near the river. 'Just wish the big excavator...' He managed a half-smile. 'Never mind. I appreciate the gesture, Karen. Thanks to you and your tent buddy.'

Stenson's visit to the commander was brief. Bob Chase dropped her off at the base camp and drove off without pausing. Starkey blocked her path towards the stationary small excavator.

'Well...?' demanded the botanist.

'Mr Starkey; the commander is going to talk to Mr Longley. In the meantime, we continue with our duties.'

'So, no guarantee of a pause.' Starkey pursed his lips, hands on his hips.

Stenson sighed. 'Wait and see what Mr Longley says,

Mr Starkey.' The botanist watched as the commander ran to meet the hovercraft. He bundled Bob Chase out of the hovercraft and drove towards the works engineer at speed. Starkey refused to let Stenson get to the idle small excavator. 'So, what are they going to talk about, Frida?'

'Okay,' she said. 'The commander is furious that Mr Longley has prioritised the pulley system without consulting him.'

Starkey's jaw dropped. 'What!? He wants to squabble with Longley! Instead of declaring an urgently needed, well overdue pause. I don't give a damn what mood he's in. I'm having it out with him.'

Stenson put out a restraining arm. 'You'll only make him angrier. Wait for him to talk to Mr Longley. Rest assured; Mr Longley won't be shifted. There will be no path.'

'So! And in the meantime? We continue. No questions asked. No!' Starkey brushed away Stenson's arm. He began jogging as the commander and Longley began having an animated discussion. For a few precious minutes, the large excavator was switched off allowing Mozart to drift unchallenged across the valley. When Starkey passed the construction crew's camp, with its trailers and huge crates, the commander gesticulated with Longley, jumped into his hovercraft and sped off. Longley shrugged and returned to the excavator.

Starkey waved down his boss.

'Not now, Ben!' the commander snapped. 'Step aside.' He sped past. The botanist swore. He swore again when the music stopped and both excavators roared back into life, simultaneously. Once more, machines clanged, gouged and bellowed. The emptied dumpster passed him.

Stenson paged Starkey. 'Mr Starkey. We need you back here, urgently. We are finishing laying down the stays. Then we must lower the food dome before the glue-cement begins to set. This must be done now.' McGowan waved frantically for him to come over.

Starkey pondered. What could he gain by confronting a man with a heart of the coldest, hardest stone? 'Okay, Frida; if you want me to come over, then switch off the excavator. Play more Mozart.'

'But... Mr Starkey—' Stenson's frustration filtered through the pager.

'You heard me, Frida. Do it now! For twenty minutes. Or I have it out with the commander. Then expect all hell to break loose.'

Stenson sighed. 'No, don't do something foolish. Okay... Okay. Have it your way. The machines will be switched off. Twenty minutes. No longer. The bulldozer driver is busy with other tasks anyway. So come right away. Please.'

Starkey walked towards the base camp to the music of Mozart. But the growls and grinding of the large excavator were ascendant. He looked across to see the commander stand stiffly to attention and glance towards the base camp. The man sniffed the air much like a rabbit before waving his arms about, to draw attention to himself. Stenson had her back to him. The man did not switch on his pager.

When the third food dome was set down, with the team now working efficiently, Starkey rushed into the second dome to fetch binoculars. From the top step he discerned many... far too many... brown patches on the fronds of each bird of paradise tree. A couple of fronds were gone. His outburst had those nearby spinning around in alarm.

'I'm going over to him now!' Starkey boomed. 'Either he declares a long pause, or I'll beat the crap out of him.'

McGowan and Stenson barred his path. 'Don't do that, Mr Starkey! Do so and you and the trees will be the losers.'

'We're already the losers!'

McGowan, her face dripping with grimy sweat and her uniform filthy with grit, grasped his forearm and looked into his face. 'Ben. Ben. I feel your hurt,' she pleaded. 'Frida is right. You can't help the trees if you get sent back to Earth. Please don't risk it.'

'Yes, Mr Starkey,' said Stenson, 'please no dramas. As much as it pains me to tell you, we must now raise the pumping station. Mr Rafferty has disconnected all of the fittings. If this task wasn't so urgent, I would call a long pause, regardless of the consequences. I'm deeply sorry but if that building isn't on new foundations by the end of the day, we'll have no fresh water and no sanitation. Cleaning the compressor will take hours. The research station will be done tomorrow. But that task will be done at our leisure.'

'So!' Starkey blurted, 'we go straight on to the pumping station. This... appalling neglect... continues.'

'Regrettably, the task will be completed,' said Stenson, as a whisper, 'with or without your help. Look, Mr Starkey; we will pause the machines when the pumping station is being raised. And again, when it is being lowered. If it's any consolation, Mr Longley will participate. He is every bit as weary as we are.'

'Nice gesture, Frida. But way too much damage has already been done.'

'I sympathise, Mr Starkey. Unfortunately, it is the best I can offer. Look: Mr Longley and his crew will not

59

operate the earthmoving machines for a few hours to-morrow morning. It will give the trees, and each of us, a well-deserved rest. The commander's path will not be discussed again.'

Starkey wasn't done. 'Frida; tell me this; if raising the pumping station is so vital, why wasn't it raised first thing this morning? In fact, why wasn't it the very first building raised?'

Stenson recoiled. 'We proceeded according to the schedule.'

Behind her, Rafferty looked sheepish. 'You're right, Ben. It should have been the first task today. I'm sorry. I was so busy racing from one job to the next, I didn't stop and think. Hell... I'm so exhausted I can't think straight.'

'No one is thinking straight!' Starkey snarled. He thrust the binoculars at Stenson. 'Take a look at the trees, Frida. See how distressed they are.'

Stenson stepped away. 'I don't doubt you, Mr Starkey.'

Starkey began waving his arms about. 'Damn it! What if the trees demand a permanent halt to our earth-works? After the way we've treated them, they well might do just that. What then?'

'I can't answer that question,' said Stenson. 'As for now, Mr Starkey, help raise the pumping station. I'm very sorry but we have no choice. I will inform Mr Longley that we have called an immediate, temporary, pause. He will comply.'

Starkey kicked the ground in agitation. 'Damn you!'

'I'm sorry. I acknowledge our lack of judgement.' Stenson grasped Starkey by the arm. 'Mr Starkey. Please go and operate a jack. Do so and I will call the pause.'

With anxious faces gazing at him, Starkey reluctantly took his place beside a jack.

Standing at the jack beside him, McGowan's head was bowed. 'You were right about the schedule all along, Ben. I should have objected. I had no idea the pace of work would be so relentless.'

'We all should have spoken up,' Rafferty added. 'I'm sorry Ben.'

'All machines are now idle,' Stenson said firmly. The workers stood in near silence. 'Let's start.' Stenson made a show of switching off her pager. 'In case the commander calls.'

As dusk descended, the heavy machinery rumbled back to Longley's camp, and fell silent. Weary in mind and body, Starkey sat heavily on the dirt as Stenson began cleaning the compressor under the glare of the botanist. Bob Chase and Rafferty hastily re-connected the extensive pipework and wiring to the pumping station, which sat on its raised foundations. Twin pylons, joined at their top by a cross beam, rose three metres above a rough, stepped, metre-high stone mound beside the second dome. The workday had drawn to a close. It had been the most hectic day of all.

McGowan sat beside Starkey. She offered him an exhausted and sympathetic smile and draped her arm across his shoulders.

'I'm going to have to speak to Zally, Karen,' Starkey moaned. 'Seeing how sick they are is breaking my heart.'

'Yes, I noticed them. You look sick as well.'

'Karen; It's my fault. I'm responsible for their welfare. But I did nothing to ease their suffering today. Nothing.'

'That's crap Ben!' she admonished him. 'You did all you could.'

'No, Karen. I didn't. I failed the trees.'

'Stop it, Ben! Hey, if it's any consolation, tomorrow, you finally get your wish. Yes, it's overdue. No heavy machinery will be used all morning. Everyone is firm in their resolve about that. We're exhausted. Longley's motives to comply may not be altruistic, but that doesn't matter, does it?'

'Karen; we might be exhausted. But that is nothing compared to what the trees are feeling. They have been subjected to a pain that dwarfs into insignificance anything we have ever experienced.' He lowered his head, crestfallen.

'Tell the trees the truth. We got our planning… badly wrong. If we'd had one iota of common sense, we would have been able to ease their suffering. At least they will get relief tomorrow morning.'

'I'm sorry Karen but I've been let down too many times to feel optimistic. Besides, the trees' ordeal won't end tomorrow. They'll be ailing for maybe months. I don't know. Healing will take a long time.'

'I hear you, Ben. We'll do better from now on.'

'Will Zally believe anything we say? After we have proven what barbarians we are, caring only about our own selfish needs.' He slammed his chest. 'I should have taken to the excavator with a laser cutter. One of the cutters was sitting right there, just a few steps away. But I didn't have the courage; I kept on working.'

'Stop blaming yourself, Ben. We got it wrong, yes. But it was the commander who refused to schedule breaks.'

Across the other side of the creek, the commander set off towards the cave. Noticing him, Starkey rose, aching, to his feet. He'd taken two steps when Mc-Gowan stood and pulled him back by the arm. 'Let me speak to him. I'm worried that you'll totally lose it. Then... who knows? You'll most likely end up in the brig back on Earth.'

He looked at her, forlorn. 'I won't go berserk. Promise. It's way too late for that. My priority now has to be to oversee and record the damage inflicted, and the recovery, of the trees.'

'Okay. I'll talk to him.' McGowan stepped away. She paged their boss. 'Hello commander. The building of a further segment of the levee and the last of the foundations should take no more than five hours tomorrow. All of us are all in agreement; the construction crew included. We must ease off. We are bloodied, bruised, filthy and exhausted. It is imperative that we bathe and take a long rest. We have no clean clothes.' She nodded at Starkey, who stood, hands on hips, behind her.

The commander's heavy breath drifted through the pager. 'But we need to make use of every hour of this favourable weather Karen.'

Starkey gaped in astonishment. He leaned over Mc-Gowan's shoulder, unable to restrain his burgeoning fury. 'No, commander! There will be a very long pause all morning. Come to the pond. Check out the carnage we inflicted on the trees today. There are way too many large brown patches on the fronds. Some fronds are floating in the pond. How many, I have no idea.'

McGowan backed away from the botanist, shaking her head while thrusting out her arm to restrain him. But Starkey kept to her shoulder. 'You told me you care for the trees,' he growled. 'But that was a lie.'

The commander recoiled. 'Those are harsh words, Ben. Can't you appreciate how vital is the work we're doing? The trees will get all the rest they need soon. I won't ask much more from them.'

Starkey swooned. 'You don't get it, do you? These are highly sensitive beings. We humans have no idea just how sensitive. I'm going to talk to Zally now. Don't be surprised if the trees will demand that we halt all work with the heavy machinery, perhaps for good. Zally only needs to make an official request. And we will have to bow to the trees' wishes.'

McGowan skipped away, cupping her hand over the pager. She shook her head vigorously at Starkey.

The commander stiffened. 'Wait there. Everyone. Gather around the steps to the second dome,' came his booming voice, echoing through all the team's pagers. 'We need to talk.' He walked briskly to the base camp, arms swinging. As he fronted up, McGowan cradled Starkey's arm firmly in hers, at the rear of those gathered.

The commander leapt atop the highest step of the food dome. After taking in the faces of his team below, his expression appeared to soften. 'I believe we all need to calm down. Rest assured; I hear what you are telling me. I can see how tired you are. I admire the dedication you have shown. But I say to you; let us press on a little longer and get the last of the foundations laid down. Build more of the levee. After those tasks are done, we'll finish early tomorrow.' Starkey was struck speechless. The commander continued. 'I give you my solemn promise. Then all of you, and the trees, of course, can have a long break with my full blessing.'

'No!' Regaining his voice, Starkey was emphatic. 'The trees will have a long break first thing in the morning.' He clenched and unclenched his fists. 'They need the morning sun to help them recoup, as best as they are able. They are hurting so badly, you can't comprehend. And we have no idea how long that pain will persist. It is imperative that they get their break in the morning. It will be a promise we *must* keep. It's your only chance of convincing the trees to allow any earthmoving machine to be used again.'

The commander gazed at each of the faces around him. He would have seen, as Starkey did, determination etched across each furrowed face. Even Stenson's. He spread his arms in an appeal. 'I'm asking you all for just one short day.' He looked intently at Starkey. 'I'm relying on you, Ben, to assure the trees that we deeply sympathise with their suffering. That is the honest truth.' Starkey shook his head. 'Ben; if circumstances hadn't conspired against us from the start, things would have been different. The cut in the budget. The rain. I was left with no choice.' He spread his arms as a plea, then jumped off his step and strode on.

'No commander!' Starkey bellowed. McGowan barred his path, arms outstretched. 'The earthmoving equipment will not be used in the morning. And don't expect Zally to allow us to work unhindered in the afternoon!'

He pushed McGowan away and ran, furious, to the pond. Three brown fronds, two only recently sprouted, floated against the dam wall. Two more larger ones drooped alarmingly. Even in the twilight, Starkey made out brown patches... many of them large... on too many fronds. Seething, he used his torch and body camera to record the damage.

With that task done, he sat heavily beneath Zally's fronds and steeled himself. 'I should have come earlier, Zally. I'm... so very sorry. I am furious with my fellow humans. We acted with unforgivably cruelty towards you today. Again, my commander had promised regular pauses. But our pauses happened too late to help ease your pain. And they were too brief. Today, I am ashamed of my kind. I failed you badly. I should have done much more. As a person, I'm too trusting.' He leaned over, clutching his legs.

'Key to the Stars…' Zally's delayed greeting lingered 'heavy' in his mind. 'We are… very disappointed… with the behaviour of your kind. This day was by far the worst of all. We expected much more understanding. I implore you; we cannot endure any more agony. With your limited senses, can you truly begin to appreciate what immense hurt has been done to us?'

'No, I can't.'

For a few seconds, there was an uneasy silence between them. 'Key to the Stars, I ask you humans to stop all of the horrible noise and vibrations. Because you refuse to show us any compassion, I ask your kind to never inflict such agony on us again. More fronds will be discarded before the morning sun shines upon us. With each discarded frond we become increasingly weaker. You humans know this full well. Our ability to generate energy becomes much reduced, as does the will to heal ourselves.'

Starkey winced. 'I feared you might make that request. I will demand that only one of the smaller machines will be used, and for it to be used sparingly. And only in the afternoon. With your consent. The nosiest machine will not be used at all. Your healing is now our sole priority.'

The answer came swiftly. 'We want all the machines to go away, and never return, Key to the Stars. Rid yourselves of them. Humans need to find other means to compensate for your restless loneliness and alienation from the world. And behave with such callous indifference.'

Starkey shut his eyes and sighed. Zally's response had come as no surprise. The commander would expect him to press for a compromise, but he hadn't the will to try. 'Okay, Zally, I will seek what you demand. I'm deeply sorry it has come to this. Rest assured; the fault is entirely due to my own kind.'

Groaning, he rose to his feet. He entered the cave with his mind in turmoil. The trees were fully justified in asking for a shutdown. But bowing to their wishes meant that tasks that could be done in half a day would take many days of mostly hard, manual toil. The commander, with the backing of his superiors, would surely never agree.

Starkey sucked in a breath and barged into the commander's quarters, interrupting a meeting between his boss and Stenson. The fierce expression on their faces made it clear that they had been arguing. The commander shifted his attention to his botanist. He leaned back on his seat, arms crossed, his mouth an angry slit. 'So, what do you have to say, Ben? Out with it.'

Starkey leaned over the commander's desk. 'Sure. Your bloody mindedness has wrecked everything, commander. Big time. The trees can't take anymore. Even a long pause in the morning won't cut it with them. There is to be a complete halt to the use of all earthmoving machines. Permanently. The trees need to begin their long and agonising process of regaining their health.'

The commander stared hard at the botanist. 'Is that the best you have to offer, Ben? Maybe it seemed like I chose to ignore you today. But—'

Starkey shook with fury. 'Don't lie to me! You deliberately ignored me. Anyway, that's irrelevant now. In accordance with the explicit demands of the trees, all earthworks involving loud mechanical noise will cease immediately. I will try and negotiate some sort of limited compromise tomorrow afternoon after we have finally proved that we care for the trees. But don't count on me being successful.'

'I'll leave you two to work things out,' said Stenson. She promptly rose and hurriedly left the room.

'Are you serious Ben?' boomed the commander. 'You're asking for the foundations of the research building, and the building of the levee, to be completed using only basic equipment and bare hands.'

'Yes. That's exactly what I'm saying.'

The commander looked up, exasperated. 'But that's absurd! It will take way too long. And all this expensive equipment will be sitting idle.'

'I fully realise that. The blame rests solely with you.'

The commander gazed at Starkey. 'Take a seat, Ben. Maybe go for a walk if that will clear your mind. Think about the massive cost of this vital work. It involves work that will benefit not just our employer but also the people on planet Earth. Think about the situation when you are more rational.'

Starkey slammed his fist down on the table. 'Don't belittle me! Take responsibility for the carnage you've caused. The trees had been co-operating. But you went and destroyed all of their goodwill.'

The commander folded his arms at his midriff. 'Ben. Realise that my responsibilities run much wider than your solely environmental concerns.'

'Your responsibilities, commander, also includes the wellbeing of the sentient inhabitants of this planet.'

'Please believe me, Ben, I recognise the importance

of conservation. Realise also that I fully intended to call an earlier pause this afternoon. But when Longley told me he had decided to waste valuable time by building that stupid platform, I admit that I became grumpy. But I do not apologise for pushing to get all of our main tasks done for the day. I worked my butt off today, Ben. No different to anyone else.' When Starkey opened his mouth to speak, the commander raised his hand. 'Ben; let us meet later and work out the best way to proceed. In the spirit of genuine compromise.'

Starkey shook his head. 'You don't get it, do you? There will be no compromise.'

The commander drew a long breath. 'Ben, I'm deeply sorry that the trees have suffered. Honest I am. But our entire mission depends on the earthworks being finished in a timely way. I refuse to waver from the only logical course of action to achieve that. Look, the research building is now our main priority. Just as you wanted all along. I'm agreeable to having that extended pause in the morning, if you insist. But, after that—'

'No. The trees alone, will decide what we can do,' Starkey growled. 'The law on sentient beings is clear—'

The commander bristled, puffing out his chest. 'I fully intend to comply with the law, Ben. But I will do so only when I'm offered a realistic compromise. All I'm asking is for one more day. A short day at that!'

'No! The trees are in a state of sheer panic. Their fronds have turned brown and are dying. That is causing their stress to multiply many times over. Understand their plight.'

The commander looked Starkey in the face. 'I acknowledge that the trees are becoming sicker, but they will survive, Ben. In time, they will prosper once more. Unhindered. It is you who needs to acknowledge that completing the earthworks is imperative. It's why we're here! Even you.'

'Our first priority now has to be the welfare of suffering, sentient beings. Ignore the trees and we will be presiding over a catastrophe. I'm certain of it. Accordingly, if you don't order an indefinite pause in the earthworks tonight, I will file an immediate claim with our Earth environmental overseers to issue an order demanding that work involving heavy machinery must desist immediately. I will submit myself to any test to establish that the request has come directly from the trees, without any prompting.'

The commander gaped, startled. 'You would go that far, Ben?' He fell silent and became thoughtful for some seconds. 'Don't you realise that such a claim could take days to resolve. We don't have that sort of time.'

'Yes, I'll do whatever it takes. If I didn't, I would need to tear up my qualifications. I'd be pissing all over what I've strived so hard to achieve for twenty-five years.'

The commander became coy. 'Don't be so sure of yourself, Ben. There is no guarantee that our overseers will back up your request with immediate effect. Or at all.'

'Are you willing to take that chance? I am.'

The commander glared at Starkey. 'If that's your attitude; I'll need to discuss these matters with Mr Longley. He will not be pleased. He has been assigned to deliver a brief. The endorsement of his superiors and his full payment depends on it.'

Starkey recoiled. 'Are you serious? That is irrelevant. Look; everyone else is in agreement. No earthmoving machinery will be used in the morning.'

The commander gritted his teeth. 'I'm telling you now, Ben; work will press on, regardless.'

'No, it won't! Not if Zally doesn't allow it. Please don't think I'm getting any satisfaction from this. I'm seriously conflicted. Believe me.'

'Really!' A look of disbelief spread across the commander's face.

'Don't doubt me, commander. I've said my piece. You must comply. That's all I have to say.' Starkey turned on his heel and stormed out of the room. He dropped on his bunk bed, his chest heaving, certain of one outcome; he would not be sharing this planet with his boss for much longer. As for the fate of the bird of paradise trees...

Sleep was impossible. An aching Starkey wearily rose from his bunk and stepped outside the cave. The planet's large moon was shining softly, just above the horizon. Thousands of stars twinkled above. The moon lit up the construction crew's camp; the machinery and the roof of their living quarters shone silver. He moved a short distance until he could make out the fronds of the bird of paradise trees, shimmering purple around the pond. He stepped inside the cave to return with a pillow and two blankets. Starkey laid down on the cold, hard and stony ground; his eyes turned towards the trees.

DISCOVERY

Next morning, the sky was a brilliant blue. The pathways were largely free of mud. The air was still. The day could not have been more perfect. The commander paced the ground, swapping furtive glances between the sky and Starkey; his hands clasped tightly behind his back. He bristled each time his eyes dwelt on the two excavators and the bulldozer, lying idle in the construction crew's camp.

Using laser cutters, two of the construction crew gouged holes for stays that would support the new research building, on an undulating slope. Another of the crew, aided by an uneasy Starkey and McGowan, set down the remaining segment of the rough retention wall using mechanical shovels and their gloved hands. Stenson applied glue-cement. Two other construction-crew workers near the Chute loaded loose stone and gravel onto the dumpster with a mechanical shovel. Longley watched on from a fold-out seat in clear sight, drinking from a flask, at the construction crew's camp. Rafferty and Bob Chase began preparing the new building's electrical and plumbing connections. There was little chatter. There were no smiles.

After about an hour, the grim-faced commander sidled up beside the botanist. 'Are the working arrangements suitable to you, Ben?' He rose up and down onto the balls of his feet.

Starkey straightened his back. 'Yes, they are. The trees will appreciate the respite we've... belatedly... given them. They have a great deal of healing to do. After lunch I'll try to negotiate some limited concessions with them.'

'Push hard, Ben,' the commander said. 'They must compromise. I refuse to have vital machinery lying idle all day.'

'I can't make any promises.' How would Zally react?

Uncomfortable under the cold gaze of the commandeer, the botanist had an idea. 'How about I use this down time to go upriver and check on whether any blockages are forming in the river. I'll take a laser cutter with me in case. I can also record how the trees that way are recovering.'

'I'll let you know,' the commander huffed. He resumed his prowling. Then he stood still, deep in thought. He tapped his pager. 'Everyone; gather around. I have an announcement to make.' Starkey grimaced, anticipating the worst. He looked on with his arms folded at his midriff.

Standing on a step of a food dome, his boss addressed the exploration team. 'Yesterday you requested a break from our vital work. This morning's enforced go-slow offers the opportunity to do just that. Organise yourselves into two shifts. Karen, Patrick and Bob will make up the first shift. Each shift will last for two hours. No longer. Go and wash yourselves and your clothes.

Rest up. The first shift begins immediately. The second shift will take their break when the first shift returns. Then we all will need to work hard.' His eyes paused on Starkey. 'Certainly, Mr Longley expects that we will.'

His words were greeted with relieved smiles by all but Starkey.

The commander's gaze returned to the botanist. 'In the meantime, Ben and I will go upriver to check for possible blockages in the river.' His smile was more of a grimace. Starkey groaned. 'That way, you will get a welcome opportunity to be rid of your grumpy commander for a time.' But not so for Starkey.

'To the river bend?' piped up McGowan. She displayed no enthusiasm, perhaps in deference to the commander's surly mood.

'I've got clothes drying beside the river,' said Rafferty. 'We'll have time to reach Waterfall Creek.'

'I've got clothes drying as well,' said Bob Chase.

McGowan rushed to her tent to fetch a bag of clothes. The three set off briskly, in good spirits, along the riverbank.

The commander turned to a despondent Starkey. 'Before we go, Ben, I need to have a quick word with Mr Longley. In person.'

Starkey forced a smile. 'Two hours doesn't give us long, but we should be able to reach the place where the blockage happened before. As long as we don't dawdle.'

'Won't be long.' The commander stepped into a hovercraft and drove to where Longley was leaning against the tread of his large excavator, sipping coffee. Their discussion lasted a few intense minutes. Longley shrugged. When the commander sped back, he beckoned his botanist to join him. Starkey dropped a small laser cutter into the hovercraft, stepped in, and they set off.

To the botanist's surprise, the commander smiled. 'You know what?' his boss said. The smile seemed genuine. 'It will be great to do some research again. And get away from the base camp. It's too easy for a man to get caught up with his responsibilities. When that happens, it can cause him to lose perspective.'

The commander steered the hovercraft to the rear of the base camp, then swung the craft around to pass the small, completed segment of the dirt levee and its retention wall. The two men headed upstream. The narrow ravine, dotted with boulders, small cascades and rubble slowed their zig-zagged progress. Starkey switched on his body camera.

'I'm amazed at how high the scarring is,' the commander said, looking at the jagged hill to their right.

'Yes, when the tidal wave squeezed through,' Starkey said without enthusiasm, 'it heaved its load up with an almighty force, scraping the side of the hills. But, as you can make out, some vegetation has begun to spring up in some of the cavities.' The commander nodded.

The two men passed by a fissure in the rock face where there were some skeletal brown fronds and chunks of pulverised trunks of bird of paradise trees. 'Dead trees?' the commander ventured.

'Can't tell. Hopefully, they've only been discarded by trees before they went into hibernation.'

The commander reached out and touched a frond. It disintegrated in his hand.

Starkey pointed ahead. 'Look; there's a green shoot on the shore, just up a bit, reaching towards the precious sun. There's another one a little further on. They weren't there three weeks ago. Encouraging.'

'Yes. Very encouraging. The trees are indeed resilient.'

'Healthy trees mean a healthy ecosystem,' Starkey said, more for the recording he was making. 'Their extensive roots bind the riverbank. Look; another green shoot. Great. No need to slow down.' The commander did not seem inclined to do so, anyway.

'There's a small coppice of trees just upriver from where the blockage happened,' Starkey commented. 'Hopefully they will give us some answers to how the trees recover. I can't draw many conclusions from the trees by our pond because they were subjected to unnatural stress when the base camp was set up. And again, over the last few days.' He stared hard at the commander.

About fifteen minutes later, at a place where the river passed between some steep, grey hillocks and fallen boulders, the commander brought the hovercraft to a halt below an unnavigable cascade. 'We need to go on foot from here,' Starkey said.

'Fine with me.' The commander grinned.

They clambered up the cascade. 'It's incredible,' said the commander. 'The trees were so ravaged here while on the other side of our hill they were untouched.'

'Different catchment area. It goes to show that the line between prosperity and disaster is incredibly fine.'

Starkey strode ahead as the surrounds broadened and became less steep. They arrived at a place where the river was formed from a convergence of a stream and a knee-high creek. 'Look here!' the botanist said, pointing at a rounded boulder on the banks of the stream. 'You see that segment of long root? The tree has gone but the root is intact.'

'Interesting.'

Starkey rushed across the boulder. 'There,' he said pointing, grinning. A green stem rose a few centimetres from the riverbank. 'It's in the sun, of course. With such a healthy root, the tree should regenerate fairly rapidly.'

The commander stroked his chin. 'But, Ben, you said that the earthworks can be done close to the stems. Wouldn't that mean we risk damaging their roots?'

'Yes, it would. Damaging their roots delays the trees regenerating, Not ideal. But realise, commander, I'm being a team player here. I'm compromising. There would be constant delays if we had to work around every root we uncovered. It's okay. The green stems only become conscious when they develop fronds.'

'Thanks, Ben. Making compromises like that is much appreciated.' The commander stared at his botanist. 'I, too, have to make compromises. My responsibilities sometimes require me to make decisions that I wish to God I didn't have to make. Like insisting that the earthworks recommence. Understand that we have a brief to complete, Ben.'

His words made Starkey freeze in his tracks. 'Hang on. What do you mean by complete?' He checked his watch. Some forty-five minutes had elapsed since the two men had set off. The commander stuck out his chin. 'But, commander, you accept, don't you, that any use of earthmoving machines can only happen after I have talked to Zally? Even if I'm the bearer of bad tidings, against my will. That is what we agreed.'

The commandeer drew a breath. 'Ben, you said that the trees most likely wouldn't object to the machinery being used in short bursts.'

Starkey sucked a breath. 'No. That's not true!' He took a step towards his boss, looking intently into the man's face. 'Zally would very likely object.' He looked the way they had come. 'If work does re-commence, in defiance of the trees, it is imperative that I closely monitor how the trees are faring.' He studied his commander's evasive face, detecting guilt. 'Tell me; have you authorised the use of a machine while we are here?'

The commander strode off along the bank of the stream. 'Should Mr Longley decree that machinery is required, I cannot prevent him from doing so. Understand, Ben, the brief is our main priority. And isn't it certain that the trees will recover?'

Starkey's hands formed into fists as he stepped in front of the commander. His boss took a step back, alarmed. 'Commander! If any earthworks have begun, forget about negotiating with Zally!' He briefly gazed at the sky. 'Don't you realise? Those trees are like children. More than that; they are sensitive, far beyond our understanding. Already they have been subjected to a level of stress and agony that we can't begin to comprehend. Right! Call Longley now. If he is using his machinery... I don't care how sparingly... he must switch it off. Immediately!' His chest heaved in anger.

'No. I won't do that, Ben,' The commander said, grimacing. 'Our work cannot be finished proficiently using shovels and laser cutters. If the trees had compromised, then...' He shrugged. 'But they chose not to. So, we must proceed regardless. I have no choice. I'm sorry, Ben.'

Starkey could not look at the man. 'Okay then. I'm going back,' he spat. 'It's vital I talk to Zally. But how can I explain another callous act? Then I'll send an urgent request to the Earth authorities. They must call an immediate halt to all earthworks. You'll have to comply.'

'Do that on your return if you wish. But I guarantee you won't get the immediate response you seek. As for right now, we continue, and check whether a blockage may be forming upstream. That's what we came here to do.'

'Another time. It's urgent that I check on the trees. And get the earthworks stopped.'

The commander stared hard at Starkey. 'Ben, I am in charge here. And I have the starter key to the hovercraft. Are you prepared to use force to take it from me? If you do, I'll have you bundled off this planet in handcuffs, within hours. Then what? Will the authorities give a damn about what a violent man tells them? No, they won't! So, let's keep going.'

The commander's response stunned Starkey. 'No! We must go back!'

'Come on, Ben. By tomorrow, all this drama will be in the past. We'll have a glass of something strong together, to celebrate getting our mission back on track. The research building will be up and running in a few days' time. With minimal noise. You'd approve of that, wouldn't you?'

'Not if means inflicting more agony on the trees and destroying the last vestiges of our tarnished credibility. Zally may never believe me again.'

The commander pursed his lips. 'You're wasting time arguing, Ben. We go on. I'll push on by myself if I need to.'

Starkey stared back at the way they had come. Walking all the way back would take far too long. 'Okay,' he simmered. 'We'll do it your way. But I'm doing so under protest. If more harm is inflicted on the trees...' He glared at the commander. 'I will make a detailed report. As for now, fortunately, I believe the place

I'm looking is just a little way further. When I get there, I'll record what we see. Then we both rush back. No delays.'

'Sure. That's a deal, Ben.'

Starkey stared hard at his boss. 'I warn you. Your promise, and your admissions, are recorded on my camera. I thought you'd want to cut your losses. But, no, you keep pushing your luck.'

'I have a duty to fulfil, Ben. It's my job. I'm sure we... us, the trees... can reconcile over this.'

'Reconcile! Crap!' Starkey snorted. 'Okay. Let's get this over and done with.' They set off in a tense, uneasy silence, as a glowering Starkey pressed forward. The commander lagged behind.

After perhaps ten minutes, the two men reached a tall, dark cascade, flanked on both sides by steep, rocky grey cliffs. Starkey scrambled up the cascade and poked his head above it. He sighed in relief. 'We're here!'

He clambered over slippery rocks to reach a wide, gently undulating patch of mostly stony land. The commander followed him. Both men leapt over a narrow, almost dry, creek that flowed into the stream.

'We are now standing where I am almost certain the earlier blockage occurred,' Starkey said. 'See this large patch of newly exposed ground between the creek and the stream? Also, look at the gouge marks and stains on both sides above the cascade. A big chunk of ground most likely became waterlogged with the heavy rain. The sodden ground gave way and became lodged between the steep sides, along with some uprooted bird of paradise trees, causing the blockage to build up.'

The commander stared wistfully at the creek and the broken ground. 'Here?'

'Yes. The blockage probably built up over a few days, restricting the flow of water. The pressure built up until it became too great. The barrier burst. It set off an avalanche and tidal wave. We know the rest.'

The commander shook his head, seemingly fighting tears. Starkey examined the surrounds. 'The newly exposed ground, and surrounds looks to be mostly bedrock. So, the ground is most likely secure. Good.' He then moved hurriedly to a gently sloping area, caked with dried mud. There, close to the stream, stood a clump of five bird of paradise trees.

The tree nearest the stream was merely a trunk. Starkey circled it, hastily filming. 'Its fronds are only beginning to re-generate, as you can see by the green stubs. It's happening very, very slowly. It must have greatly feared for its own safety, and grieved for the loss of nearby trees, so it kept dropping fronds until none remained. Having no fronds is severely hindering its recovery.'

Starkey moved on. The other trees had two or three full-sized fronds, all of which had large brown patches, and a few stubby, green fronds. Starkey examined each tree, careful to record their state of health.

'I'll compare the progress of these trees with the video I took soon after the tidal wave. There are dark-green patches surrounding the brown parts on the fronds. Good sign. They are healing. They are renewing quicker than the stump. But slowly, nevertheless. Again, suggesting that they have endured severe stress. Fortunately for them, the blockage gave way before they too dropped all of their fronds. The next stage for a stressed tree without fronds is to collapse into hibernation.'

The commander pursed his lips. 'Ben. Doesn't this

finding prove our trees will also recover after being stressed? In time?'

'Commander, please don't think we can ignore the wishes of our trees,' Starkey growled. 'The unnatural stress we inflict may kill them. I don't know. I have no intention of finding out. Our machines terrify them. And because we humans are also mobile, they fear us. We have a responsibility to protect them. Can't you appreciate that?'

The commander nodded. 'Ben. Believe me. I do not wish to cause the trees… undue harm.'

Starkey faced his boss, his hands on his hips. 'Really?' He slapped his thigh. 'Okay. We found the trees I was looking for. The ground here is stable. There is no sign of a blockage forming. Now we head back. Fast as we can. Page Longley now. Any earthworks need to be stopped.'

'I won't do that. Our work must continue.'

'Damn you!' Starkey snapped, 'Be aware that I am recording this trip. You will face the consequences when I send my report to the authorities on Earth. Right. Let's go.'

The commander was unmoved. 'Do that, if you wish to.'

'Yes, I do. Very much.' Starkey glared at the commander and strode on. He took only a few steps when he started, causing him to stop, stock still, and overbalance into the small, shallow creek. His ears had begun to ring. He tried to clear his head. 'Zally?' he said, perplexed, looking back at the coppice of trees. 'Are you trying to reach me?'

Suddenly, Starkey was filled with desperation to be back at the pond. So far away. He clambered, half-slipping in his haste, down the high cascade. The commander followed, a distant expression on his face. At the bottom, the botanist heard a dull thud. He spun around to find the commander on his knees, his hands cupping his head. Starkey squatted beside him. 'Commander. What's the matter?' The commander's eyes stared vacantly ahead; his mouth flapped uselessly.

The ringing in Starkey's ears intensified. 'I'll get help.' He tapped McGowan's number on his pager. But got only static. He tapped the all-contacts number. Static. He laid the commander on the ground and tried his boss' pager. Again, static. 'What?' he wailed. 'I can't stay here!' He looked at the sky. 'Zally, if you are causing this to the commander, and can hear me, somehow, please desist. Understand; I can't leave my commander here.'

Groaning, Starkey lifted the commander onto the man's wobbly feet. He wrapped his arm around his boss' armpits. 'Commander. I can't contact anyone. You need to help me get back. We must move fast.'

The commander lurched forward and collapsed in Starkey's arms, bringing both men crashing into the stream. Starkey dragged the unconscious commander to a rounded rock. He turned off his body camera, fearing the evidence it held would become damaged. By bending his knees, Starkey hoisted the commander over his shoulders with a grunt. He set off, straining with the weight, cursing; his feet shifting. 'This is taking too long,' he cried out. 'Zally. I'm coming. But I can't get there any quicker. Help me out if you can.'

He fought a strong urge to set down his heavy burden and flee to the pond. But he struggled on, the weight buckling him at his knees. He kept having to stop and re-set his load.

Starkey hadn't gotten far when his left foot slipped on a smooth, wet rock, slamming the two men hard onto a cascade. A stab of pain shot through Starkey's left ankle as he struggled to his feet. He sat beside the commander and awkwardly draped his boss across his shoulders once more. Screaming with agony, Starkey lifted himself and his load to his feet. Each step came with sharp stabs of pain. When the terrain was rough, he laid the commander down gently, placed his arms under the man's shoulders, and dragged his boss forward.

'It's taking too long!' Starkey screamed, in pain and frustration. He barely heard himself. The ringing in his ears was becoming louder, more painful.

Starkey's exhausting exertion, over slippery rocks, seemed to never end. He gave a whoop of sheer joy when he finally reached the cascade, with the hovercraft parked below. Grasping the commander's wrists, he carefully lowered his boss down the wet, rocky slope, then he slid to the bottom, gripping his ankle in pain. Starkey hoisted the commander roughly onto the hovercraft, and tied the man down with grubby straps. He placed a dirty, scrunched-up raincoat under the commander's head to keep it as still as possible.

He started the hovercraft and took off, steering a perilous passage through rough terrain while slamming the hovercraft's pager. More static. The speeding craft glanced off rocks and boulders, and skipped off the water like a tossed stone, flinging the commander's arms all about. Starkey yelled in triumph when he broke out into the familiar wide valley.

Pounding his fist on the horn, he drove around the back of the base camp, to come to a shuddering halt at the site for the new research building. No one rushed to greet him. If any heavy machinery was being used, he couldn't tell. None were in sight and the ringing in his ears masked all noise.

Baffled, Starkey looked around. The site was not only deserted; it was untouched from when he and the commander had set off. 'Where are you all?' he screamed, unable to hear his own words. His sight began to dim.

He sped off in a panic, slamming the hovercraft hard into the steps of a food dome. For a few seconds he sat, rattled, before speeding off again, desperately honking the horn. He passed the food dome where two pylons, destined to be set up by the cave, leaned. Still, no one was in sight. Nor any earthmoving machine.

'Where are you?' he yelled at the top of his voice. 'Someone! Anyone! This is an emergency!'

Starkey caught sight of vehicle tracks where none should be. The tracks headed up and over the small, completed segment of the dirt levee and towards the wide gully. He followed the trail to the top of the levee. There, he gaped in utter disbelief. His blurred vision made out a tangled and broken brown mass around the pond.

The dumpster, its cabin facing him, blocked Starkey's path down the other side of the levee. He staggered, tripping, from the hovercraft, feeling faint. Was it Zally's doing or was it shock? On the dumpster's trey were two large cement pipes, strapped down by rope. 'This can't be happening...' he yelled at the young man in the cabin. But the man's bulging eyes were unseeing; his body slumped against his seat. The dumpster stood on a small segment of a newly and hastily constructed, downward-sloping path. The rough, raised path, glistening with glue-cement, led towards the narrow, rocky gap that separated the gully from the river. Rocks near the gap had been partially smoothed by laser cutters. The bank of the gully to his left bore a large, grey-brown gouge. Within the ugly gash was the bulldozer; its driver slumped across the controls.

Starkey fell to his knees, disbelieving. The act of treachery and evil before him was beyond his comprehension. He caught a glimpse of two pairs of legs, unmoving, across the opposite side of the pathway. He moved in that direction until a terrible noise permeated through the ringing in his ears. It was the sound of a bull bellowing; attacking, then retreating. He spun around. On the far side of the wide gully, below the pond, the large excavator, splattered with dark mud, jerked wildly as it bucked impotently up against a large, rounded boulder. It let out a burst of noise as it rose, then it slid back into the gully before resuming its fruitless attack. In the cabin, Longley rode the crazed bull, his head and arms flailing.

'Turn it off! Turn it off! Now!' Starkey shouted. But the works engineer was beyond responding.

Swooning, Starkey ran into the muddy waters of the gully, crying out as stabbing pain cut at his ankle. He grasped hold of the cabin door and dragged himself upwards with shaking hands, to duck past Longley's lurching body and flaying arms, and switched off the engine. Longley had a pulse. Starkey felt a callous sense of satisfaction. Longley, along with the commander, would answer for the heinous crime committed this day.

The ringing in his ears subsided a bit. His eyesight improved. To his relief, he heard no machine. That was little comfort; abject carnage had been unleashed on the trees. The terror and agony they had to be enduring was unfathomable. Starkey spun around, to give full vent to his fury. But Longley remained prone across the controls. No one stirred in the gully.

He had to front up to Zally. To say what? No! He felt faint and his mind was a torrent. Go to Zally and he'd crumple, a quivering, blubbering mess. He'd need to regain some vestiges of his shattered composure. Even if able to think straight, how could he possibly convey to Zally the boundless depth of his shame and anger? No such words existed. If, somehow, he could convey some hopelessly inadequate apology, he would then be confronted by the equally daunting task of convincing Zally to release the trees' hold over the perpetrators of this terrible crime. *If* Zally could be reached. With so many fronds discarded, drooping or turned a horrible brown, the trees had to be severely debilitated. Could they... would they... divert their dwindling energy reserves to aid those responsible for ravaging them? Worse, the trees may be collapsing into hibernation. If they were, Starkey's fellow humans were almost assuredly doomed. For he knew they had been struck down by a force that dwarfed normal unconsciousness.

Until he could stabilise his tumultuous emotions, Starkey fell back upon his training as a scientist. He switched on his body camera and began recording the crime scene before the guilty had an opportunity to meddle with the damning evidence. Starkey first turned the camera to the large excavator with Longley collapsed inside, careful to include the gouge marks on the boulder and the muddy trail the excavator had forged as it crossed the gully. His commentary, spoken as a faltering whimper, could not disguise his contempt. The commander's confession, made upstream, would seal the case.

Starkey waded back through the mud, dragging his injured leg, to film the new segment of the still glistening pathway, the dumpster with its load, and the large gouge extracted from the bank of the gully. He limped across to the bulldozer. As he filmed its prone driver, he caught sight of McGowan, her arm extended upwards across the male driver. Her hand was grasped tightly around the machine's starter key. Rafferty and Bob Chase lay at her feet. All three, thankfully, had a pulse. Other humans lay spreadeagled on the opposite side of the new pathway, along with the small excavator, the glue-cement compressor, the compacter, a couple of laser cutters and mechanical shovels. The betrayal was total. Starkey staggered to the top of the levee to pan the camera across the full scene, culminating in the filming of the stricken trees. He burst into tears. 'We humans did this bastard act to these highly sensitive and intelligent beings,' he sobbed. 'I make this recording having no idea what to say to... the trees. But I must go to them now.' He sucked a few breaths. 'Perhaps I will be struck down like my fellows... I don't know. I cannot blame them if they punish me. We are all guilty.'

He sobbed as he clambered up the dam wall to reach Zally's pond. He could not raise his eyes to witness, at such close quarters, the utter carnage inflicted on the trees... trees which had been breathtakingly beautiful and joyful as they greeted the rising of the sun. The ugliness could not be blotted out entirely; at least eight brown fronds floated against the pond wall. Other fronds drooped haphazardly. Starkey's legs gave way; he dropped heavily to his knees before Zally.

He found it almost impossible to speak. 'Zally!' His throat choked up. He *had* to keep speaking. 'Zally. Zally,' he uttered, steeling himself. 'What happened today can never be forgiven. I will not insult you by trying to apologise. Never have I witnessed such insensitivity and outright evil.' Starkey cringed, waiting for a response, perhaps a burst of outright hostility sent hurtling through his mind. But he felt only the iciest of silences. He had to persist. If Zally could not be roused... If the trees had descended too deeply into hibernation... his colleagues... his wonderful companions... would rot where they lay. Along with those of the construction crew whose offence was to act, some reluctantly, upon orders issued to them. He had to save them all. If it were possible.

'The machines should never have come this way,' he stammered. 'Those responsible will be severely punished. I give you my solemn guarantee; they will leave this planet immediately. And they will take their terrible machines with them. The humans who did this to you will never return. Nor will any machine that generates such hurtful vibrations and noise.'

Zally was silent. Perhaps the tree was in too much agony... to hear him. Or perhaps a furious Zally had cast him aside. The botanist had no choice; he had to somehow reach Zally. 'Okay; I'll promise more. The machines will never be started again. Ever. They will be left where they are to rot over time. I will destroy their engines to ensure it happens.'

No response. He craved for a reply. Any reply... No matter if it blasted through his mind with the coldest, fiercest fury. Starkey blubbered on. 'Every human will be sent back to my planet. Everyone. Our mission on your planet has now ended. They will take to my planet a message forbidding any human to come to your planet again. They... we... have witnessed how capable you are of defending yourself. They will gladly leave.'

Starkey paused. His shattered spirit was descending into a maelstrom. 'To ensure no humans return, I will remain behind so I can destroy the Chute that brought us to your planet. After I destroy it, be aware that I will be unable to leave your planet. I hope I can stay here with your blessing and oversee your recovery. I look forward to seeing you fully healed. And to witness your greeting to the sun. Rest assured that when I die, I cannot leave behind a seed from which another human can be created. Is that acceptable to you Zally?'

Silence.

'Please Zally.' Starkey was despairing, drowning. 'Give me an answer. Say something. Anything.' He had nothing more to offer. But, with the other humans facing doom, he could not desist. 'The danger has passed. You and the other trees can now devote all of your energies to healing. *Please* begin healing. I realise it will take a very long time. And you will have to endure considerable pain as you do. But take comfort; there is nothing more to fear. There is no reason for you to hibernate. I am so sorry. I cannot begin to describe the depth of my sorrow for what my kind has inflicted on you. Please do not discard any more fronds. I tell you again; I beg you; do not sink into hibernation, Zally. Begin healing. Your ordeal is over.' He swooned, steadying himself with an arm.

Only a terrible silence followed. Keep persisting! But he was impotent. 'Never will such an evil deed be inflicted upon you again. Never. There are no words to convey the guilt and shame I am feeling. I offer you no excuses. There can't be any.'

Struggling for breath, quivering uncontrollably and

barely able to utter any words, Starkey waited, frantic for a reply. But only his laboured breathing and the gentle gurgling of the spring disturbed the silence.

What more could he say? 'Zally. The threat is gone. Forever. Please… please talk to me. Just a few words. Let me know you are about to begin healing. Your anger is fully justified. Tell me; how much are you hurting? How angry are you? Please. Say something.'

Silence.

Starkey leaned back to scream in frustration into the blue sky. He lifted himself on wobbly legs, to return to the dam wall and gaze upon the guilty and the innocent who lay prone below him. 'What have you done?' he wailed. 'You've destroyed something so incredibly wonderful! Why?' He bowed his head.

It was imperative he allay his feelings of self-recrimination and self-pity; Zally had to be convinced, somehow, to release the trees' control over the humans. *If* it were possible. He returned to face the tree once more, and dropped to his knees, head low and hands clasped together in supplication. 'Zally, you defended yourself as you are entitled to do. We deserve the full force of your wrath. But I beg you nevertheless; please show us some pity. As undeserved as it is. Allow my people to wake so they can leave your planet. They will leave immediately. They will never hurt you again. They wouldn't dare try. Believe me. Please.'

He listened. No one stirred in the gully.

His chest heaved. 'I acknowledge that we don't deserve any mercy but *please* let them wake. And leave. Please.'

A terrible, cold emptiness resonated throughout his body. It may have been Zally's response. Or maybe his own draining emotions. Was the tree listening? Was it capable of hearing? 'Please Zally. I'm begging you.'

Starkey grasped at straws. 'Zally, my fellow humans must be conscious to leave your planet. When they get to Earth, they will tell the humans there to never come to your planet again.' He was rambling. 'If you allow it, I promise I will stay behind to destroy the Chute.' He took a breath. 'Zally. My kind can't tell other humans to stay away if they don't go back. So, you *must* release them.' This was a blatant lie. He was perfectly capable of sending a message. But he was floundering.

He ached, craving to feel Zally's words. Or hear any human voice. A terrible loneliness was overwhelming him.

Silence.

'Zally; I'm pleading with you; let the humans leave.' He took an anxious breath. 'I cannot stand by and allow my fellows to die like this. We humans do not hibernate. They will die if left as they are. Leaving behind no seed. Please release everyone, even those responsible for your suffering. They will be punished severely. I promise.'

For an indeterminable time, he was unmoving. His breath came in gulps. He steeled himself again. 'Please show us human beings some mercy. Release them. Please Zally! Tell me; what more do you want from me?' he moaned. 'From us? I'll do anything you ask. Anything. But let my people go home. Zally, *please*.' His chest heaved.

He heard only the sound of the gurgling spring.

'Zally. *Please*. Your world is yours, and yours alone. Forever. Please Zally! *Please*!' He wiped the tears that streamed down his cheeks.

Starkey's eyes stayed fixed on the lower trunk of the tree which had magically come into his life, enriching him beyond anything he could possibly have desired or dreamed of. He could not bear to glance at the tangled ugliness surrounding him. He would rather die.

'*Please* Zally…'

'Zally…'

'Zally…'

POPSICLE

EARLY NOVEMBER

S pike's mobile phone rang at his bedside. It was his 'other' mobile phone. The one that had to be answered.

'What?' Spike wasn't one for niceties.

It was his right-hand man, Hargraves. Everyone called him Harry. The man's voice bubbled with excitement. 'Have you checked out the charts this morning?'

'This early?' Spike yawned. 'Course not. You woke me up just now. So, what's so damned urgent?'

'Get this; the Pops... Gary's hit is number one.' Harry was almost breathless. 'How about that?'

Spike sat up. 'Number one! In the first week? Jesus! Are you serious? Gary's heap of crap is number one?'

'I'm not kidding. Amazing huh.'

'Wow! What can I say? Okay; this means we're in for a hectic time. I better get to... err... Gary's place right away. I'll be there soon.'

'It's great news, sure, Spike. Cachink, cachink and all that!' But Harry's mood was more subdued. 'Won't it complicate things more than we anticipated?'

'Hmm. Yes, a bit. Don't get flustered, Harry. Leave this to me. I'll make some refinements to our plan by the time I get there. Basically, our strategy doesn't need to change. We keep on message. We'll definitely need to beef up security, though. Get Slasher onto it. Essentially, it's more a matter of deciding when we bring everything to a head.'

'That's what I figured. Bring our plans forward, eh.'

Spike scratched the stubble on his chin. 'Hmm. Not keen on that idea, Harry. To my thinking, that's our last option. Hey... we're about to be drowning, neck-deep in cash. I reckon we do the opposite; we push our plans *back* a few weeks.'

Harry sucked a breath. 'That's very risky, Spike.'

'Harry,' Spike said, with his most reassuring voice, 'Just relax. I'll handle our strategy. But I don't see why we shouldn't chance it.'

'But if someone finds out, we—' Harry sounded anxious.

'Don't fret, Harry. I'll come up with some contingencies. Trust me on this. One thing; this is important. Get the recording engineer... Tim ... over there as well. This very morning. Pronto. Got that. Buy him a bottle of Champagne. Tell him he's in line for a bonus. If that doesn't convince him, tell him that Slasher gets annoyed when people say "no". We need Tim to put together a follow-up hit, urgently. Make hay while the sun shines.'

Spike heard Harry gasp. 'But that might take months.'

'We only need something quick. I'll monitor the situation day by day. Any garbage Tim can churn out will keep the cash registers running hot. We can skip a video this time. Harry; just get him in, okay. He starts straight away. Oh, tell Slasher that no one is to get past the front gate unless I say so. Double check the security cameras and the alarms.'

'On to it. Okay, Spike. We'll talk more when you get here. But—'

'Relax Harry.'

There was a pause. 'I'll try.'

Spike switched off his phone and leaned back against the wooden bed post. 'Wow! The Popsicle's single is number one. Well… screw me. You know what, Spike, old man? I reckon this could deliver you a country estate in Essex. With a bit of luck.' He tossed the bedsheets aside and rose to his feet, pausing to glance at his image in the full-sized mirror, clothed only in black Y-fronts. Spike was short and scrawny, and slightly bow-legged. He looked every bit of his fifty-five years. His chest was a mat of grey hair; his legs and arms were equally hairy. The coverage on the top of his head was sparse. He scratched his balls. 'Can't be greedy. Best settle for a small estate.'

The grey stubble on his chin was spiky. 'Shave? Nah. Unshaved looks great in the papers. Shows how dedicated I am to my work.' He let out a loud chuckle and ran a hand through his thinning hair. 'A trim maybe. Later.'

His personal mobile rang. The one that didn't need to be answered straight away. He lifted it out of his black dressing gown, which lay crumpled on the carpet. 'Spike.'

'Hi, Spike, It's Tony from Hits 1,2,3, the nation's number one music channel. You must remember me.'

'Oh yes, I remember you,' Spike said with not an iota of enthusiasm. 'What do you want?' He had a pretty good idea…

Tony exuded enthusiasm; a media man seeking favours. 'Spike, are you aware that Gary Fortune's new track has reached number one?'

'So, I've been told. Great result. Let me say that it's a deserved reward for the rough journey he's taken the last few weeks. I tell you Tony, he put his heart and soul into that single. And what a truly ground-breaking production it is, don't you agree?'

'It certainly is... a departure... from his other material, for sure. Hard to describe really. But it clearly struck a chord with the public. Anyway... the reason I'm calling is obvious. Gary isn't answering his phone. Hasn't for some time now. With his new-found success, Gary's fans and the general public will be expecting him to do a round of interviews to discuss the single and tell his fans about the journey he's taken to get it out. What do you say I get to do the first interview with him? I'm talking about the nation's number one music channel after all, Spike.'

'You need to—'

'I can do it by person or by video link. I'm easy either way. With his fame about to explode, I'd say world-wide, the timing is perfect. Don't you agree? The interview will be a fantastic promotion. Win-win, I reckon.'

Spike sucked a breath, 'I hear what you're saying. But, Tony, you're no doubt aware that Gary's been doing cold turkey at his home for the last few weeks. He's shut himself away from the heartless world that treated him so cruelly. Everyone turned on him at a time when was incredibly fragile. He wasn't shown the slightest mercy. Right now, he is totally focussed on making a full recovery.'

'Sure, I know he's going cold turkey. He must be hurting bad. But won't that make him want to jump at the chance to promote his new single even more... his first entry into the charts in more than two years... by agreeing to an interview with me. Just a short interview will do.'

Spike sucked a deeper breath. He couldn't tell the guy to piss off, as much as he ached to. Should Hits 1,2,3 stop playing the single… No. He had to offer the guy some crumbs.

'If I get to be first cab off the rank,' Tony droned, 'I'll make it well worth his while. Like I said, I won't keep him long. Trust me; I'll present him in a positive light. We'll talk about his big hit, then briefly move on to how he's dealing with his drug addiction. I realise that might be awkward for him, but I'll be empathetic.'

'Tony; by all means report to your listeners and viewers that Gary hasn't touched drugs for weeks. He hasn't even taken an aspirin. True. As for an interview. Hmm. Afraid not. Sorry. Gary's not ready to front up to the public yet. Not just because his health is delicate right now. Understand that he still thinks you people in the media are shit. Or have you forgotten the hatchet job you people did on him?'

'Okay, we were tough on him, yes. Look, Spike, we couldn't turn a blind eye, could we?' Tony drew breath. 'He kept disgracing himself. In pubs, clubs, shopping centres. That crazy road-rage incident. We had to report them. He's been banned from so many places. He's lost his license. How he dodged jail time is a matter of conjecture. What could he expect?'

You guys don't know the half of it, Spike thought. He had to bust his arse (and his wallet) to keep some of the Popsicle's worst excesses hidden.

Tony wasn't done. 'Spike; accept that Gary went way off the rails. I promise I won't dwell on those events in the interview. Hey; I think it's great that he's taken the plunge. I applaud him. His encouragement can be a true inspiration to others facing the same challenges. That's how I plan to end the interview.'

Would the media treat the Popsicle with compassion? Any praise would surely be fleeting. Readers and viewers crave for stories of infamy. Gary Fortune's obituary would be already prepared.

'You know what, Spike? I reckon Gary's notoriety contributed to the success of his new single. It made people curious about where he is right now in his life.'

Tony would have flinched if he'd seen the glare on Spike's face, reflected in the mirror. 'Maybe. But there's no way he'll change his mind. I'm telling you now; he will not talk to you people. No way. Going cold turkey is a very tough battle. He needs his space. Free from hassles. My task at the present time is to make sure he gets to concentrate on his battle. His ex-wife, Julie, is helping. Yes, Julie. There's some breaking news for you; the two of them are seeing one another again. Have been for a couple of weeks now.'

'Really!' Tony was incredulous. His outburst had Spike jerking the phone away from his ear. 'After such a spiteful bust up?'

'Yep, it's true. There's a scoop for you. Gary decided to go cold turkey after he finally took a good, long hard look at his excesses. He had to admit that he'd hurt many people dear to him. Me included, I tell you. But Julie especially. He confessed his misdeeds to her, got on his knees and begged her to forgive him. As you'd expect, Julie was reluctant at first. But, in time, she relented. Now, she's become his rock during this challenging time. Of course, he's also getting professional help from a doctor. Who wishes to remain anonymous by the way. Please respect that wish. I'll look on you more favourably if you do.'

Tony sighed. 'Okay, Spike, how about you give me a short grab with Gary instead? You do the interview and send it to me. That way you have full control over the content. I only need a short grab for the time being. What do you say?'

'Sorry. No. Get it into your skull, Tony. He's bitter and disillusioned with the world. He feels rejected. Abandoned. He blames you people for encouraging his recklessness. There's some truth in that. And he's pissed off that not one of his hangers-on bothered to offer a steadying hand when he badly needed it. So, for now, Gary's music... and Julie, of course, are the only two things that matter to him on his long, rough road to recovery. Report that to the public.'

'But—'

'Got to go, Tony. Sorry. Busy day ahead. Lot's happening. I'll be in touch when and if circumstances change. Okay?'

'But can I—'

Spike ended the call. He switched the phone off, swore and looked at the mirror again. 'This is going to test me big time. But Jesus! Number one! Who the hell would have guessed? Cash registers must be going absolutely berserk. Damn it! I'm not stopping until I get what I deserve.'

As he dressed, Spike figured a way to get the wolves off the trail for a while. He would write a media release on behalf of... Gary Fortune. The wording would be straight-forward. Am deeply honoured. And humbled. (Humbled? Gary? Hell, some might fall for it.) Thanks to the fans who stuck with me. Who never stopped believing in me. Crap like that. It'd take an hour, tops. He'd done it before. The media release wouldn't appease the wolves for long, though. He'd need other ideas. But, bugger it, he was going for broke.

⁜

S pike drove his seven-year-old gold (coloured) Mercedes to Gary Fortune's house. The dwelling itself was a nondescript orange-brick affair in the suburbs. The rock star had bought it (on mortgage) after the messy divorce had decimated his finances. The house had three simple bedrooms, one of which had been converted into a small recording studio. That room, as well as the entire outside of the house, had been soundproofed. The house block was surrounded by a high, light-grey concrete-brick fence, topped by razor wire and equipped with security cameras. They were Spike's recent touches. The building was surrounded by neglected lawns and gravel paths, ensuring the security cameras had an unhindered view of the yard.

When Spike got out of his car, he found two photographers and a couple of journos peeking through the tall, black wrought-iron front gate. The heavy, fawn-coloured drawn curtains offered those gathered nothing. Slasher and his equally big mate stood, tight-lipped and tattooed arms crossed, on the other side of the gate. The press spotted Spike and jostled to take his photo. Over the years, he'd perfected his pose of casual distain. Then came the questions, delivered with the energy of a semiautomatic. 'How has Gary responded to his single reaching number one?' 'Can he come out and have a word with us?'

'I'm about to see him. My guess is that he'll be quite laid-back about it.' He grinned. 'Expect a press release around lunchtime.'

'Ask him to come out for a couple of photos. Please Spike.'

Slasher opened the gate and glowered at those gathered. Spike rushed through, ignoring the questions and requests hurled at him. He sped inside the house, locking the door behind him.

Spike stepped into the garish, red-and-black walled loungeroom. A screen on the wall showed images projected from the six security cameras around the property. He found Harry, small and chubby and dressed in a well-worn blue suit, looking harassed, his face ruddier than usual. 'Been fielding many calls, Harry?'

Harry sighed. 'It got nuts, Spike. Had to take the phone off the hook. My mobile's off now as well. I figured we need to work out how we're going to deal with the extra unexpected attention.'

'Good man. My phone's off too. No great problem. I'm refining our plan. The key is; tell them only what we agreed.'

'You want to stick to the strategy?' Harry wrung his hands, anxious.

'Oh yes. We're about to be showered by riches beyond our wildest dreams, Harry. So, yes, we must stick to the strategy. Hell... we've earned it.' Harry's long face showed that he didn't seem convinced. 'Don't you agree?'

Harry winced. 'I understand your logic. But Spike, how can we keep the media at bay? Some will stop at nothing to get to Gary.'

'I know. I know.' Spike fanned down Harry's doubts. 'First thing; tell Slasher and his mate they'll get a big bonus when this challenging time is all over. That'll make sure they clam up. Not that Slasher would blab. Someone needs to monitor the security cameras twenty-four seven. Our priority right now is to buy time. Keep strictly on message. Tell the sticky-beaks that the Popsicle is still disillusioned with the whole planet. He's isolating. And needs his space. Tell everyone to listen to his single. If they do, they'll detect the depth of his cynicism and his disillusionment with the world.'

Harry looked at Spike, puzzled. 'You can work that out, listening to the song? Seems like he's just rambling to me. With some special musical effects tossed in.'

Spike tut-tutted. 'Of course, the single is a heap of trash, Harry. Self-indulgent, incoherent, unadulterated trash! True to form for Gary Fortune.' He shook his head. 'I'm just reiterating our official take on the song. Get it?'

'Oh, right. Love the video, though. The Popsicle dancing around that ugly industrial estate, under the dim streetlights.'

Spike grinned. 'He wasn't dancing. That was him walking home, totally off his brain. Computer enhanced and edited, of course. Julie filmed it from the back of a car when their divorce was raging. She intended to use it, with other footage, as blackmail for the divorce settlement. But after his lawyers saw a sample of her accumulated material, they went belly-up quick-smart.'

'I have to say that Tim is a genius. The way he put together that video is truly remarkable.'

Spike pursed his lips. 'Tim is most certainly multitalented, Harry. How he faked the times when the Popsicle opened his mouth to spew so as to make it look like he was bursting into song is incredible. After spewing, the Popsicle collapsed in the gutter. None of that made it to the video, of course. Talking about Tim, I need to speak to him urgently. We must get a follow-up hit out the door, Harry. Pronto. Is he here?'

'Yep. He agreed, but it took a quick chat with Slasher over the phone to… err… convince him. He's in the recording studio.'

'Good. As he's working on the new track, you and I will need to promote Gary's first two albums. We have to grasp this golden opportunity to claw-in whatever income we can get our hands on. Especially with our time likely to be short.'

Harry gazed at Spike with admiration. 'You're always one step ahead, Spike. One thing, though. You know what? I thought Tim would be over the moon, with the praise the recording and the video are attracting. State of the art, the media are describing it. But he seems quite depressed.'

'No problem.' Spike smirked. 'I'll cheer him up. Before I do, though, give me the keys to the pantry.'

Harry recoiled. 'Why? Is that wise with Tim in the house?'

'I'll keep the door locked behind me. I'm feeling a heap of gratitude towards our Gary Fortune right now. You and me are about to get a deserved reward after he blew all that cash to buy that supposedly newly discovered diamond finds in… that place.'

'Lake Cobb. It's in Western Australia. Even the most rudimentary research would have shown there are no diamonds there. It's a barren wasteland in the middle of nowhere. The lake is dry much of the time. Gary had to be off his head when he signed the deed papers.'

'Of course, he was. Fucking idiot! Anyway, hand me the keys.'

Harry hesitated. Reluctantly, he reached into his pocket and pulled out a set of keys. He used one to open a drawer in a cupboard. From that drawer, he took out another key, went to a drawer beneath a small work bench, and unlocked it. From that drawer, he produced a key and handed it to Spike. 'Bring it straight back.'

'Sure. I always do.'

Clutching the key tightly, Spike snuck past the recording studio to a nondescript wooden door. After glancing around to be sure no one was watching, he unlocked it. He stepped inside the unlit pantry and hastily locked the door behind him. The varnished wooden shelves in the narrow room were almost empty; since the divorce, no one had bothered to re-stock it. The last of the wine and spirits had been plundered a month ago, and the beer weeks before that. Much of the room was taken up by an industrial-sized freezer, humming softly. Spike checked the temperature inside it and nodded. All was as it should be. He wiped the moisture off the lid of the freezer and gazed inside.

'Hello, Popsicle,' he said to the emaciated body, still in the red robe, with matching slippers, from the day he died. 'You look terrible.'

The body was lying face up inside the freezer, the exposed skin an awful purple and black. The cadaver had dark, sunken eyes and sunken cheeks. His collar-length dyed blonde hair was a myriad of tangled icicles. The Popsicle's arms were flayed against the sides of the freezer. He was curled up at the knees; otherwise, he would not have fitted inside.

'Got some great news for you. You're number one in the charts. Who could have believed that a third-rate, drug-crazed has-been could have pulled that off? Well, it wasn't because of your input, was it? Tim's the miracle worker. You might have stuffed up bad with that land deal in Western Australia but you fluked it when you bought the rights to that sound-mixing program. It's worked a treat. The public love the new single…

don't ask me why... Just shows what a bunch of idiots they are. But it's whether they get drawn in that matters, isn't it? Congratulations, you useless bastard!'

Spike didn't linger. After tapping the cover of the freezer and giving the cadaver the thumbs up, he left the room, careful to hastily lock the door behind him. He handed the key to a pensive Harry who began the process of placing each key in its rightful place.

Spike made a beeline to the recording studio. He found Tim sitting on a swivel seat, looking absently at YouTube on his laptop. Tim was dwarfed by banks of computers on benches and recording equipment. He was a short, slender lad in his mid-twenties who wore a haunted expression on his pale face. His short, black hair was unkempt. Tim wore thick, black-rimmed spectacles.

There was a faint smell of paint; the black walls and ceiling had needed many sky-blue coats before the black no longer seeped through. Gary, no doubt off his brain, never took notice of the change of colour. He enjoyed the smell, though.

Smiling, Spike reached out his hand, which made the young man recoil. The lad looked at Spike with trepidation. 'Tim, it's great to see you again. You've heard the fabulous news, eh? Gary's hit has reached number one on the charts.' He fist-pumped the air.

Tim shifted uncomfortably. 'Mr Hargraves told me over the phone.' He took a breath. 'He also told me that you want a follow-up hit.' The young man shook his head, tight-lipped.

'That's how this business operates, Tim. When things fall your way, you build upon the successes. You can't delay. The track you produced for Gary, and the video, are being acclaimed as state-of-the-art, I've been told. You've given us a fantastic platform for taking the next step. Yes, by producing another single.' He smiled.

Tim's chest heaved and he glanced at his feet. 'I don't want to do any more work for Gary.'

'What do you mean you don't want to?' Spike snorted. 'We paid you well, didn't we? And, with the song hitting number one, you're in for a big, fat bonus. You deserve it Tim. Really, you do.' He placed his hands on his hips and stared hard at the idle recording equipment. 'All I want you to do is produce one more song. Just one. You don't need to go to much trouble. No need for a video. Why is that a problem for you?'

Tim gritted his teeth. 'You have no idea what I went through to get that song out. I kept telling you it was wrecking my health, but you wouldn't listen. You didn't give a shit about me.' He looked about to burst into tears.

'That's being a bit harsh, Tim.' Spike sat on the corner of a table beside the young man.

'Oh, I don't think so,' said Tim, shaking his head. 'The tracks Gary handed me were the product of a slurred, drug-fuelled psychosis. I had to sift through so much rubbish to select a few bits that were barely usable. Then I had to hammer those fragments into some sort of shape, tone down the weirdness, and infuse the program with computer-simulated analyses of rhythms from The Beatles and The Stones. It was the only way to get Gary's song into some semblance of being musical. Even then, my ordeal wasn't finished. I had to go through the track syllable by syllable to hammer the vocals into some sort of coherent shape.'

'And what you did was sheer brilliance, Tim.' Spike beamed. 'All you need to do now is the same thing one more time. Like I said, no need to go to as much trouble. Gary's fans will snap up anything.'

Tim opened his mouth to protest. Spike lifted his finger; he hadn't finished. 'It's always easier the second time around.'

'Look, Spike, there isn't enough of Gary's material left that's even remotely usable. And that's saying something.'

'Use whatever bits you can. Blend in some stuff from of his first two albums. His first album is not all that bad. The track can represent him revisiting his past when his life was simpler. Mix in consolidated sounds from a couple of other groups. Amalgamate it all in your special program like you did before. Then, before you know it, you've got another single.'

Tim's mouth twisted into a snarl. 'It's not that easy, Spike. Last time you convinced Gary to redo a few lines. Remember how you pinned him against the wall to get him to agree? But what he did was still crap. I only got a couple of grabs from it.'

'But it helped.'

'A little bit, yes. Look, Spike, I'll tell you again. Listen to me. There were too many days when I slept on the floor here, totally spent. Lots of times I couldn't sleep at all. When I finished the track, I was a mental wreck. As for making a new single, Mr Hargraves told me that Gary isn't even prepared to make any new inputs whatsoever. That's insane!' Tim slammed the table beside him with his fist. 'How can you expect me to do something for you under such impossible circumstances? If you want a recording engineer… not me… to work on a new single, you'll need to drum it into Gary's head that he needs to offer some new, remotely usable material.'

Spike wondered what sound the Popsicle's frozen head would make if he drummed on it. 'I'm offering you twice the money I did the first time. For something that only needs to be half as good.'

Tim looked at Spike's face, visibly becoming distressed. But underlying the young man's expression, was… possibly… the faintest look of interest. Or maybe that emerged from Spike's imagination. If Tim was smart, surely he'd be acutely aware that a dork like him needed heaps of money to get women to show the remotest interest in him. 'I'll only consider… consider making the track if you can get Gary to co-operate. Much more than he did before. If he's breaking free from his drug-taking like I've been told, surely, he'll be amenable to contributing more. If he refuses, I'm out of here.'

Spike fixed the sound recordist in the face. 'I fully acknowledge the torture you went through. But it was my firm belief at the time that it was best that I shouldn't interfere with the thought processes of a genius. Didn't I make the right decision?' he said, almost as a plea. 'The end result proves I made the right call. What you achieved is the music equivalent of the Sistine Chapel, Tim. That is why Gary, and I, have total faith in your ability to produce this new song, without his input.'

'That's nuts. Why won't he help me out?' Tim's face was contorted in exasperation.

'He figures his genius is already out there in his tracks. All it needs is for you to bring it out and present it to the public.'

Tim's jaw fell, incredulous. 'You call his contribution genius? You're delusional.'

'Tim, you're a technician. Don't get me wrong. You're a damned good one. But you obviously don't fully appreciate Gary's subtle genius. I, as his manager and promoter, am able to recognise that genius, even if you can't. Have a go at a new single. I prefer you do it, rather than having to find someone second rate.'

'No way, Spike! I won't do it. No!'

Spike became conciliatory. He smiled and stroked his chin. 'Why don't you go home and think about it overnight? I'm happy to talk generous terms with you.'

Tim jutted out his small chin. 'No. My answer is no. No!'

'All I'm asking you is to think about it. That's all.' Spike shrugged, palms out.

Tim glared at him.

Spike opened the door. 'Tell you what. Just bring me the track by this time early next month.' He shut the door behind him, leaving the recording engineer wide-eyed, mouth agape.

Spike stepped back into the loungeroom. Harry looked up from his chair. 'How did you go with Tim?'

'He'll do the track, Harry. There are ways to convince him if he drags his heels. Right!' He clapped his hands. 'Next item. Is Julie coming in again today?'

'She's already here. If you want to chat to her, and I think you should, she's resting in the main bedroom. I told her to not leave the room until Tim has gone. She understands that Tim must not find out about Gary.'

'Good. I'll talk to her.' Spike hesitated. He lifted a curtain by a couple of inches and pressed his face close to the window. A minute later, the front door slammed. He watched as Tim rushed to the front gate, then out on the footpath, with his laptop and a briefcase. The media people surrounded him. Their body language revealed their disappointment. A shrugging Tim had nothing to tell them. And who gives a damn about a recording engineer, even one who had staked his claim as a genius? The lad stepped around the scrum and walked briskly down the road.

Satisfied that the coast was clear, Spike wandered over to the main bedroom. He barged in without knocking to find Julie lying full-length on the bed, watching a soap opera on a flat-screen TV.

'God, you're a rude bastard, Spike,' she hissed. 'You think you can just barge in like this.' Julie was in her early thirties. Six years before, she still turned heads whenever she entered a room. But years of Gary's excesses had taken its toll. She'd put on weight; her rouged face was puffed up. Her peroxided hair only partially covered the brown underneath. The gleam in her eyes had dimmed. 'It's bad enough having that scary guy with the tattoos stalking around the house.'

'Oh, him. Don't fret; that's Slasher.'

'He ducks through the nearest door whenever I come across him.'

'He's very shy.'

'Shy? With a name like Slasher.'

'Oh, that's just us having a little bit of fun with him. Actually, he wouldn't hurt a lamb.'

'Well… he looks really mean. He scares me. Anyway, what do you want? You're not one for courtesies,' she said, sour-faced.

Spike wrung his hands and spoke briskly. 'Sorry for barging in, Julie. But I'm juggling a lot of balls. More than I'd like to. The Popsicle's song getting to number one is great news but it means I'm having to fend off more pressure than I'd anticipated. It's important that I sort out something with you.'

'Oh?' Julie looked at him with suspicion. 'What?'

'I should have asked you first but, this morning I

started a rumour that you and... Gary... are back together.'

'What?' Julie became wide-eyed, dumbfounded. 'Are you joking? That's crazy. You said that without asking me?'

'Yes. I've gone as far as claiming that the two of you have been together for weeks.'

Julie's eyes bulged. 'Ridiculous! What the hell are you trying to pull off?' she demanded.

Spike was unfazed. 'I'm trying to keep the media at bay, Julie. So, I'm spreading a story that you spend a lot of time at his house. Usually, you sneak in, unseen. You're giving him support as he grapples with his agonising struggle to free himself from the scourge of drugs. And, miraculously, the time you have spent with him has rekindled the love between the two of you. He has pleaded with you for forgiveness. He seemed genuinely remorseful. Look Julie; just go along with it, okay. It will be worth your while and mine if you do.'

Julie glared at Spike, indignant. 'But I hate his guts. Alive or dead.'

'That hardly matters, does it? Just concentrate on the here and now.'

When Julie left her rock-star beau for good, the guy went berserk. His rage became incendiary when handed the divorce papers. Julie did him over good. No one would disagree that she deserved what she gouged out of him. It ended up with Gary needing a mortgage to move to his current, modest, house. Julie kept the flash house. In a fit of drug-induced psychosis, he had all the rooms in his new abode, except one, painted with dark or garish colours, with some uncomplimentary words scrawled on a few walls. Yet, he'd had the main bedroom painted lilac, Julie's favourite colour.

Perhaps a semblance of humanity still remained in his heart.

'Why should I go along with you?' Julie pressed.

'Self-interest, Julie. I'm talking about getting you a better deal with his estate. Your only hope of getting a slice of the cake is if your relationship with the Popsicle is seen to be re-ignited.'

Julie frowned. She slammed her fist on the bed. 'Spike; Let's get something straight. I might hate him but he's not a Popsicle.'

Spike slapped his thigh in annoyance. 'Would you feel better if I shoved a stick up his arse?'

Julie's hands formed into fists. 'He's a human being, Spike.'

Spike bristled. 'He's dead, Julie. He was a crap human being when he was alive. Nobody knows that more than you. Okay, I'll call him Gary, if that makes you feel better. Look, if we push this romance angle, we keep the press off our backs for a bit longer. And throw a spanner in Gary's parents' plan to get control over his estate, like they've been trying to do. Understand; if they do get control, they'll close down Gary Fortune Music. So, no more income for me, for Harry, and your payments will end as well. That's why we need to keep Gary alive for the time being. It would help if you play your part and tell whoever asks that you and Gary are together again. Do you see where I'm going with this?' He gazed hard at her.

She nodded. 'Okay. I see your point. But I still can't believe you've kept him in that freezer for weeks.'

A memory flashed before Spike. Julie had dropped into the house to retrieve some appliance she believed was kept in the pantry. Gary had been missing for five days, which was alarming but not unusual. He and Julie had stepped into the pantry together. And there was the Popsicle, lying in the industrial freezer. Julie had run out of the room screaming. Spike stood there, frozen. But not frozen in the way the figure before him was. It had been Harry who had held Julie tight in the lounge room until her screams turned into tears. And then into sobs.

Spike sighed. 'Like I said at the time, Julie, I wasn't the one who put him there. You and I found him. Remember. I'm prepared to swear to that fact on a stack of fivers.'

'Can I believe you? You lie all the time.'

'I'm the manager of a rock star,' Spike said, with hands on hips. 'Of course, I lie all the time. But I wasn't lying then. And I'm not lying now.'

'But you decided to keep him in the freezer.'

'Sure. It was a very tricky situation. When he'd gone missing, I tried his phone lots of time, I phoned you, checked his usual haunts and his hangers-on. I tell you, when I saw him there in the freezer, I nearly pissed myself.'

'I know you. All you're trying to do is keep your precious gravy train from crashing.'

'That's true, yes, Julie. Not only that but think about it. If I'd brought in the cops, it would have been very tricky to explain. And, if his death was made public back then, we'd all be shafted by now by Gary's parents. Yes, you too, Julie.'

Julie stiffened. 'His parents always hated me. And I hated them back! They were nasty to me. Bastards! And there was me doing everything I could to get Gary on the straight and narrow. I nursed him back onto his feet so many times.' She was verging on tears.

'Exactly. And how did he reward you? And how did he reward me for all the things I did for him as well? He laughed in our faces, that's how. He bragged to his mistresses and hangers-on how we were running around after him like demented slaves. And he bragged about how clever he was when he hid from us when he was out of his brain.'

Julie sucked in an angry breath. 'He was never going to change. Oh sure, he promised over and over that he would. Hand on his heart. But he was bullshitting me. Even when the magistrates demanded he go to a clinic, he'd escape a day later.'

Spike pressed his advantage. 'Exactly Julie. With the success of the new single, can't you see why we need to keep Gary alive, so to speak, for as long as we can. Gary Fortune Music is about to be flooded by cash. The alternative is that his parents get the lot.'

'But how long will you keep him in the freezer?'

'I'm thinking the end of the year. Maybe. Depends on how the royalties are flowing in.'

Julie was puzzled. 'How do you plan to announce his death?'

Spike became evasive. 'I've got some ideas. Best I don't tell you. So, like I said, we keep Gary alive for now. We make lots of cash from the new single. And maybe from another single we're planning. Think about it. How would you cover the bills with your payments cut off?'

Julie became quizzical. 'So, I'm getting a cut from his single?'

Spike shook his head. 'Any increase in your allowance would need to be approved by Gary. Getting that approval at present will be highly problematic.'

'That's not fair!' Julie growled. 'I deserve a better share. The allowance I get barely covers my essential bills.'

Spike glared at her. 'It's not possible, Julie. Maybe you shouldn't have such expensive habits. Your settlement money should have set you up for the rest of your life. But no. You've spent… what? Well over a hundred thousand on plastic surgery and beauty treatments alone.' He glared at her. 'What a bloody huge waste of money that was.'

Julie gaped, offended. 'You have no idea of the trauma I went through being Gary's wife. His drug-induced psychosis, his wild temper, the affairs, the all-night drinking and drug-taking, me having to go out all hours to find him and try to bring him home. I forked out bail money. Bribes. It wore me down, Spike. I'll never get over it. I still get nightmares.'

Spike bowed his head. 'I'm sorry I said what I did, Julie. I know how tough it was for you. All the things you did, I had to do as well.'

'No, Spike, you have no idea what it was like for me. I had to act as his dutiful wife. I had to stand beside my man and make crap excuses for him over and over. It was me who had to nurse him when he was more dead than alive. And there was him, yelling abuse at me. Cheating on me. Not giving a damn. It was all one big charade for him.' A tear formed under an eye.

'I know, Julie. I'm sorry. Look; I'm under pressure. I want to do what's best for us all, financially. Realise that I'm the one taking the biggest risk by keeping Gary alive.'

Julie nodded. 'Okay. I'll go along with your plan. For now. But it's risky for me as well. What am I supposed to tell the press?'

'Just tell them you're spending a lot of time with him. You've fallen in love with him again. He's off the drugs and alcohol. His health is improving. Slowly. He has his bad moments. That's to be expected. There's colour in his face again. Just don't tell them what colour.'

Julie gave a shrug. 'What if the drug-dealer guy who put Gary in the freezer contacts the police?'

'He's gone missing.'

Julie blinked. 'Missing? Do you know where he's gone?'

'Vanished without trace, Julie. Most likely to never be found. Forget him. You and me have a lot more important things to keep us occupied. And we need to keep our wits about us. Be very careful what you tell the press. Don't chat to them for any length of time.'

'I won't be able to keep this up for long, Spike.'

'I don't know if I can either. But, for now, stick to my plan. We might get Gary's parents to negotiate a cut from his estate for you, to keep you from taking them to court. Can't guarantee anything. But if all goes well you might end up being able to build your dream home overlooking Lake Cobb in sunny Western Australia.'

Julie went sooky, like a five-year-old. 'You're not funny, Spike.'

Spike sat on the bed. 'I'm trying my best for both of us, Julie. You know what's a pity, though? If you'd had a child, the estate would be passed over to you as guardian.'

'Yes, I know. I so much wanted to have a child.' Julie looked downcast.

He snapped his fingers. And again. 'Julie, I've got an idea. Tell me to get stuffed if I offend you. But consider this.' He took a stance before her. 'Why don't you go and get pregnant while Gary is still alive? So to speak. That'll be proof that you and him are back together.

And, more importantly, you'll produce an heir to his estate.'

'But Gary never preserved his sperm. He was paranoid that he'd get paternity claims one day.'

Spike snorted. 'Yes, I know. Umm… there is another way…' He took a breath.

Julie eyed him intently. 'Are you suggesting…?'

'I'm not suggesting anything, Julie. I only ask that you consider the positives of having a baby. The child inherits the estate. With you as guardian. Surely there's a couple of guys you fancy. I bet a few of them would leap at the prospect of having it off with Gary's missus.'

Julie stiffened. She became lost in her thoughts for a few seconds, then licked her lips. 'Well, there are a couple…'

Spike's mood lifted. 'That's the spirit, Julie. Great time too, to get pregnant, with Christmas parties and New Year's Eve just around the corner.'

'What if someone challenges the baby's paternity. And demands a test?'

'We'll rip them to shreds in the media. Think about it. How despicable would it be to seek a paternity test on the child of a loving partner and a father who has only recently passed away?'

Julie's eyes gleamed. 'You're right, Spike. What more noble way can a woman declare her love for her man than to have his child?'

'Absolutely, Julie.' Spike pumped his fist. 'I'll leave you to work out the details. Right now, I have some other business to attend to. Be sure to pop into the house regularly. Stay some nights. Make sure you're seen by the photographers outside the gate. Let them film you opening the front door with a key. Talk to them from time to time. Don't dwell. Just crap on about how

Gary is making progress. And, especially, how much in love you are.'

'Spike, I'm worried. We might end up getting thrown in jail.'

'Not if we all work together. Think about it. If you don't go along with my plan, we walk away from Gary Fortune Music with only the shirts on our backs.'

Julie leaned forward, looking determined. 'Okay. I'll give it my best try.'

Spike grunted and smiled. 'You're a real trooper, Julie.'

He left the room. So far, so good.

In the loungeroom, Harry beckoned Spike over. He whispered in Spike's ear. 'Doctor Jones has sent in an email. He wants to know whether you're still refusing to let him check up on his patient.'

Spike snorted. 'He can't come into the house. Isn't that obvious?'

Harry glared at him, indignant. 'Of course, I'm well aware of why. I brought it up is because Jones wants us to cough up for the two consultations we've cancelled.'

'No problem. Send him the cash.'

'But that's not all. He's nervous. Remember the document you got him to sign stating he examined the Popsicle two days before he died, and that he found his patient to be in reasonable health but in need of being regularly monitored.'

'Yes, reasonable health. That's what he signed.'

'Jones says he's since become very concerned. He hasn't seen or heard from the Popsicle since that day.'

'Obviously.'

'He wants to get in touch with Gary immediately. He suggested a video call to begin with. What should we do, Spike?'

Spike shrugged. 'That depends, Harry. But the Popsicle will be kept alive and out of sight until… January.'

Harry stared at Spike, agape. 'January! Jesus! Are you out of your mind? We'll rot in jail for sure. We can't possibly get away with it.'

'Harry, we're talking about income. Truckloads of income.' He rubbed his hands. 'Besides, I made a special deal with the Popsicle, remember. I get an extra cut in the royalties to cover the expenses of doing the single. But I only get it if he's alive.'

Harry gave Spike a knowing smile. 'That was very generous of him to offer you that deal.'

'Enough of your sarcasm, Harry. I've earned every penny I'm about to get.'

'Well, if that's your plan, there's a major complication. Doctor Jones told me that, should you refuse to allow him to examine his patient, he wants a cut of the revenue and for you to issue a disclaimer. Otherwise, he'll go to the authorities and state that he believes the Popsicle is being held here against his will. And is being denied receiving vital medical treatment.'

'He wants a cut? Suits me. Get Slasher and his mate to go see Doctor Jones. They can negotiate just how big a slice the good doctor would like to get.'

'That's a bit drastic.'

'No other option, Harry. There are too many hangers-on as it is. I'm the one paying these people. We have to put a lid on it. As for right now, I need to put together a sugar-coated press release from the… ahem… talented and so very grateful Gary Fortune.'

Harry looked at Spike, his eyes filled with admiration. 'There's nobody even remotely like you, Spike.'

'That's the absolute truth, Harry.'

'Just understand; I'm uncomfortable about this.'

Spike wasn't listening. He clicked his fingers. 'I've just got another great idea. I need to speak to Julie again.'

He ran to the bedroom door, this time pausing to knock before going inside. Julie wasn't there. He found her in the pantry, looking down on the Popsicle, hands clasped at her chest. She had demanded having her own key to the pantry from Harry. Spike had not been pleased at the gesture. Julie had switched the light on. Being bathed in light did not suit the cadaver's complexion.

He sidled up beside her. 'I've just had another idea that I'd like you to consider Julie.'

She eyed him suspiciously. 'I'm not sure I want to hear it.'

'I think you should. Just listen. You and Gary went on a holiday in an expensive resort on the south coast of Spain, two years or so ago, didn't you?'

A wide smile crossed Julie's face as she turned her gaze to the cadaver. 'Yes, I remember it well. We had a fantastic time. The good times pretty well ended after we got back.'

'You had photos taken of the two of you when you were there, yes?'

'Yes.' Julie frowned, suspicious. 'Why do you ask?'

'How would you like to go to the same resort again? As a reward.'

'Just me?'

'No. You'll fly there with Slasher's son. In a private plane, travelling incognito after dusk. Don't worry; once you check in to the resort, he'll go and stay in a cheap pension. The guy is roughly the same build as Gary. He can pass if he's wearing a good disguise. Dark glasses, hat and stuff. He'll keep mostly out of sight. Leave the arrangements to Harry and me.'

'What's this all about?' Julie scowled at Spike.

'Here's my plan. At the resort you get some photos taken of you. In the same spots where you and Gary hung out. When you get back, we'll do some Photoshopping using snaps of Gary from two years ago. He looks the same as he did then.' Emaciated. It was Julie who looked different. 'We'll release the photos to the media. They'll lap it up. The photos should keep the bastards off our tails for a while.' Hopefully, Doctor Jones as well.

Julie blinked, perplexed. 'But the people at the resort are sure to tell the press they never saw Gary.'

'Of course, they will,' said Spike, beaming. 'These flash resorts always deny celebrities have stayed there. If they're asked nicely.'

'It means taking another big risk, Spike.' But her expression suggested agreement.

'It'll all work out fine, Julie. Just be discrete. Trust me on this.'

'Trust you!' But her mood softened. 'Well… to tell the truth, a week at the resort will do me a power of good. I've been under too much stress for far too long.'

Spike shrugged. 'Great! You go there maybe next week. Sooner the better. But you can only stay for three days. You just need to get the photos done. We don't want to rack up too much unnecessary expense.'

Julie stamped her foot and screwed her face. 'If it's not five days, I won't go.'

Spike shut his eyes. Hopefully, Julie, who was gazing wistfully down upon the Popsicle, didn't hear what he whispered under his breath.

MID JANUARY

S pike's doorbell rang. It wasn't nine, so the visitor was no friend. He swore. Groaning, he lifted himself from his bed, Spike peered under the curtains. A new-model black car was parked across the road. The doorbell rang again. Twice. Mumbling, he donned his dressing gown and sauntered to the front door. On the doorstep stood an unsmiling, clean-cut young man dressed in an expensive black suit, neatly pressed white shirt and thin black tie. The man hugged a large orange envelope to his chest. 'Good morning, Spike. You know why I'm here. I'm—'

'I know who the fuck you are. What do you want?' As if he didn't know.

The man pressed the envelope into Spike's chest. 'I'm here to present you with these documents. By the way, my colleague in the car on the other side of the road is taking a video of our interaction.'

'Couldn't give a shit.'

'For the record, I have just served you with legal documents, countersigned by a judge, demanding that you produce Gary Fortune for the purposes of being medically assessed and interviewed by independent experts acting on behalf of Mr Fortune's parents. As we have stressed to you for some time now, we are deeply concerned that Mr Fortune may be being held against his will or is otherwise incapacitated and in need of professional intervention. If you don't present him to us, we have been granted legal access, under a police escort, to gain entry into his house, or any other place he may be, and take him away to be assessed. You and your lawyers have exhausted all avenues to further delay proceedings.'

Spike shrugged, nonchalant. He lifted the envelope above his head to show it to the man in the black car. 'I'll tell you people again. We're not forcing Gary to do anything. If he walked outside, I wouldn't lift a finger to stop him. Honest.'

The young man sneered. 'We'll let the medical and legal experts decide on his physical and mental state. And whether he is capable of making his own decisions.'

'Julie will be pissed off big time when I tell her about your visit. She's been tending diligently to his every need for months. You must have seen the photos of Gary and her, now happily together again, holidaying in Spain. Don't you think they make a happy couple? But you don't give a damn, do you? You lot are hell bent on making them miserable.'

The clean-cut man met Spike's scowl with a smile. 'The photos did nothing to convince my clients of Mr Fortune's state of health. I repeat; we require him, in person, to prove to independent medical experts, that he is mentally competent. Realise that Mr Fortune's parents have not had any communication with their son since last September. He has not responded to their, or our, phone calls or to other written requests to make contact.

In fact, he hasn't contact anyone we are aware of for more than two months now. His parents are understandably very concerned about his welfare.'

'Can't they take a hint?' Spike said gruffly. 'He wants nothing to do with them. Gary despises them. They want to control him so they can get their grubby hands on his finances. They've been harassing him, and me, ever since the divorce.'

'Mr Fortune's erratic behaviour has greatly disturbed them for some considerable time. His escapades with drugs and alcohol are well documented. Their concerns are perfectly legitimate.'

'Gary put out a second single at Christmas. It's number twenty-six. Listen carefully to the underlying themes in it. The song condemns hard drugs and excessive alcohol, albeit expressed in his own, understated, way. Strains of his first album also come leaping out at the listener. It's Gary's way of admitting to the world how much he had strayed.'

The man in the black suit returned a bored expression. 'Whatever. I have presented you with these documents. As such, you and Mr Fortune are required to respond, in person, within twenty-four hours.' He glanced down at his watch. 'That is all. Good day, Spike.'

The man smiled formally and left.

'Blood-sucking bastard!' It had started to rain. Spike grinned as he watched the guy dash across the road to the car, drawing his jacket over his head.

Spike shut the door. He absently tossed the envelope on the carpet and tapped out a SMS to Harry.

After dressing, he drove to Gary Fortune's home. He paused at the front gate where five journalists were gathered, huddling from the teeming rain, beneath large, black umbrellas. They'd obviously been briefed about the court documents. None wanted to take his photo, so he didn't lower his umbrella. Each of the journos barked much the same questions. 'When will Gary Fortune step outside? Is he now going to front the media?'

Spike wasn't fazed. 'It appears he has no choice but to leave his home, despite him showing no inclination to face this uncaring world. Julie, his devoted partner, will be upset by this unwelcome intrusion into their lives.'

'When will he appear in public?' the wolves pressed, even as he spoke.

'That's a decision for him and Julie to make. Oh, by the way, what do you think of the statue that Gary set up on the front porch last week?' The white-clay statue, which stood in clear sight, depicted a seated old man, dressed in flowing robes. It was about a metre and a half in height.

A barrage of questions followed. Mostly about Gary Fortune's state of health and his first appearance. Spike selected the one he deemed the easiest to answer, though he needed to glance at a piece of paper from his pocket first. 'The statue is a copy, of course. It's of a guy called... if I remember correctly, Sophocles. Some ancient Greek guy who wrote some tragic stories. Gary feels as if the man was writing about his own life.'

'Does Gary identify with the plight of Heracles then?' said a young woman. There's always one smart arse in every crowd.

Spike was stumped. 'Dunno. That stuff is not my thing. Maybe try asking Gary.'

He ignored other questions fired at him, and strolled past Slasher and his big mate, dressed in thick raincoats that made them look even larger and more menacing than they were. As he approached the house, he heard a comment from the other side of the gate; 'it's like a prison.'

Spike stepped inside the house. 'It's time for the Popsicle to do a runner,' he said to Harry as he waved the orange envelope about in the lounge room. 'We have no choice and, besides, we seem to be losing the PR war. In a way, I'm glad. All this pretence has worn me down.'

Harry nodded gravely. 'Just as well the Socrates statue finally arrived.'

'Yes, it took its time bring delivered. It's of Sophocles, Harry. Anyway… we act tonight. You clear on what you need to do?'

'Sure. Place a cover over the statue under the pretence that Gary wants it removed before he steps outside. It reminds him too much of the pain he has endured for months now. And the pain of complying with the court papers.'

'Perfect. And then?'

'Me and Slasher will put the statue in its container at 3am, lights off, security cameras switched off, when no one can see us. We get the Popsicle out of the freezer and put the cover over him instead and leave him on the porch until the early morning. He's frozen solid so he should stay intact. When morning comes, Slasher and I will squeeze the Popsicle into the container with the statue. We load the container in a covered truck. Slasher and his mate drives to a boat waiting at a small, very isolated, pier. He'll have a couple of bags of quick-drying cement ready.'

'Great. What happens to the statue?'

'Slasher drops it off at your place.'

'Yep.' Spike nodded. 'That should eliminate any possibility of any awkward questions.'

Harry continued. 'Tonight I take a ladder to the side fence.'

'Using gloves.'

Harry looked offended. 'Of course, I'll use gloves the whole time. Then... after Slasher takes away Socrates—'

'Sophocles...'

Harry waved the comment away. 'Whoever. I climb the ladder and cut a segment of the razor wire on the side fence. I leave the ladder. Make a scrape on the wall and a leave couple of muddy foot marks as well. That should convince the police that the Popsicle has done a runner.'

'Perfect. Can't see how the plan can fail. Have you forgotten the shoes?'

'No, I haven't.' Harry glowered. 'I wear his shoes when I cut the wire. In case I leave behind some footprints in the dark. Particularly with this rain. The shoes get dropped off in a thick plastic bag, deep in a bin at a fast-food outlet.'

Spike clapped. 'Yep. You've got it. Gary Fortune will disappear and never be found. Guaranteed.' He spread his arms, letting the moment wash over him. 'My God! It's all about to end. At last. I'm going to make myself a stiff drink after I get that phone call from Slasher when he gets back to the pier. Maybe I'll have two or three.'

'Have one for me as well,' Harry growled. 'After all, it's me who's got to do the dirty work?'

'Harry; you're not being paid good money just so you can sit on your arse and monitor the security cameras, do the vacuuming, and fetch beers and tea and coffee for Slasher and his mate.'

Harry became sheepish. 'Okay, but I refuse to do anymore dirty work after this. One thing, with the Popsicle missing and not declared dead, won't we have to wait maybe years before his estate gets doled out?'

Spike grinned. He gave Harry a wink. 'Not a problem. Until the Popsicle is declared dead, with any luck, we all keep being paid. Sure, his parents will keep trying their damnedest to get their hands on his money. But we'll cross that bridge when we get to it. God, what an ordeal it's been, eh?' He snapped his fingers. 'Oh, is Julie here?'

Harry sucked a breath. 'Yes, she's here. As usual.'

'Great! The loyal, devoted partner. I better break the news to her.'

'Spike, I need to tell you; she's pregnant.'

Spike gave a fist-pump as he leapt into the air. 'Brilliant! She'll get to collect the Popsicle's estate when Gary Fortune is declared dead in absentia. It bodes well for our future as well, Harry. There's no way she'll reveal the true identity of the father of her child.' He grinned.

Harry sighed and looked at his feet.

Spike's grin faded. 'Why the look of concern, Harry? Nervous about tonight? Feeling relieved, maybe? Can't you see? The last piece of my plan has fallen neatly into place. Some claim Tim to be the genius. But I now stake my claim as the genuine, undisputed, genius amongst us. Please excuse me, Harry, I must phone my real-estate agent.' He moved towards the door.

'Don't get too far ahead of yourself, Spike. Let Julie say her piece first,' Harry announced with a sigh.

'You still can't bring yourself to relax, can you Harry?' Spike said calmly. 'I can handle Julie, no matter how she takes the news. It'll all be fine. You'll see. A couple of weeks after the Popsicle does a runner, I'll organise the release of an EP. We'll include the two singles, then add a re-mix and a live track as well as a re-issued single from his first album. It'll be just the perfect job for Tim after he gets discharged next week.'

'Like I said, don't get too far ahead of yourself, Spike. Talk to Julie.'

Spike shrugged. 'Of course. But my important phone call… comes first. Later, I'll put out a press release stating that Gary Fortune is preparing himself for the daunting task of fronting up to the world again. He'll heap praise on Julie, expressing his deep love for her. Then he'll have a swipe at the legal firm and his parents.'

He made his phone call from the recording studio. When it was done, he went in search of Julie with a spring in his step. She wasn't in the bedroom. He found her in the pantry, with the light on, looking down into the freezer, her eyes glistening. It was definitely time to dispose of the body. It was showing increasing signs of deterioration.

Spike approached her, adopting a sombre expression. 'Hi, Julie. I hope what I'm about to say doesn't come as a shock, but Gary has to leave the freezer later today. You'll need to say your farewells in the next couple of hours. Then go home.' He placed his hand gently on her shoulder.

Julie took a breath and stood tall, brave. 'Don't worry about me, Spike. I'm thinking positively about it. After all, I got to spend all this time with Gary while he's been lying there in the freezer. It's given us time to talk about all the pain and letdowns he caused me.'

'We?' Spike blinked.

'When he was alive, he'd yell at me whenever I complained. Or he'd storm out of the house and go ape.

Since he died, I've been able to get all my hurt off my chest, talking to him.'

Spike rolled his eyes. 'I'm happy for you. Now about—'

'But we also had our happy times together, Spike. Not just these couple of months.' An expression of rapture spread across her face. 'We've been remembering our holidays. Days by the seaside. The parties. And the outrageous celebrities we knew. Thinking back, we had many happy times, Spike.'

'I'm glad. For you both.' He broke into a wide grin. 'And I've also been told the excellent news; you're pregnant, Julie,' he said. 'More joy for you. And, as I told you back then, you'll produce that vital heir to claim Gary's estate.'

Julie burst into a smile. 'Yes, it is a joyful time.' But, almost immediately, her smile fell. She became more circumspect. 'But you might end up being disappointed with me.'

Spike blinked. 'Don't see how. Your pregnancy makes the inheritance a done deal. You should be thanking me. After all, it was my plan.'

Julie spoke, measuring her words carefully. 'It may still work out. I was careful to choose two married men to take to bed with me. I mean, married men are guaranteed to keep quiet about their playing around. But before those men...' She looked at the floor.

'What? Something happened before you bedded those guys?'

Julie hesitated. 'Remember when you sent me to the south coast of Spain?'

'Of course. The media went bananas over the photos we released.'

'Well... I went to a show in Malaga. There was a

band from Senegal playing. The lead singer rushed on stage, all bare-chested; his body so shiny, taught and trim. His thighs seemed about to burst through his shorts any second.'

Spike raised his hand. 'I'm catching an uncomfortable drift here Julie.'

'I'd had a bit to drink. He knew who I was. Later, we both got swept up in a moment of wild passion. Never have I—'

Spike raised his hand and Julie fell silent. 'I gather you didn't have time to fit a condom.'

Julie folded her arms at her midriff. 'Are you disappointed with me?'

'Jesus Julie!' Spike exclaimed. 'You did that. With the inheritance at stake? The child in your womb is supposed to be fathered by Gary. After you give birth to his child, you can have as many babies as you so desire. And who cares if those children are black, green, or blue. I wish you well, but—'

Julie became adamant. 'I don't care if the baby isn't white. I'm having this child. I've wanted a child for so many years and I'm not giving it up. Not for anything. It might not even be that singer's child. It's too early to be sure.'

Spike leaned against the pantry door. 'Well... all we can do is wait. Everything is up in the air until we know, Julie. As for right now, I need to go and work a few things out.' He half-smiled. 'Okay. Enjoy your child, Julie. It's what you've longed for. I'm happy for you. True.'

Julie gave a faint smile.

Spike wandered back into the recording studio. He slammed the wall and flopped onto one of the swivel chairs to lean back and stare at the one blank wall in the room. He remained, unmoving, and shut his eyes for many minutes. Then, slowly, he brought out his mobile phone and tapped some numbers.

'Hello, Bob. It's Spike again... I'm good, thanks. How's your day going? Good to hear. Look; I want to cancel the offer I made for that place in Essex. Yes... I'm deeply sorry. No, no, my mind is made up. I've decided to go and live in the Ilha de Tavira in Portugal instead. Went there two years ago. Loved it. The holiday did me so much good. Came back so relaxed. Should never have allowed myself to get sucked into this crap business again. Look, I'm fifty-five. I've been playing this game for way too long. I need to get the hell out before I totally lose my sanity and whatever's left of my soul. Do you have an office in the Ilha de Tavira by any chance? Didn't think you did, but I thought I'd ask. I'll send you an email straight away to confirm the cancelation. Yes, I'm certain I no longer want to buy the place. Like I said, I'm deeply sorry to do this to you... Thanks for being so understanding... Yes.'

Spike sighed. 'Bye. Yes. Bye.'

He leaned back in his seat and gazed at the blank wall. He noticed that the underlying dark paint had begun to seep through once more.

FROM LITTLE
ACORNS GROW

THE EXPERIMENT

Deborah Challen took her daughter by the hand, gave it a gentle, reassuring pat, and led her into a small, square, and softly lit, cream-coloured room. Three walls were bare; the fourth had a sizable one-way inward-viewing window. The girl needed some coaxing. It was the fourth time that twelve-year-old Jilly had been brought there. Years of visiting clinics and doctors had made her wary. Also, she did not like enclosed rooms. Lollipops, soft toys and many smiles usually eased her anxiety.

Jilly had Attention Deficit Syndrome. Her IQ was that of a six-year-old. The young girl was thick set, with plump, rosy cheeks. She spoke little. While Jilly generally had a sweet, gentle nature, she could also be non-co-operative, and throw tantrums, when frustrated.

Deborah placed Jilly on a green padded seat beside a small, lightly varnished table. Jilly's eyes focussed on the viewing window opposite. 'Yes, Jilly. Daddy is sitting behind that mirror even though you can't see him.' Deborah took out a lollipop from her shoulder bag and offered it to her daughter. Jilly clapped her hands. The session was off to an encouraging start.

Smiling in relief, Deborah slipped into a swivel seat across the opposite side of the table. On the table was a roughly constructed, mostly grey metallic box, similar in size to a large briefcase. A microphone on a low stand was attached to one side, while a narrow, direction-specific speaker rested on a similar stand on the other side, facing Jilly. The young girl had a dislike for headphones.

'We're going to listen to some music you love,' her mother said softly as she adjusted her dark-rimmed glasses. Deborah was in her late thirties. She was of medium height and had flowing brown hair. Deborah stood up and used a tissue to wipe some spittle off Jilly's chin. 'I'll play the music soon.' She returned to her seat and placed her shoulder bag on the table. 'You love music, don't you, Jilly?' Jilly grunted assent. Deborah took out a USB from her bag and attached it to the metal box. She turned to where her husband sat behind the one-way window. 'Say something to her, John.' She fiddled with the makeshift dials on the crude metal box.

'Hello, Jilly,' came John Challen's disembodied voice through a small, square speaker next to the window. 'It's great to see you. I'm glad that you've come to where me and your mother work again. I'll be staying behind this window for now. But I'll be with you real soon. I promise. Your mum and I want you to hear the lovely music first. We've changed a few things from last time.'

With her eyes fixed on the window, Jilly began thumping the table in protest.

'Come out for a minute or two, John,' said Deborah as she fine-tuned the dials and began scribbling on a paper notepad. 'Jilly has hardly seen you these last few weeks.'

John sighed. 'Okay, I'm coming Jilly. Just for a short while.' He came through the door, beaming. John was about the same height and age as his wife. He had short black hair, a neatly trimmed black beard and a trace of a paunch beneath his pressed blue shirt and grey trousers. 'Here I am, Jilly. Here I am.'

The girl broke into a smile and bobbed up and down. She ran over to her father and hugged him, burying her head into his chest. John stroked her hair and led her back to her chair. 'Right now, Jilly, I want you to listen to the music. We won't be here long. I'll be behind that window all the time. After you hear the nice music for a while, we'll all go home. Together. Won't that be good?' He turned to his wife. 'Deb; let's get started. Fingers crossed it'll work out this time. We must be close.'

Deborah shrugged. 'Well, if it doesn't work, I have no idea what else I can do to fine-tune the calibrations. The partial run-through on Thursday was promising. But if the Pacifier doesn't work this time...' Her lined forehead revealed her anxiety.

John smiled sympathetically and brushed his hand on his wife's shoulder. 'I'll be back soon, Jilly.' He dashed from the room. Seconds later his voice came over the speaker. 'Ready. I'm switching on the recording device.'

His wife took a deep breath. 'Right. I'll start.'

'We're on.'

Jilly moved about her seat and grinned. 'Nice music! Good!' she stuttered.

'Sit still, Jilly. Keep listening to the nice music. If you move around a lot, you won't hear it properly. This is much better than going to a clinic, isn't it? Much nicer. Now please stay still.'

Jilly grunted in satisfaction.

'Can you hear the music, Jilly?'

Jilly bobbed up and down gleefully, clapped her hands and grunted her approval.

Deborah smiled broadly and slipped on a set of headphones. 'Good. Can you hear someone whispering when the music is playing, Jilly? Is someone talking to you through the music?'

Jilly looked dully at her mother for a few seconds before immersing herself again in the soothing sounds of classical music.

'You can't hear my recorded voice mixed in with the music, can you? Great.' Deborah smiled. She glanced briefly towards the window. 'That's good, Jilly. You're happy, and when you're happy, we're happy too.' She could hear the USB recording of her encouraging, whispered voice through her headphones but not the music.

Deborah watched and listened, fascinated, as Jilly's reactions kept transforming. One minute Jilly sat in quiet contentment, then she bounced about in glee, only to look serene soon after. Moments later she clapped and waved her arms. A few times, her mother had to persuade Jilly to stay still on her seat. With each change of reaction, Deborah leant over the table to view the dials on the Pacifier. She wrote brief notes on the notepad.

'I've definitely made progress, haven't I, Jilly? Maybe one day soon I will be able to teach you better. And bridge the gap between us a bit more. Wouldn't that be great? Maybe we'll be able to help other kids who have the same problems than you—even grown-ups—as well. I hope so.'

Some twenty-five minutes later, Deborah glanced over her notes, flicking from one page to another, then back again. She did a double-take and gasped, then pulled the USB from the machine. 'It's done, John.' She gazed at the grey machine before her; running her fingers over its metal; her expression grave.

Her husband burst into the room. 'I can barely believe it. We've done it, Deb! We've done it.' He floated about the room, immersed in his glee. Then, aware of the look on his wife's face, he became puzzled. 'What? Don't you agree? Jilly reacted perfectly. She was happy and well-behaved throughout. The Pacifier works. I feel like screaming from the top of the highest building in town.'

'Don't do that, John. I believe that we have a problem.' Deborah took off her headphones.

'Problem? What problem?' John stared at his wife. 'Why are you looking at me like that? The Pacifier works Deb!' He ran over to Jilly, beaming. 'Wasn't the music fantastic, Jilly?' His daughter burst into a wide grin. He glanced back towards his grim-faced wife. Preoccupied with her thoughts, she absently rolled the USB between her fingers. 'Okay Deb, tell me. What's the problem?'

Deborah considered her words. 'I've been monitoring the calibration between the music and the subliminal messages. When the subliminal message suggested something, Jilly did exactly that. One example; she clapped her hands on cue, just as my subliminal message suggested she do to show her appreciation. It was my way of being certain that she was engaged in the experiment. But…' She shook her head and stared at the grey machine on the table.

'So?' said John as Jilly rose from her seat to bury her face into his chest.

'Did she do those things because she wanted to, John? Or because she was commanded to?'

'Commanded?' Deborah's words shocked him. 'What are you talking about?'

'John; she kept doing exactly what I suggested she do.' Deborah looked her husband in the face.

'What? Are you suggesting...?' His voice trailed off. 'Surely not. Jilly's reactions looked perfectly genuine and spontaneous to me.'

'You think so? I don't. Before we take this project further, we need to be absolutely sure one way or another. Put Jilly back in her seat. I'm going to try issuing direct subliminal commands using the microphone, while the music plays.' Jilly was delighted to be seated, facing the directional microphone again. Her mother re-inserted the USB, pressed a button and adjusted dials. She flicked the microphone on.

Jilly licked her lollipop. Her father, watching on, bit his lip.

'Right,' Deborah whispered into the microphone. 'The music is on. Clap your hands, Jilly.' Her daughter duly clapped her hands. Both parents sucked an involuntary breath. 'Put up your hand, Jilly.' Jilly did so. 'Cry, Jilly.' Jilly wept. 'Stop crying now.' Jilly stopped. Deborah dropped the microphone heavily on the table and looked up at her husband, aghast.

For some seconds the two parents were struck silent. 'Jesus.' John's mouth was agape. He shook his head as if warding off a fly. 'Okay. We've seen how it affects Jilly. But we also need to find out if the Pacifier affects other people the same way.'

Deborah nodded. 'I agree. Let's do it.'

John's chest heaved. He ushered the protesting Jilly from her seat and led her to her mother, who sat her on her knee. Jilly struggled but Deborah held her tight. 'Just sit with Mummy and give Daddy a turn to hear the nice music. It will only be for a short while.' Her husband adjusted the speaker and nodded. Deborah turned the music on. 'Clap your hands, John,' she whispered into the microphone. An icy bolt shot through her spine; John had clapped his hands. 'Raise your right hand.' He did so, a look of incomprehension across his face. He had not heard his wife's voice but guessed exactly what she had said.

'One last thing, John. I'm going to let you hear exactly what I say with the subliminal dial on as well and music playing. Try and resist.'

Her husband pursed his lips, deep in thought. Deborah adjusted a dial.

'Scratch the back of your left hand,' she said into the microphone. Her husband did as he was asked.

'Oh my God!' exclaimed John, leaping up as if the seat held upturned pins that dug into him. 'Our Pacifier can... can...' He stood, immobile, in disbelief. Jilly ran to hug her father. 'I don't believe it. I just...' His face became pale.

Deborah looked at her husband; her downcast expression revealing her shattered spirit. 'There's one more experiment I need to do to round things off. Bring Jilly to me again. I'm about to make a subliminal suggestion to you, John. The difference this time is that I'm going to switch the machine off after I make the suggestion. I want to see how you react.'

John shrugged, blinked. 'Whatever you say. Sorry. I'm too numb to think right now.' He took up his seat as Jilly sat on Deborah's lap. His wife took a half-empty plastic water bottle from her shoulder bag and placed it in front of her husband. Jilly struggled, but Deborah held her firmly once more. She played the music for her husband, then whispered into the microphone. 'I'm going to issue you with a command. When I say your name with the machine off, tip the water from the bottle on the ground. I'm switching the machine off now.'

John looked intently at Deborah, an agonised look on her face. She flicked the switch and took a deep, lingering breath. 'John,' she whispered.

Her husband reached for the water bottle. He undid the lid and tipped the water onto the ground. He stared, uncomprehending, at the water spreading beside his foot. Baffled, he looked at his wife. 'Oh my God. Did you tell me to do that?'

Deborah could only nod. There was a lump in her throat.

'Oh my God!' said John, his face twisted in dismay. 'I did what you told me to, even with the machine switched off. I can't believe it.' Jilly ran to her father and sat on his lap.

His wife stood abruptly. She walked towards the viewing window before turning to face her husband. 'This means we have no choice, John. We must abandon this project. The machine has to be destroyed and all of our notes need to be burnt.'

John lowered Jilly to the ground and stood. 'Deb; that's surely an over-reaction? You did the software. All you need to do is amend it. Hopefully, it won't involve anything major. Look at how Jilly responded to the Pacifier. It did exactly what we wanted it to do. With that one glitch.'

Jilly dropped into the seat and grunted. Deborah switched on the machine and adjusted some dials. 'I'll play some music for you, Jilly.'

With Jilly preoccupied, husband and wife stared at one another. 'Deb; we can't simply turn our backs on the immense potential of the machine. You only need to eliminate the suggestive aspects of the programme. Look at how happy Jilly is.'

Jilly bobbed up and down, smiling, on the seat. She seemed to be straining to listen to something more than the music.

'No John!' Deborah was adamant. 'Even if it were possible to fix it, and it isn't possible, it would only be a matter of time before someone said, "let's try this small adjustment," and the genie will be released from its bottle. Then, God help us all.'

John paced the room. 'Okay. How about we use the machine with Jilly. Only Jilly. We keep the Pacifier locked up.'

'No John,' Deborah said firmly. 'Even doing that is too risky.'

'But we can't just throw the Pacifier on the scrapheap,' John pleaded with his wife. 'Not after all the work and money we've put into it. And knowing how much good it can do.'

'We have no alternative, John. It's way too dangerous. What if I'd asked you to kill someone?'

'But doesn't the research show you can only hypnotise someone if they are predisposed to that action.'

Deborah shook her head. 'We can't predict what someone under the influence of this machine may or may not do. It's taken us to uncharted territory. We can't take any chances. I'm going to delete all my files dealing with the Pacifier when I get home. There's no alternative, John.'

With Jilly bobbing up and down, husband and wife stared at one another in stunned silence. Their labour of love… a labour that had consumed innumerable hours and the bulk of their already diminished savings, and which had finally achieved what it was intended to do, lay on the table, consigned to be flung into oblivion.

John sighed deeply and stared at the floor. 'Okay. As much as it hurts me to say it, I agree. I understand the situation.' He looked up. 'But how about making a small concession? We keep the Pacifier until Jilly's birthday in ten days' time. Surely, she deserves the chance to experience the joy she felt here one more time. It would be her birthday treat.'

Deborah, looking drained, snatched the USB from the machine and flicked the switch. She glanced sadly at Jilly who shifted in her seat and grunted, impatient for the music to restart.

'Also; you never know, Deb,' said her husband. 'Maybe a solution will magically come to you during those ten days. It happens. Even coming up with an idea that we can explore.'

Deborah looked at him and grimaced. She shook her head. 'No, that won't happen, John. Okay, I tell you what; we keep the Pacifier locked away. We keep the USB locked away some other place. We bring the Pacifier out for that one special day. For Jilly's sake. But only for that one day. After Jilly's birthday treat, we'll take the machine apart and dispose of it in small pieces at different locations.'

John's face fell. He looked about to burst into tears. 'We're agreed.'

'Thanks. I realise what a huge disappointment this is. For you and for me. Oh; are you still recording this?'

'Yes,' John said sullenly. 'I'll go and switch it off now.'

'Erase the record of this experiment for good measure,' Deborah called out as he hesitated at the door. He left the room, shoulders slumped.

Jilly's mood on the journey home was buoyant. Her parents were sullen, silent, their mood gloomy. The future development of their daughter, and their wonderous machine, lay in shreds. The Pacifier sat in a locked metal box on John's lap, the USB taped securely underneath the lid.

Huddled on the back seat, John momentarily reached into the side pocket of his jacket.

THORNTON BONNEY

The following morning, John Challen, who hadn't slept the entire night, did not want to get out of bed.

'Then take the day off,' said Deborah, standing beside the bedroom door. 'Ring Brigitte at work. You're exhausted, John. You've been running on empty for weeks.'

John rose onto an elbow. 'No, Deb; I have to go in. I've got to tell Thornton that I can't extend his contract beyond the end of the month. The guy needs time to look for other work.' He sat up. 'As for us, don't ask me how we'll pay our debts. I haven't gone through the accounts, or checked the bills, for weeks. Haven't had the courage. Or energy. We've been focussed solely on the Pacifier.'

'We've battled through rough patches before, John.' Deborah offered a sympathetic smile.

'Not on this scale, Deb.'

'Whatever happens, John; all that effort we put into the Pacifier was worth the risk. I don't regret making the sacrifice. Even if it breaks us financially. It's just…' Her husband looked away. 'Anyway, I'm going to ring my contacts. I'm sure I'll pick up some freelance work. As for Thornton, when people sign contracts, they do so knowing full well they may not get an extension. If you don't let him go, we don't stand a chance.'

'I know.' John leant his head against the bed post and shut his eyes. Deborah hesitated before slipping out of the room.

John couldn't stomach breakfast. He dressed quickly, pecked his wife on the cheek, and drove to work, dreading the day. Walking through the front door, he paused to examine the fading beige paint in the hallway. There were scuff marks on the doors and walls. A makeshift handle hung loose on the grey stores' cupboard. If it came to selling the building... His own office was compact, nondescript and cluttered with stacks of printouts, books, computer discs and trays of USBs. Some lay on wooden benches, some on the floor, leaning against the walls. Clutter had never bothered him. He could always find what he was searching for. Besides, it reminded him of his dedication to succeed sixteen years earlier. So what if a few visitors or prospective clients had poked their heads into his office to ask the bearded man inside where they could find John Challen's office? Since Jilly was diagnosed, Deborah had worked mostly from home.

John hung his jacket on the umbrella stand beside his office door. He dropped into his seat and shut his eyes for some time before wincing and slamming his fist on his desk. He made his way into the lab. The lab was spacious, with four long, varnished wooden work benches (now somewhat worn), their tops covered by green rubber. Around the sides of the lab, military-green metal shelving held mostly equipment, devices, technical manuals and binders. Two years earlier, the benches had been a hive of activity, with five employees working alongside him. He wished Deborah stood beside him, to wrap her arm around his shoulders after he broke the news to his remaining two employees. Both looked up from their tasks when John entered the lab. Their faces dropped; the deep concern on their boss' face had to be obvious.

'Brigitte. Thornton,' John sighed. 'I have an important announcement.' His two workers drew close. Squat, with blonde hair and white-rimmed spectacles, Brigitte was aged in her forties. Thornton Bonney was a boyish-looking man in his late twenties. He was of average height, carried a little baby fat, had soft, pink features, thinning brown hair and wore gold-rimmed glasses. 'I have grim news to tell you. Deborah and I ran another test on the Pacifier last night. Regrettably, once again, the machine did not work. After a lengthy discussion about the future of the project, we came to the heartbreaking conclusion that the Pacifier can never be made to work.' He paused and swallowed. 'As you can understand, coming to this conclusion was a massive disappointment to us. Especially after the enormous effort we put in.' He forced a pained smile.

There was silence. 'Bugger!' Thornton exclaimed.

Brigitte did not react. She was close to Deborah and probably was aware that the Challens had doubts about achieving success.

'Deborah and I wanted to make the world a better place,' John continued. He was conscious of Thornton's eyes upon him. 'But… no. So, I am left with an unpleasant duty to perform.' He drew a breath, looking pensively at Thornton. 'Thornton; I need to tell you; due to the dire situation with our finances, I cannot extend your contract, beyond the end of the month.'

Thornton rubbed his chin. 'And Brigitte?' the young man asked, his face grim. 'What about her?'

'Brigitte's contract ends in ten weeks' time. She'll be working to finish the Roston contract. I'll help her out after I've sorted our finances.' Thornton pursed his lips and glanced at Brigitte, beside him. 'Thornton; if it's okay with you, how about you help Brigitte for your remaining time here?' The younger man pursed his lips. 'But should you prefer to leave right away, I will understand. If that's what you choose to do, I will pay out your contract tomorrow. I'll give you a glowing reference. You've earnt it.'

Thornton gazed hard at his boss. 'This is a major blow, John. Gee. I thought we were close to a breakthrough. The government had expressed interest in the project.'

John winced. 'Yes, but with no promise of funds. Deborah and I hoped we could swing this. Believe me. I'm deeply sorry how things have panned out. But we have no choice. If I can manage to win a suitable contract sometime in the future—'

'Are you absolutely sure the project can't be rescued? This has come as quite a shock.'

'We don't have the slightest doubt. Sorry, Thornton. I truly wish it were otherwise.'

'How about you just shelve it for now,' Thornton said, grimacing. 'When you get some financial backing, we can examine all avenues thoroughly.'

John shook his head. 'No point. The problems with the Pacifier are clearly beyond anyone's capability. I'm deeply sorry. All I can do is to thank you from the bottom of my heart for your tremendous contribution and dedication to the company, Thornton. I'll do all I can to find you other work.'

Thornton cleared his throat. 'So, John, you're casting me adrift. With no warning.'

His boss sucked a breath. 'I realise this is hard on you, but please understand that Deborah and I re-mortgaged our home to finance the project.' He nervously gripped the table before him. 'I won't hold it against you if you walk out of here right now.'

'So, that's it?' sneered Thornton. 'For me, who's been a major player in the development of the Pacifier.'

John straightened his back, gobsmacked. 'I acknowledge your contribution to the project. But to claim that you've been a major player is, if you pardon me, quite an overstatement. You sourced and fabricated many parts, true, but you mostly worked on various other projects as well. It was Deborah and I who worked on all the key aspects of the project.'

Thornton glared at him. 'Don't belittle my contribution, John. I put my heart and soul into that project.'

'I acknowledge your work, Thornton,' John said, testily measuring his words. 'But what I told you just now, stands.'

Thornton fumed. 'If that's your attitude, then, stuff you. I'm through.' He turned on his heel and stormed out of the room. John heard him slam the front door behind him. He hadn't the energy to chase after his employee and try to appease him. Maybe he'd contact him later. Right at that moment, he needed to muster whatever energy he could to try save the company.

John turned to his other employee. 'How are you feeling, Brigitte?'

'I'm okay, John. I understand. You and Deb must be hurting badly.'

'We are. Very much. Thanks.' He tried to smile. Then, with a sigh, he returned to his office. Inside, the in-tray was overflowing; bills, some still in their envelopes, covered much of the desk.

Two hours later, John still struggled to marshal the will or discipline to focus on the task of arranging the bills into some order of urgency. His mind too preoccupied, he opted to take a stroll in a nearby park and stop at a café. As he sipped his coffee, he was suddenly struck by a realisation. He leapt to his feet and rushed back to the office. When he arrived, he checked the pocket of his jacket, still hanging on the umbrella stand. He sighed in relief; the disc recording was still there. He admonished himself for his carelessness; he should have locked the disc in the safe. No. More than that. He should have destroyed it. Any risk, no matter how miniscule, was too great. He donned his jacket. He'd lock away the disc later.

John brought out a sandwich from his briefcase. After taking a few bites he tossed the remains in the bin and locked his office door. He took out the recording and inserted it into his laptop. And pressed play. While John did not hear the music, he heard Deborah's recorded voice. She had her back to him, concealing her reactions. He saw only Jilly. Jilly wore an almost perpetual smile. She laughed, clapped and waved her arms about. When she wasn't animated, she sat, serene and expectant. Watching her happy face lifted her father's spirit. All the time knowing that Jilly's joy would be fleeting. Only on the day of her birthday would she respond with such delight once more. Afterwards, the incredible machine would be destroyed. Jilly would not understand. He could barely come to grips with it, himself.

John watched on as the images of the horrible realisation of the Pacifier's fatal flaw dawned on him and his wife. He couldn't continue watching; he rewound the recording to watch Jilly being happy once more. Then, reluctantly, he switched off the disc and locked it deep inside his safe. With a deep sigh, he forced himself to tend to his financial woes. There were so many bills. So many reminders. Final notices. The most urgent ones were placed in one pile.

There was a loud rap on his door, startling him. He cleared his throat. 'Just wait. I need to unlock the door.' He did and Thornton strode inside, almost knocking his boss over. The younger man no longer wore his technician's uniform, having changed into an expensive blue sports coat and black trousers.

'Hello Thornton,' John greeted the young man with little enthusiasm. 'Going out on the town?'

Thornton spread himself across John's visitor's chair and grinned broadly. 'You betcha, boss. No better way to get over being told you've been sacked.' John opened his mouth to speak but allowed the man to continue. 'What are you doing tonight, John? Surely, you're not working back again. There's no reason to do that anymore, is there?'

John sighed. Thornton clearly had no idea of the immediacy of the company's financial predicament.

'Tut tut, boss,' Thornton admonished him lightheartedly. 'You really should unwind, you know. C'mon, it's almost six o'clock. Let's go and have a couple of drinks at Rowan's. It's been a long time since you've been out drinking with your dedicated employee. And besides, I feel really bad about my outburst when you… made the call about my job. I want to make it up to you.'

John's first inclination was to make some excuse. He would have welcomed having a few drinks with a sympathetic friend. But not with Thornton. The thought of making conversation with the dapper young man made him wince. Thornton could be intense; Deborah, in particular, found him to be uncompromising and argumentative. She didn't like the guy, but he never refused to take on work that needed to be done. Thornton stayed with the company when two others quit to take on higher-paid jobs. Thornton's request placed John in a bind. He felt he owed Thornton some friendly gesture after sacking the man. Perhaps, with some sympathetic words, the younger man could be convinced to see out the last three weeks of his contract. Maybe help John search for tenders. Also, John was fully aware that he'd been overdoing it for far too long. Nor was he ready to face an impatient Jilly and a neglected Deborah just yet. And what was one more day neglecting the bills?

John nodded, cobbling together the remnants of a forced smile. 'Okay. I'll come. But only for a little while. Just give me five minutes. I'll meet you in the tea-room.'

'Sure, boss. I'll wait.' Thornton seemed satisfied. 'I'll lock the front door.'

John shuffled some papers on his desk as Thornton left the room. He became tense as he turned his attention to the tricky task of ringing Deborah to tell her he would be home late.

'Jilly has been pining for you all week,' came his wife's tired and resigned voice over the phone. 'She's been fretting. You realise that don't you, John?'

'Yes, I do,' he whispered, his forehead resting against the palm of his hand. 'But I feel obliged to spend a little time with Thornton after sacking the guy. I'll be home in an hour. No more. Promise Jilly I'll spend time with her later. I better go. Sorry. Bye for now.'

John dropped the handset and swore. He snatched his briefcase and marched to the tea-room, regretting having agreed to the get-together. 'Ready?' he asked Thornton who was pacing the floor. The two men left through the rear of the lab and headed into the chill of an autumn evening. In silence, they drove down the road in John's ten-year-old Ford, with its small dent on the passenger's side.

U ntil around seven, Rowan's Bar and Bistro was a handy place to go and find a small table in a quiet, faintly lit corner for a snack, a drink, and a chat. On three days in the week, after seven, Rowan's began steadily transforming into a nightclub, at times with live music. The bar was roomy, with enlarged photos of singers and visiting celebrities on the fawn-coloured walls. The folds of a heavy, dark-crimson curtain covered the front of a small stage. 'Go find us a table. I'll buy the first round,' John volunteered. Thornton had already begun drifting to a table beside the edge of the stage.

As the men sipped their beers, Thornton commented on a recent sporting result. No doubt sensing his boss' disinterest, he cleared his throat. 'Brigitte took the news really well.'

'Well… Deborah and her are close.' He gave a nervous chuckle. 'She's probably more attuned to my wife than I am.'

'Yeah. And being set adrift won't be much of a problem for her. Her husband's on good money, isn't he? She can put her feet up.'

John blinked. 'Brigitte enjoys working. There's no way she'll be sitting idle. She mixes in much the same circles as Deborah, so I imagine she'll find something.'

'Lucky for her. As for me; I might as well get straight to the point.' Thornton laid his beer on the table. He looked directly into his boss's face.

John sighed. 'Please do.' He sank back into his seat, anticipating the conversation was about to become uncomfortable.

Thornton pressed forward. 'I'm sorry to have to bring it up but—'

'Particularly as there is nothing more that can be said, Thornton. Sorry. If you aren't satisfied with my offer to pay you out, I'll give you some extra cash, to cover a bill or two. But I can't afford any more than that.'

'I am aware of your money problems, John,' Thornton said, quaffing the rest of his beer. 'It's more about the Pacifier. It's bugging me. You ditching it, just like that.' He snapped his fingers. 'It's okay for you. You've made it in this world. You can bin the Pacifier and move on. But what about me, John?'

John gestured for Thornton to keep his voice down. Thornton continued in a whisper. 'Look, John, I'm a very good technician. You can't dispute that. There is so much I could achieve if I got a genuine break. But, instead, I've spent the last seven years chasing short-term contract after short-term contract. Sending in so many applications. Going to annoying interviews. I deserve better. And, at my age, I need stability in my life. I believed I finally got my break when I started work on the Pacifier.' Thornton waved to the barman to fetch him another beer.

John looked intently into the man's face. 'I'm sorry for you, Thornton. I truly understand how you're feeling. But there's nothing I can do. Sorry.'

'But I'm convinced the Pacifier can work. Just let me look into it with you.'

The older man checked that no one was in earshot. He whispered testily. 'Thornton, no one knows the workings of the Pacifier as Deborah and I do. We slaved away trying all sorts of options. We're the ones able to judge whether the Pacifier has a future or not. Remember that when you're out partying tonight—again.' It was time to leave.

Thornton sipped at the beer the barman placed before him and frowned. After an awkward silence, the younger man leaned across the table, his hands held outward, palms up. 'I can't figure out why a compassionate man like you would want to throw the Pacifier on the scrapheap so easily. I'm certain you've jumped to a premature decision. We're talking about a device that can do so much good for so many unfortunate people.'

John simmered. 'If there was even a remote possibility of success, no matter how unlikely, we would pursue it. I'd sell the shirt off my back if it were a possibility.'

'But John...' Thornton begged.

John brushed away the appeal with a flick of his hand and a glare. 'Thornton. For Christ's sake, the project is finished. Get over it. I refuse to discuss it with you anymore.'

'You're prepared to give up helping your own daughter, John?' Thornton's expression was cold.

John took a deep breath, checking his fury. He looked the younger man square in the eye. 'There's nothing I wouldn't do for Jilly.'

Thornton looked intently at John, perhaps to sum the man up. He sucked in a breath and raised his hands as to surrender. 'Okay then. I thought it was worth a try—appealing to you—that's all. So, I'll call it quits. Don't worry, John, I mean it. Let's just enjoy our drinks, shall we? After all, we came here to unwind.' He raised his glass as if to toast his boss.

John pursed his lips. He became more conciliatory. 'Thornton, I need to be certain you'll put the Pacifier out of your mind. You need to move on.'

'Believe me, after our little discussion here, the whole issue is dead and buried.' Thornton brightened up. 'Come on, John. Smile. It's okay. Really.'

John quaffed the rest of his drink. 'I'm sorry, but I need to be on my way. I've hardly seen Jilly for days and I promised Deborah I'd spend some time with them both tonight. If you'll excuse me…'

Leaning back, Thornton shrugged and smiled as he drained the rest of his beer and tapped his empty glass. 'Sure, John. I understand. You have a good night.'

The older man was already on his feet, counting out notes from his wallet. He dropped a few on the table. 'I'll have your payout placed in your bank account by tomorrow lunchtime.'

Thornton simmered as his boss disappeared out the door. Sneering, he scooped up the money from the table. He ordered another drink, something stronger this time, and swore at the empty seat opposite him.

Thornton was still drinking at eight thirty. The atmosphere now hummed with the chatter of smartly dressed patrons. 'My lasht one. Then I'm off. Promise.'

The hovering waiter pursed his lips. 'My apologies sir, but I won't serve you any more alcohol this evening. Maybe a meal and a coffee or two instead? That way you can stay until Audrey Brockhurst begins her performance.'

Thornton was perplexed. The waiter explained. 'I thought you came early to get a good seat and avoid paying the entrance fee.'

Thornton's eyes widened. 'Audrey Broshhursht here?'

'Yes, Audrey Brockhurst is singing here tonight. She lives in the next suburb. She'll be on stage in about half an hour. So, stay if you wish, as long as you order a meal and have a couple of black coffees. No more alcohol.'

Audrey was a petite and lithe singer with long, jet-black hair and a resonant, husky voice. During the past few months, she had risen to become a national sensation, swamping the TV stations and You-tube. The prospect had Thornton rubbing his chin. The waiter was right; seeing the sultry singer perform was way too good an opportunity to let pass. So immersed had he been with his dark thoughts after John Challen's departure, and the drinks before him, that he only realised at that moment that some activity was taking place behind the curtain. The tables in the room were fully occupied. Someone had taken the seat opposite him. Many people were sitting or standing beside the bar.

Thornton nodded. 'Right. Maybe I'll shtay a while

after all and shtart on the lemon shquashes and coffee. Oh, menu please.'

'Remember, just food, coffees, and lemon squashes. Okay?' Thornton gave a thumbs up. Seemingly satisfied, the waiter wandered off to return with a menu.

More people piled into the venue. Before long, the crowd had spread to stand all around the walls of the room, two or three deep. Thornton checked the time on his phone. The husky singer was late. Otherwise, his luck was in. A young waitress, who wore her black hair in a ponytail, had arrived about twenty minutes earlier. She brought him his meal and a large coffee. Perhaps because she was busy serving patrons, or because of his tip, she fetched him the double whisky he requested. The chatter in the room would have disguised his slurred voice.

Thornton got in another drinks order with the young waitress before the neatly suited owner of Rowan's stepped in front of the curtain, to the sound of some cheers and clapping, and a smattering of jeers. Audrey was quite late. 'Without further ado,' the man announced. 'Rowan's presents someone who all of us are very proud of; a local huge success story, Audrey Brockhurst!' The crowd burst into a loud bout of cheering, clapping, along with a couple of catcalls.

The curtain parted. Three slick band members, dressed in black, dashed onstage and took up their instruments. The music sounded up. With a swaying flourish, there she was—Audrey Brockhurst—strutting before him in a skin-tight black leather pants and low-cut black singlet, to thunderous applause and whooping. She pounded out her first song. The patrons lapped it up. Each song she sang was greeted with a rapturous glee that reverberated throughout the room. No one was more enthusiastic than Thornton. One time, the pouting singer briefly and politely acknowledged the over-whelming encouragement she was getting from him. When Audrey walked off the stage at the end of her first (all-too-brief) set, Thornton had never wanted a woman more.

A table at the opposite side of the stage had been set aside for Audrey's entourage; two trendy-looking young men, two stylish young women in evening gowns and one tall, very muscly, bald man in a black suit. When the sultry singer came from backstage to chat to her entourage, Thornton decided to make the singer's acquaintance. Stumbling towards her, two bouncers dashed forward to block his path. One was young, tall and thin and had what Thornton considered to be an oafish expression. The other man was broad and squat, about forty, and balding. His scowl sug-gested him to be a man who wouldn't retreat from a fight.

'Sir. The lady doesn't want to be disturbed,' growled the shorter bouncer.

Thornton placed a congenial hand on the man's shoulder. 'Ah, c'mon pal...'

The bouncer bristled. He brushed Thornton's hand off roughly, puffing out his chest. 'Keep your hands to yourself, sir.'

Thornton raised his hands. 'C'mon guys. I'm Aus-trysh's greatest fan. Honesht. I'm shoo she won't mind me saying hullo to her. Jush hullo. I'll be er good boy.'

The bouncer turned to the singer. 'Miss Brockhurst. Excuse me. Do you know this man?'

Audrey gave one short, disapproving glance and shook her head.

The reaction of the singer left Thornton with his mouth agape. 'Wha...? I just—'

The older bouncer placed a restraining hand on Thornton's shoulder. 'Sir; it's time you left this establishment. You've had more than enough to drink for one night. I'll call you a cab.'

Thornton was still staring at the woman who'd rejected him so abruptly and coldly, despite the unabashed adulation he had endowed upon her. 'What a bish.'

'Right. That's it for you mate,' the older bouncer snarled, gripping Thornton painfully by the right arm and pulling it up hard behind his back.

'Come on, sir,' chimed in the younger bouncer, with a smile. Thornton thought the smile made the man look even more of an oaf. 'We'll have you safely home before you know it.' The younger man took Thornton's left arm. The two bouncers spun him around and led him somewhat forcibly towards the door. Everyone in the darkened room turned to watch. Some pointed. A few chuckled.

Embarrassed, Thornton became livid. 'Hey. Let go 'uv me.' The bouncers took no notice. At the front door, Thornton was shoved roughly outside. He turned to face his adversaries; the two bouncers were joined by two colleagues, who were manning the door. They looked ready for trouble.

'There are taxis just around the corner sir,' one of the doormen said. Would you like me to phone one for you?'

Thornton studied their faces. He was contemptuous of their brazen, glaring faces. 'Bashtards!' he yelled. 'I'll make yosh all pay fer shish.'

The older bouncer took a menacing step towards

Thornton and shoved him in the chest. 'Don't threaten me pal. Piss off or I'll scatter your teeth all over the footpath.'

'Bashtards!' Thornton sneered. 'Yer dunno who I em? Eh?'

The bouncer sneered. 'No. And I couldn't give a stuff.'

'Oh yer. Well ... I invented a machine that'll chansh th' whole whirl. The whole whirl! Thash who I am, bashtard! What yer shay 'bout that? Eh? Eh?' He jutted his chin as he staggered.

'I don't give a damn. Piss off.'

Thornton contemplated the wall of bouncers. It struck him then that the oafish bouncer was familiar. But from where? There was no time to think. The balding bouncer fronted Thornton, menacing for a fight.

Prudence prevailed. Thornton tottered off in search of a taxi, muttering oaths and threats. He found a taxi rank and clambered inside the first one in line. 'Where to, pal?' The taxi driver took one look at Thornton's face and winced.

'Penshley,' Thornton answered testily.

The taxi driver nodded and drove off.

In the back seat, Thornton was stewing; his breath coming in snorts and gulps. First John, then Audrey Brockhurst and, finally, the bouncers had snubbed and humiliated him.

Thornton had bragged openly at university that he was destined to achieve greatness. They'd sneered at him. He'd had a dream back then: being chauffeured along a wide avenue in a black limousine; a cheering, adoring crowd waving at him. Some of their faces, filled with wonder, pressed against the windows as they ran along-side. That dream remained, vivid, in his memory.

He'd recalled it many times over the years. It had to be a premonition.

As the taxi passed through the dark streets Thornton twisted his lips in anger. 'Na more,' he growled. 'Won't take shis no more.'

Grim-faced, the taxi driver drove on.

THE DESPERATE GAMBLE

Thornton spent the afternoon of the next day, a Friday, drinking the contents of a bottle of whisky. Neat. John had deposited the money owing to him by lunchtime, as promised. On Saturday, Thornton slept much of the day, waking only to vomit into a bucket beside his bed. In the evening, he bought another bottle.

Next morning, Thornton found his work reference from his boss attached to an email. A note appeared with it asking if there was anything Thornton believed needed to be added. He printed off the reference and tossed it on the kitchen table without reading it. He paid a visit to a man he knew at a certain pub. A nod of the head and they drifted discretely to the toilet. Thornton passed over a wad of money; the other man reached into his sock and handed over a satchel of white powder.

He woke up the next morning, nauseous and resentful. It was then that Thornton Bonney made a sneering decision. He would become a stalker.

W hen darkness fell, Thornton donned black clothes and black gloves and drove a block away from the Challen's home. There he donned a black balaclava. He snuck into the Challens' back yard, carefully opening the side gate. He crouched to peer through a narrow slit of light beneath window curtains. Thornton was familiar with the layout of the modest house, having attended a barbeque the Challens had held during the summer. From what he could make out from his limited view, husband and wife were showering Jilly with attention in the lounge room. Jilly giggled, eliciting laughter from her parents.

Thornton returned to spy on the Challen's each night. But it was Friday evening that presented a possibly tantalising prospect. It was Deborah's bridge night. Both husband and child would be home by themselves. It was a long shot but...

By Thursday, Thornton's resentment had risen to the point where he struggled to contain it. He shocked his drug dealer when he asked to purchase a revolver and a packet of bullets. 'You sure about this?' the man said, examining Thornton's face. 'You're not planning to do anything stupid, are you?'

'No. It's for my protection. I've got enemies. I'll only use the gun if they try and do something to me. Don't worry; I'm not planning to kill anyone. Or rob a store.'

'Okay then,' the man said, unsure. 'I'll meet you out the back in two hours' time. I won't mind if you change your mind.'

The deal was made in a seedy alleyway. When he arrived home, Thornton, now a little more sober, regretted making the purchase. Yet, on the evening of Deborah's bridge night, the loaded revolver rested heavy in a deep pocket of his overcoat. The weapon would only be used if he had no choice.

Thornton sat, impatient, in his car on a tree-lined avenue. He straightened in his seat when an early-model blue Mazda came out of a driveway, turned into the adjacent street, and drove off. Deborah Challen was behind the wheel. She was alone.

When he was sure the coast was clear, he donned his black balaclava and leather gloves, and carefully made his way to the back of the Challen's home again, to crouch beneath the lounge room window.

The heavy curtains were fully drawn. He barely made out the muffled voices of father and daughter inside. When Jilly suddenly chanted "music; music; music," Thornton acted on a hunch. He tried the back door. To his surprise, it was unlocked. He took a breath and slipped quietly inside, amazed at how easy it had been. Thornton was in for more luck; the lounge room door had been left ajar by the width of a handspan, giving him a wedge-thin view of father and daughter. The walls of the room were painted a colourful pink—no doubt to please Jilly—with a few posters of cute animals and cartoon characters hanging on the walls beside some family portraits. Some soft toys sat on tables, bookshelves, and cupboards.

Thornton heard approaching footsteps. He scurried through the nearest door, which happened to be Jilly's bedroom. Lying behind Jilly's bed, his hand on the gun, Thornton heard John's footsteps and the sound of a door being locked. Then John slipped into an adjacent room as Jilly, in the lounge room, started pounding the table with her fists, calling out for her father. 'I'll only be a minute,' John replied. When Thornton heard John re-enter the lounge room, he crept to the ajar door once more. Peering through the gap, he covered his mouth with his hand to smother a triumphant gasp. John lifted a familiar grey metal machine from a metal box and placed it on the lounge room table. As Jilly became rapturous, her father plugged in the microphone and directional speaker. Her excitement masked Thornton's exclamation of glee.

'Stay still in your seat, Jilly. I'm going to play some nice music for you again,' John pointed the speaker at his daughter. Jilly became more animated. 'Mummy would not be happy if she knew what we're about to do, would she? So don't tell Mummy about this.' He inserted a USB in the machine, pressed a button and began adjusting dials with Jilly bobbing up and down. 'You need to sit still Jilly to hear the music properly.'

A few metres away, Thornton watched, wide-eyed. Providence had delivered him an opportunity too good to resist. From his jacket pocket, he took out the loaded revolver, flicked off the safety. He did not hesitate. Kicking open the lounge room door, he strode into the room.

John spun around in shock. 'Who are you? What are you doing in my house?' He stepped between Jilly and the intruder, with the Pacifier behind h im.

Seeing the man who had dismissed him, cringing, only emboldened Thornton. 'Well, well, here we are, the three of us. And here is the magic machine as well.'

John gritted his teeth. 'Thornton! What the hell do you think you're doing?' He reached towards the Pacifier.

'Don't touch that machine!' Thornton bellowed, brandishing the gun.

'Get out of my house right now!' boomed John. 'Go!' He thrust his arm towards the door.

'Nice music!' Jilly cooed.

'I came here,' Thornton mocked him, 'because I've got nothing to lose. It only takes a minute to copy a disc, John. You see; I returned to the office soon after I left the building that day, to pick up a few items. After seeing that you weren't there, I went into your office and checked your jacket pockets, hoping to find some cash...I often found bits and pieces there... you never noticed. And, incredibly, I found a video recording. 'What could this be? I said to myself And, to my great surprise I found something far more useful than money. What an amazing disc it is. You and Deborah conducting experiments. Move away from the Pacifier, John. I'm in no mood for niceties.'

Thornton's words made John reel. 'What do you want, Thornton? I'll give you everything I have in this world if you promise to keep quiet about the Pacifier.' His voice tremored.

'Nice music. Nice music,' chanted Jilly, clapping her hands, oblivious.

'Ah, but John, I watched the disc. I know what the Pacifier can do. It truly is the most amazing device. Who would have envisaged just how magical it is.'

'Oh Jesus! I should have...' John sighed; his shoulders slumped. He glanced at Jilly, who was smiling. 'Name a sum, Thornton. Any sum. And I'll bring it to you. Somehow. I'll sell my business. This machine must never see the light of day. Surely you must realise that.'

'What a discovery, eh, John? A machine that can command even normal, healthy minds. Remarkable. You and Deborah are geniuses. No question.'

John stared back at Thornton. 'What's your price?' He sidled up beside the Pacifier.

Thornton's wide grin from the slit in his balaclava resembled the disembodied smile of the Cheshire Cat from one of Jilly's story books. He spoke calmly, assuredly. 'Let us both enjoy this moment, John. I guessed right. I figured you couldn't resist making your daughter happy. You old softy.'

John gave Thornton a searching look. 'Look, Thornton. Be reasonable. Just let me—' He reached beside him towards a dial.

'Back off! Keep away from that machine! Now! Or I'll kill you. I will. Don't push your luck.' Thornton screamed.

Jilly jumped and looked at her father. John stepped back and held up his hands in surrender.

Thornton stood, simmering. 'You have no idea what I plan to do now, do you John?' He was soaking in the exhilaration of power. It stirred a longing that had always been within him.

John remained calm. 'Thornton… Please. If you understand what the machine can do, you must also know—'

'There's no way that I'm going to let you destroy such a fabulous machine. It's mine now.'

'No. Don't do this. For Christ's sake.' His voice tremored in fear.

'Don't moralise with me. Not after you cast me adrift like an old rag. I gave you a chance to make things simpler for us both when we went to Rowan's. Oh yes, I was going to get my hands on it no matter what. It just depended on how I would do it.'

John steeled himself. 'You have no idea how to operate the Pacifier. It's more complex than you might think. You're only familiar with some technical components of the machine. You can't get it to work. Believe me. So, give up, Thornton, while you can.'

'I might not know exactly why it works,' Thornton said, grinning, 'but I know enough to get it to work. Yes, the calibration between voice and music must be a very delicate operation. But I'm a patient man, John. Not always, though. And definitely not now.'

'Music! Music!' Jilly chanted.

John swallowed and stared deep into the younger man's eyes. He made a sudden dive at the dials of the Pacifier. He fiddled with one of them before death's cold gaze stared at him. He took a couple of involuntary steps back. A moment later, three bullets blew his chest apart.

Distressed by the noise, Jilly leapt from her seat. She stared, uncomprehending, at the stranger in black. Then she noticed her father, on the carpet. And the blood.

Thornton casually bent over the crumpled body and sneered. 'You should have used the machine on me, John. But you were too gutless. This is what happens to gutless people.' He pointed the gun at Jilly, then lowered his weapon. 'No need,' he said without emotion. Thornton moved swiftly. As Jilly gazed at him, cowering in fear, he wiped the gun carefully on John's sleeve. Finding John and Deborah's bedroom, he placed the gun beneath the bed. The keys for the house were in John's trousers pocket. It was all so easy. He switched off the Pacifier and placed it, with the USB still attached, in its box.

Jilly's eyes were fixed on her father's limp body. She ran to him, bursting into tears. She lifted her hands, finding them drenched with blood. She began screaming.

'Shut up, you idiot,' Thornton yelled as he moved towards the back door, his precious new acquisition safely tucked under the crook of his arm.

Walking quickly along the footpath, keeping to the shadows, he could still hear the girl's cries echoing along the street.

T wo days later, the police brought Thornton in for questioning. With his arms folded across his waist, he vehemently denied being anywhere near the Challen's home that fateful night. Where was he that night? Why, at home watching a DVD. Alone.

The police were suspicious. 'A neighbour has given a very good description of a car parked near the scene on the night of the murder. The description fits very closely with your own car. You know the Challens. You were sacked a few days earlier. That gives you a possible motive.'

Thornton shrugged. 'Wasn't me. Wasn't my car. Didn't you say the killing happened at night? The neighbour made a mistake. Understandable in the dark.'

The net began closing on Thornton. He was greatly relieved when he received a phone call from the police a few days later, notifying him that Deborah Challen had strolled into her local police station and admitted to the murder of her husband. She brought the murder weapon with her, dropping it on the inquiries desk as if it were a set of house keys. The duty officer had stepped back in disbelief.

'She's a cold one,' a detective told the local police. 'Won't give us a motive. We established that she seemed distracted when she played bridge earlier in the evening. After they packed up, she calmly drives home and shoots her husband. Get this… She keeps insisting that she has no idea how it happened. Some sort of brain snap maybe. Can't tell. But I'm absolutely certain that she's not being truthful with us. It's one the weirdest cases I've come across.'

G etting the Pacifier to work proved problematic. Working in Thornton's favour, John Challen had only been able to adjust the dial that calibrated commands with the music. So he needed to guess the settings. Thornton's first experiment with the machine failed dismally. From his car, he'd directed the Pacifier at the older, balding bouncer who'd harassed him that humiliating night at Rowan's. The bouncer was sitting on a public bench opposite Rowan's smoking a cigarette, before fronting up for work. The bouncer did not respond to Thornton's spoken directives. Neither did he respond to his colleagues, who found him, unmoving, on his seat, staring dully before him. Annoyed, Thornton drove off. He was not about to give up, even if he needed to scramble the brains of dozens of people. With the police on his back, he could not delay.

He felt more assured when he chose his second guinea pig; the younger bouncer who Thornton considered to have an oafish expression. Before he'd conducted the failed experiment, it had dawned on Thornton where he'd seen the man before their confrontation at Rowan's. The young man worked as a gardener in the city park, close to the Challens' laboratory. It was in this park that Thornton set up his second experiment.

Thornton had placed the Pacifier in an oversized briefcase, with meshed holes inserted for a concealed microphone and a directional speaker. His luck was in; he arrived at the park and caught sight of the oafish man preparing a garden bed for two oak seedlings. Thornton sat on the grass, behind a colourful garden bed of flowers and short shrubs, close to where the young man was toiling. He set up the Pacifier with the speaker strategically pointed between the branches of a shrub. Thornton sat, pretending to read a book as he waited for the gardener to become sufficiently immobile. He cursed softly in frustration, when the gardener was approached by a colleague. Fuming, impatient, Thornton had to wait as the two men became involved in a discussion.

The thin, oafish gardener did most of the talking. He complained bitterly about 'the people who run the country.' According to him, these untrustworthy people were able to cling to power by spreading lies to confuse and subjugate an ignorant public. A compliant media was all too eager to peddle their lies.

'Sure, these people lie,' his colleague said. 'They all lie, Ron.'

'Yes. But some won't stop at anything to stop the public from finding out the truth. Take my mate, Harry. He was on to them. He taught me most of what I know about what these people have done. He knew too much, so they scrambled his brain. That's what. He's a vegetable now, Ben.'

'I don't know, Ron. My guess is that he probably popped a pill that he shouldn't have taken.'

'No way,' Ron said, indignant. 'Harry never did drugs. There's no doubt in my mind; the bastards got to him. He was too great a threat to them.'

At last, the oafish gardener's colleague wandered off, shaking his head. As Thornton had hoped, the young man became suitably still as he began digging a hole one for one of the oak seedlings. Then the man followed up by placing wooden stakes and a plastic protective barrier around the new tree. Thornton sprang into action. Passers-by were most likely surprised to see a man sitting, seemingly speaking to a large, black briefcase that was balanced on the branches of a shrub. Thornton took no notice of them. He was too desperate for his experiment to succeed.

Later that evening, Deborah Challen walked into the police station to surrender, after having dinner outside at a restaurant.

From the day Deborah made her confession, a self-satisfied Thornton became a regular visitor to the city park. Whenever he approached the young gardener, the thin man was obliged to stop whatever he was doing and bow deeply to the man whom he'd come to believe was the cleverest man in the entire world. The gesture gave the dapper man carrying the oversized briefcase a huge buzz. So much did Thornton revel in the experience that not only did he visit the park regularly but, at times, he also attended Rowan's bar to receive his homage.

It was with deep regret that his rising ambition convinced Thornton to move to the more affluent side of the city. As he set ever more lucrative plans into motion, he found little time to visit the city park. By that time, the gardener was of little consequence to him. Thornton's plans involved receiving favours from far bigger fare; rich people who insisted on giving him, a complete stranger, large wads of cash and other generous gifts.

AUDREY

Audrey Brockhurst awoke, bleary-eyed. A spring-
time shower tapped a gentle rhythm against her
bedroom window. Beside her, Bobby was fast asleep. He
was a tall, balding professional bodybuilder. Audrey
checked the digital clock beside her. Startled, she sat
bolt upright. It was a few minutes past nine. She rarely
emerged from her bed before ten, but this morning she
hurriedly shook off the blankets.

Her stirrings woke Bobby. Yawning, he instinctively
reached out a tired arm to curl around Audrey's waist
as she sat on the edge of the bed. 'Piss off Bobby.' She
flung his arm aside.

'What's up, Aud?' Bobby lifted himself onto one elbow. 'Are you okay?'

Audrey snorted. 'I thought up this great tune last
night. When I woke up this morning that tune came to
me again. But damn it! It's gone again. It's right there
at the front of my mind. I know it is. But—' She
tapped her forehead.

'It's okay, baby. Don't force it. It'll come.'

'Shut up!' Audrey snapped. 'You're making things
worse.'

'Okay. Settle down.' Bobby lowered himself, glancing pensively at her.

Audrey swore. Angry, she slipped out of her lacy nightie and pulled on a pair of jeans and a T-shirt. She strode into the kitchen, poured herself a carrot juice and drank it in one gulp.

Bobby, wrapped in a dressing gown, appeared at the kitchen doorway. For a brief time, he found Audrey gazing at rivulets tumbling down the window. 'Hey, Honey; what's up? You know I'm always here for you.'

She did not glance his way. 'If you really want to help, Bobby, just leave me alone.' Bobby watched on as Audrey snatched up her handbag and dashed outside, slamming the door behind her. She jumped in her car and sped into the street, tyres squealing.

THE CAFÉ

With rain teeming down, Audrey rushed from her car, leaving behind an umbrella. After pausing to check the fading black letters above a small and nondescript inner-suburban café, she ran inside. The café was empty apart from a burly barista, clothed in black, who leaned against the counter, reading a newspaper. The man was aged in his mid-forties and had flopping jowls like a bulldog. He glanced casually at the woman who had rushed through the door; but his eyes quickly widened as he jumped to attention, dropping the newspaper. 'Good morning, Miss Brockhurst,' he stammered. 'You are Audrey Brockhurst, aren't you?'

'Yes, I am.' Audrey said coldly. She steeled herself, being in no mood for conversation, nor adulation. The café was small and narrow with ten mostly small, dark-varnished tables in two neat, parallel rows. The tables were covered by clear plastic held down by metal clips. A coffee machine and a cash register took up most space on the small counter. Beside the counter was a fridge revealing a variety of drinks. Pastries and snack items lined a shelf, visible beneath the counter. The furniture was old and weathered. The off-white walls extended to a cream-coloured ceiling from which two stained, long neon lights hung.

'A large black coffee, please. No sugar.' Unsmiling, she brushed some of the dampness from her shoulders and hair as she critically scanned the room.

'Black coffee? Sure. My pleasure.' The barista jumped to attention. 'Wow. I can't believe it. Audrey Brockhurst. In my cafe. Would you mind if I took a photo of the two of us? Please.'

'I would mind. Sorry.'

He shrugged, disappointed. 'I understand. Everybody must ask you for photos all the time. Anyway, take a seat. Anywhere.'

Audrey moved to the rear of the café.

'I've got your album,' the barista enthused as he took his place behind the coffee machine. '*Bittersweet*. It gives me goose bumps every time I hear it. I play it all the time in the café. But damn it, just the other day, my wife took it home. Bugger!'

Audrey offered a fleeting smile. She shifted her focus to the fading paint on the ceiling. When she was a schoolgirl, she had often frequented places such as this with her friends. But no longer. 'Thank you. Black coffee. No sugar.'

Expectant, she faced the door.

'Black coffee. On the way,' the barista said brightly.

As he worked the coffee machine, a stranger with gold-rimmed spectacles and thinning brown hair walked briskly inside. The stranger wore a heavy grey jacket and sported an umbrella, which he shook dry. In his other hand he held a large briefcase that seemed damaged, and poorly repaired.

The stranger flashed cold eyes at the barista. 'Large black coffee. Strong. Two sugars.' He did not dwell. The stranger strode confidently and took up the seat facing the young starlet. After leaning his wet umbrella against a seat opposite, the man placed his briefcase carefully on the table, tapped it, then leaned towards Audrey. She examined his beaming face. Her major hit *Bittersweet* began playing, though the volume was faint. She thought it odd; hadn't the barista told her that his wife had taken the album home?

'Hello, Audrey. Nice to meet you at long last,' the stranger said with a disarming smugness. 'It took me a while to catch up with you, what with you... and me... being so busy. But, since that day when I first laid eyes on you, I've been determined to get together with you. I'm a very determined man, Audrey.' He briefly stroked the briefcase. 'You probably don't remember me. I caught your act one night in Rowan's a while back. I had to... leave before making your acquaintance.' He smiled. 'Besides, I wasn't ready to meet you back then.'

'I admire your persistence. It's a shame that I've been so busy.' Audrey had a deep aversion to strange men approaching her wanting to chat. Invariably, she disposed of them swiftly and icily. Bobby usually kept them well away. But the man sitting before her was... somehow... different to the numerous creeps who sought to pester her. This man was special. Instantly, she knew that they shared an unique and intrinsic mystical understanding of one another. Yet, to look at him, he wasn't her type. He looked more like a boffin, maybe an accountant. His suit seemed expensive, his hair was styled, so he had to be successful at whatever he did.

'I saw you perform again at Rowan's three nights

ago,' continued the confident stranger. 'I enjoyed your show, oh so very much. You are one hell of a sexy lady when you strut your stuff. I nearly asked you to come home with me right there and then. But prudence prevailed and I decided to wait patiently until today.'

She nodded at him. 'Thank you. I'm very flattered.'

'I look forward to you and me becoming an item. We will, as you are fully aware. This morning marks our joyful beginning.' He glanced around. 'Believe me; I didn't choose this place because of its atmosphere,' he whispered. 'I chose it because it gives us the privacy that I need to discuss some important matters with you. In the future you and I will visit some of the most exclusive venues in town. I can't wait.' His smile broadened.

'Yes, I remember performing at Rowan's. Thank you for your interest. Again, I'm flattered. What do you do for a living, Mr...?'

The dapper man grinned. 'I'm the campaign manager for Geraldine Hughes. As you probably know, there's an election coming up in a couple of months' time.'

'Yes, I know. People ask me to help with campaign fundraisings all the time. For different political parties. But I keep clear of those sorts of things. Geraldine Hughes...? Isn't she the old lady who's always going on about the banks?'

The barista brought them their coffees. The look on the stranger's face signalled that the man should not linger. The barista slunk to his counter.

The stranger's attention returned to Audrey. 'Yes, that's Geraldine all right. Mind you, she would be deeply offended if she heard you calling her old. She's fifty-six actually. I can fill you in on a little secret about her. Of course, you won't breathe a word of this to another soul…' He checked his briefcase as Audrey nodded absently. 'You see, she's certain to be re-elected. It's a safe seat for the government after all. But not long afterwards, Geraldine will unexpectedly quit politics for a reason she will steadfastly refuse to explain. No one will be able to convince her to stay on. And, when she does leave, I'll be nominated as her replacement. By then, I'll have garnished plenty of support within the Party. Of course, the voters will need to vote for me. But, as I said, it is a safe seat.'

'That's very interesting.' Audrey winced as she tasted the coffee. It was very ordinary.

'Yes. I think so too. Audrey, for me to be truly successful in politics, and I'm talking about reaching the highest level, I need a wife that will increase my profile in the eyes of the electorate and, particularly, in the media. My public profile will become increasingly important as my political career continues to rise. Which it will.'

'What you say makes sense.'

'I fully agree. I will carefully plan my strategy to ensure that nothing and no one will get in my way. That's not as simple to achieve as I would like.' He smirked as Audrey took in his words. 'But I will succeed. It is important to me. You see, I have an unsatiable desire to be admired. In fact, I'm prepared to go as far as to admit it; I crave adulation. And I lack the willpower to deny those cravings. Anyway, I'm babbling.'

'Oh no. Not at all. I find you fascinating.'

He grinned. 'I was sure you would feel that way. You are so kind, Audrey. What I want to say is; I need you, Audrey. So, after this tedious, but necessary, election of Geraldine takes place, you will marry me. Start looking for a dress. The wedding will take place immediately before my endorsement as the Party candidate. Choose a dress that will attract maximum press coverage. But not overly revealing. Money is no object; I have very rich benefactors.'

'Yes. I will marry you,' Audrey said, without a moment's hesitation.

'Perfect. I knew you'd agree. After all, I'm irresistible.'

She blinked. 'Yes, you are. And you've come up with a very clever plan.'

The confident stranger leaned back in his seat. 'I'm almost embarrassed by your praise. But, yes, I am very clever. You know, Audrey, you'll reap some wonderful rewards by teaming up with me. Believe me, I'm a very good catch. Rich people give me money all the time. And I'm not just talking about political donations to the Party either. Then they conveniently forget they ever gave me any money at all. Isn't that remarkable? And it's all completely fool-proof.'

Audrey smiled faintly. 'You are the most incredible and clever man that I've ever met. I look forward to our wedding.'

'Oh, Audrey, you flatter me again. Of course, you'll forget what I just said about how people give me money all the time, won't you? And forget my political ambitions.' He gazed at her, with a smug grin.

'Of course.' She looked at him, confused. She'd already forgotten.

'Oh, it goes without saying that you'll have to dump your boyfriend immediately. Let me know if he causes you any trouble. If he's stubborn, I'll be able to persuade him. Trust me on that.'

Audrey's eyes stared blankly at him.

He took a pen and sheet of paper from the pocket of his jacket. 'Write down your mobile phone number. I'll be in touch soon. When I do, I'll bring your engagement ring. And I may well take my bride-to-be home with me.'

'That's fine with me.' She scribbled on the sheet of paper.

He glanced at the paper, then tucked it and the pen back in his pocket. He hastily drank the rest of his coffee, scooped up his belongings, and rose to his feet. 'Got to dash. Unfortunately, I have lots to attend to.' He turned to leave.

'I understand. Oh, who are you by the way?' Audrey inquired.

The stranger turned around and smiled wryly 'Oh yes, I should tell my future bride that, shouldn't I? My name, my dear, is Thornton Bonney. It has been a great pleasure to meet you, Audrey.'

'I feel the same way... Thornton.' She studied his face, curious as to what it was about this man that so attracted her. 'Don't keep me waiting.'

A look of mock surprise came over Thornton's face. 'How nice it is to hear those words. Have a little patience, my dear. But, as much as it grieves me to tear myself away, I must say bye for now.'

'Yes. Bye... Thornton.'

Thornton strode out of the café as if he owned it. The barista frowned as Thornton strode past. Audrey stared at the dull, fading paint on the wall beside her. She didn't like the colour. The barista drifted over to pick up the two empty cups and drop off the bill. He didn't smile. Nor did he speak. Audrey avoided making eye contact.

She dropped off some cash on the counter to pay for

the coffees. In the corner of her eye, she saw the barista gazing intently at her. There was a look of concern on his jowled face. Did the guy believe that she'd been uncomfortable in the presence of the confident, flashy young man?

ELECTION NIGHT

Thornton made his triumphant entrance into the large hall to the sound of a wave of loud clapping and cheering. Slowly, pausing often to soak in gushing words of congratulations, he made his way through the throng of well-wishers. The people crowded around him, joyous in the thrall of victory. His victory. Some raised glasses of champagne. These people adored him. Many shook his hand or patted him on his back. Thornton loved it. It took some time before he reluctantly tore himself away from the crowd to join the bigwigs of the Party, who had lined up on the stage.

The cheering and clapping became thunderous as he stepped to the podium with a fist pump. His jacket and tie had been discarded in his car; the white shirt, top button undone, was the image he sought to present to the world this night. The man who was just one of them. Thornton hesitated, soaking up the energy in the room and to admire the huge posters of him that lined every wall. The posters carried no message; only his name in large letters and the Party name in smaller letters underneath. It had taken numerous photo snaps before the photographer came up with one Thornton approved of.

Thornton raised his arms, fists clenched, in acknowledgement of the crowd that gazed adoringly at him. Someone thrust a very full glass of champagne in his hand. Some of it spilt as he drained it in one gulp. The crowd cheered louder. The Party big-wigs kept their distance. For this was Thornton's night; the culmination of a slick, carefully micro-managed and expensive campaign. Someone rushed to refill his glass and dashed just as quickly away. He gulped it down and tossed the glass aside to more cheering. He could have stood at that podium, basking in the cheering and adulation of the crowd, for much of the night. Pure exhilaration pulsated through his veins. Never had he felt so alive.

It was time to speak.

'Thank you all. Thank you so very much. Can I say a few words?' he yelled into the microphone. His every word was greeted by tumultuous applause and cheering, almost drowning out his voice. He feigned embarrassment. 'If I can be heard, that is. Please.' The crowd laughed. 'Thank you. Thank you.' The happy people before him burst into a verse of 'for he's a jolly good fellow'. He waited patiently for the singing and the cheering to subside. To his disappointment, which he tried to disguise, apart from the Party's photographer and cameraman, only two TV cameras were visible—an unfortunate consequence of winning a by-election for a safe seat. It was his one lowlight of the evening.

'I'll just—I'll just say a few words and then we can all get back to the celebrations.' He couldn't stop smiling. The constant interruptions delighted him. These people loved him. He wished there were even more of them.

A deep and loud voice bellowed from the front of

the crowd. 'Bit of shoosh. Thank you.' The noise softened into a murmur. Thornton glared at the man.

'First of all, I want to thank everybody here,'
Thornton said, beginning his well-rehearsed speech.
'And to all those who helped the campaign who are
unable to be here...' There was loud applause. 'I can't
tell you how honoured and proud I am to be standing
before you as your new member of parliament.' There
was more cheering. 'I can tell you truthfully that this is
the most wonderful day of my life. But I have to say—'
He waited for the cheering to subside once more. 'But I
have to say that I wouldn't be standing here if it hadn't
been for the hard and dedicated work of all of you.
Thank you all from the depth of my heart.' The wild applause kept coming. 'There are two people in particular
who I must offer a special thank you to, for everything
they've done for me. And I need to let them know right
here how much they mean to me. The first person to
thank is my predecessor, my good friend and brilliant
adviser, and altogether fantastic human being: Geraldine Hughes. Where are you, Geraldine?'

Geraldine Hughes made her way through the front
of the crowd and stepped onto the stage to stand beside
Thornton on the podium, and wave. The middle-aged
matriarch, dressed in white, was tall and slim, with
shoulder-length, grey hair. Thornton was none too
pleased by the overwhelming response she received. He
placed his arm around her, an action that became a
gentle nudge to move her further from the podium.
Geraldine smiled and bowed, waved some more and
blew kisses to the crowd before standing beside the
Party bigwigs. Thornton resumed his moment in the
spotlight.

Beaming, Thornton yelled into the microphone as

the applause for Geraldine took time to ease. 'I—Thank you—Thank you—I can tell you, filling Geraldine's shoes in parliament will be one hell of a tough assignment. Why she chose to retire so soon after the general election, despite her being capable of achieving much, much more, I will never know.' There was wild cheering. Again, too much for his liking. 'I, and all of you here, I'm sure, feel she still has a lot to give to the Party and to the country. Yes, I'm sure. Geraldine, I will always treasure the advice you gave me these past few weeks. But pardon me if I ignore one piece of that advice. You told me that I shouldn't go looking for a post in the Ministry within my first couple of years in parliament. But I can tell you all now, here, I'll be giving the Ministry my best shot as soon as I can.' The crowd cheered. A few of the big-wigs, and Geraldine herself, looked blankly at him. 'I am fired with too much passion to hold back from delivering the very best I can give for my constituents, and for my country. And, to best achieve those goals, I need to be in the Ministry.'

Thornton let his words sink in. He gazed at the Party officials, assessing those who seemed to disapprove of his bold statement.

'The second person I need to thank, and please come and join me, my dear, is my dedicated, hard-working, and extremely talented and ravishing wife, Audrey.' A huge cheer broke out. Audrey was standing near the edge of the stage, dressed modestly in an ankle-length, glittering silver dress and with her hair styled and trimmed, in the manner expected of the wife of a member of parliament. Albeit a somewhat stylish one. She gave the crowd a bashful wave. 'Please, Audrey, come and join me,' She smiled shyly as she stepped up to the stage. Thornton butted in as the cheering and some raucous hooting dragged on. 'Such is her dedication to see me serve my country that she chose to put on hold her own highly successful career. She did this for me, and for the benefit of the Party. Most of all, for the benefit of the country. I feel humbled and privileged by her selfless act.' He reached out his hand towards her.

Audrey Bonney made her way hesitantly to the podium. She may have been dressed as a consummate politician's wife, but her presence sent the photographers into a frenzy. Her husband moved swiftly to her side as cameras whirled, clicked and flashed. He shuffled about to ensure he kept facing the crowd and, in particular, the publicists and the press. Thornton kept a firm grip around Audrey's waist, a broad smile on his face. He burst out in a fit of laughter.

SCANDAL

On a dark, late-winter's evening in a fashionable, leafy, inner suburb, three television crews and a few press reporters and photographers huddled together in clumps outside the front gate of the stately double-storey home of Geraldine Hughes. The tall trees lining the street swayed gently in the breeze. Impatient and cold, the crews sipped coffee and made small talk to kill time. Periodically, they speculated on what machinations had to be taking place inside the house.

From behind the high, black wrought-iron fence, three sour-faced, plain-clothed policemen faced the media contingent, standing shoulder to shoulder like guard dogs, toting walkie talkies, guns holstered. Two strongly built men in black suits and thin ties flanked either side of the front door, arms crossed. Inquisitive neighbours, some draped in blankets, had gathered in twos and threes along the street, craning their necks over cars, fences, and gates, curious about the goings on.

Gail Leslie, a tall, athletic reporter for one of the TV crews, paced back and forth along the footpath, her hands buried into the pockets of her heavy knee-length coat. She drew the coat about her for extra warmth. Twenties-something, she had long blonde hair, tied back. Bored and longing for another hot coffee, she strode towards her colleague, Mike Wardlow, who peered out from the front seat of the parked news van.

'Think it'll go until late?' she said. 'It would limit the coverage. The network might have to keep running with the crackdown on that anti-vax demo that got out of control, as the lead.'

In his forties and sporting bushy black hair, Mike shrugged. 'Don't know. Simpson's advisors must be pressing him to act. He needs to put this disaster behind him. The discussion is more likely to be how he'll break the news. And the aftermath.'

'Roberts goes,' Gail replied with a diffident shrug. 'No doubt. If not for the deed, surely for the cover up. What on earth was he thinking? Must have panicked. Can't work out why Simpson didn't ditch the guy this morning, and taken the flack. This way, the sordid mess gets dragged along.'

Mike stroked his chin. 'Yeah, very strange. Even the sections of the press who'd been sympathetic to Roberts are baying for his blood. Maybe what the delay is about... is deciding who will replace him. Until the scandal, he'd been feted as being quite competent. So, what now? I reckon Stella is the favourite to take over. What do you think?'

Gail pursed her lips. 'She's tough enough. But she has her detractors.'

Mike grinned. 'You for instance?'

'Just doing my job. She can be abrasive.'

'You women are so hard on one another, aren't you? Well... apart from maybe Stella no one stands out. And who'd want to be standing in Roberts' shoes.'

'True. It's going to take someone with credibility to push through Roberts' amendments to the taxation laws. Right now, it's a mess. Obviously, he had other matters on his mind.' The two of them shared a smirk.

Someone from a rival crew, standing beside the front gate, raised an alarm. All heads looked towards the front door. Someone inside had peered out to speak to the two huge men on either side of the door. The movement sent camera crews leaping into action, scooping up their equipment to jostle with one another around the gate. Mike donned his headset. 'Studio. Mike here. You guys standing by?' he barked into his mouthpiece. 'Good. I think something is about to happen. Be ready to switch over to Gail on short notice.'

Gail flung her warm coat onto the back seat of the van. Shivering from the cold, she sighed, patted her hair into shape and adjusted her bright-blue pant suit as she joined the other crews. Mike mouthed the words 'be with you soon.' A microphone was thrust into her hand, an assistant performed a sound check, and each of her crew members nodded their readiness. The timing was good. That moment, the white Prime Ministerial car came into sight; its sole occupant being a chauffeur.

Wardlow yelled into his mouthpiece. 'Cross to Gail now! Now!' A wave to his crew, and portable lights were switched on. TV cameras were hoisted on shoulders. The car pulled into the driveway, ushered through the tall, wide gate by the police. Gail stood straight as the go-ahead came over her earpiece: 'We're crossing live to Gail Leslie at the home of Geraldine Hughes. As we can see on the screen, the Prime Minister's car has just pulled up. We expect Mr Simpson to come and address the media any time now. Over to you, Gail.'

'Thanks, Marcie.' She faced the camera. 'There has

been movement in the house behind me. The police will not let us get any closer. As you can see, they appear to be taking instructions through their walkie talkies. The feeling here is that the Prime Minister will finally make a brief but decisive announcement.'

A policeman stepped over to the gathered camera crews. 'Keep the driveway clear, please.' The man looked edgy.

'Is the Prime Minister about to speak to the media?' a reporter from another crew got in. 'The public is waiting to be informed about the events of the last two explosive days.'

'That is for the Prime Minister to decide,' replied the grim-faced policeman.

There was an awkward lull for a couple of minutes, as the cameras focussed on the closed front door of the house. To fill in time, Gail reminded viewers about the scandal in which Minister Roberts had become embroiled. She cut her report short when four assistants of the Prime Minister spilled out through the front door. They winced at the sight of the salivating hyenas poised outside the front fence. The door shut behind them.

The assistants were bombarded by much the same question. 'When is the Prime Minister coming to provide an explanation for the behaviour of Mr Roberts?' "No comment" was the reply. The cameras continued to record. Something needed to happen, or the TV stations would pull the plug on the live coverage.

The front door opened again. 'There's some activity at last,' said Gail as the crews jockeyed for the prime position. 'We are now expecting the Prime Minister to address the media.'

Suddenly, there he was: George Simpson, Prime Minister. Flashes ignited like strobe lights. With a nod,

Simpson stepped behind the two burly men who had been guarding the door. The three dashed towards the Prime Minister's car, without acknowledging the gathered media. One of the burly men opened the back door. Simpson jumped in. Those on the other side of the fence gave a collective gasp. Simpson's minders slammed the door behind him, and the car began to reverse, escorted by the police.

'What?' Gail exclaimed. She very nearly added a few words on live TV that would have gotten her sacked.

'He's making a runner,' someone called out, in seeming disbelief.

'He must be kidding,' another gasped. Someone swore.

Most of the gathered contingency glanced at one another, too stunned to react. But not Gail. As the car reversed out of the driveway, she reached its back door and thrust her microphone towards Simpson, her camera man filming over her shoulder. 'Prime Minister,' Gail yelled as she ran beside the car. 'What do you have to say about this extraordinary scandal? And the botched cover up?' Prime Minister Simpson, his profile rendered as a cringing shadow by the tinted glass, averted his eyes. 'What took place at the meeting that just broke up?' someone behind her barked. 'Have you demanded the resignation of Minister Roberts?' Microphones and cameras were thrust as the car as pulled into the street.

'Is your leadership now under threat?' yelled another reporter as the car accelerated down the road. The question was merely a lingering moment of media theatre.

The attention turned to the Prime Minister's principal secretary who strolled, pensive, to the front gate.

She was a thin, short woman in her late thirties, dressed in black. She stopped at the front gate, valiantly trying to appear calm before an agitated gaggle, who hurled questions her way. She stood, defiant. 'The Prime Minister has no comment to make at this time,' she said with a quivering voice.

'Why has he refused to address the media tonight?' Gail asked. It was one question interspersed amongst many.

The principal secretary did not flinch. 'He will be holding a press conference at the front of Parliament House at ten o'clock tomorrow morning. At that time, he will make a full statement and answer any questions you care to raise.' Amidst the barrage of questions that followed, she spun around and briskly walked to the front door, stepping inside. The two burly men at the door resumed their stance, arms crossed. TV cameras filmed her every step.

Gail looked directly into the camera before her, trying to mask her indignation. 'I stand here before you in a state of utter disbelief. I am struggling to find the words to describe what we have just witnessed,' she said. 'The Prime Minister has chosen to slink away like a fox into the night, rather than inform the viewing public as to what is going on.' Her mind was whirling. She had endured the cold for hours only to be treated with disdain. She needed to press on, if only as a lead up to the morning's press conference. 'It was thirty-six hours ago that Minister Roberts's reputation lay in tatters. Yet the Prime Minister's lame and evasive response to this crisis has left me shocked, and most likely you out there as well. His actions tonight were sheer cowardice. We are left to speculate whether Mr Simpson's own career may be in jeopardy. Did he play a part in the cover up?

Tomorrow morning, at the promised ten o'clock press conference, Mr Simpson will need to justify why he should remain as Prime Minister. His reputation may be perma-nently damaged. For now, I'll pass you back to the studio. This is Gail Leslie, reporting outside the home of former MP, Geraldine Hughes.'

The camera was switched off. 'Got the whole thing, Gail,' said the camera man, as Gail dashed to the van to seek the warmth of her coat. 'Right up until the car dis-appeared around the corner.'

'Brilliant summary, Gail,' said Mike, smiling.

She shrugged, simmering. 'It was ad hoc, Mike. I can't believe this. The opposition and the media are going to want his head tomorrow.'

'For sure. Who would have figured he'd go belly up? He's lost the plot. There must be more to this scandal than we know.'

'Drop me off home please.' Gail longed to escape the cold air. Suddenly, Mike's hand shot up, seeking silence. His other hand cupped over his headphones. A message was being relayed to him. He gasped. 'Can you confirm that…? Really? Wow.'

'What is it?' Gail pressed as Mike snapped off his headset. He stared at her, wide-eyed, bewildered. 'Just heard from my source in the building. You won't believe this. Simpson has cut Roberts adrift. No surprises there. Why he didn't make the announcement tonight I don't know. Roberts' replacement is going to be… and get this… Bonney.'

'Bonney!' the entire camera crew gasped in unison.

'Yup. Bonney. Apparently, it's a done deal. My source knows his stuff. Simpson will make a joint an-nouncement tomorrow morning.'

'What Ministry will he get?' an incredulous Gail

blurted. 'Can't possibly be Treasury. Maybe a new Ministry of Worthless Babble and Arranging Photo Shoots. Hell… Simpson must be delusional if he believes that Bonney is up to the job. Are you sure about that tip?'

'Positive.'

Gail shook her head as if warding off a fly. 'All he's proven since he was elected is what a lightweight fool he is. And he has form. Those reports about his bouts of drunkenness and temper can't all be false.'

'True. Don't ask me to explain.'

'It's not about talent, obviously. My guess is that Simpson is being pushed by Bonney's backers. The man has some very influential people on his side. God knows what they see in him. Whatever. I'll take bets that we'll be reporting Bonney's demise very soon. He's a certainty to fall flat on his face.'

Mike shrugged. 'Couldn't agree more.'

The sound recordist called out. 'Speak of the devil. Bonney's stepped outside. He's coming this way.'

'Go get him, Gail,' growled Mike. 'Press him about the rumour. See how he responds.'

Gail nodded. 'He'll be sure to brush it aside. But he can't resist another chance for a photo shoot, can he? So true to form.' The crew picked up their gear and jostled their way towards the front gate behind Gail, who reluctantly tossed her warm coat at the van window for Mike to catch.

Thornton ambled towards the gate, stopping opposite Gail. No advisors or minders accompanied him, though a couple of his colleagues peered, anxious, out from the front door. He felt snug. The police drifted close but kept to one side. The government was disintegrating, but that was irrelevant. The next election was some time away; he could get a lot done by that time. Even if the Party lost the election, myriad possibilities awaited him. Perhaps turn his hand at becoming a TV presenter. Or an actor. He could lead a cult with a following of tens of thousands of devotees. Regardless, he'd be very, very rich and powerful. But those considerations were for a future date. For now, he was the sole focus of the gathered media.

He smiled, prepared for any question fired his way. The tricky ones he'd leave for a floundering Simpson the next morning. With the cameras directed at him, and bulbs flashing, the reporters pressed against the fence. All posed much the same question. 'Mr Bonney; what can you tell us about the events of this evening?'

It was Gail who Thornton chose to face. He stroked his chin, unperturbed, and eyed the eager reporter with a steady gaze. Her subtle body movements as she flinched ever-so-slightly from the cold wind gusts, tantalised him. Perhaps… another day… He needed to show the world what a statesman he was. Thornton cleared his throat. 'As you are aware, the PM will give a press conference tomorrow morning. I will not speculate on what he will say at that time.'

The faces on the gathered crews dropped. A few looked away. He was off to a bad start. 'But you may be speculating if me standing before you here indicates that I will be elevated to the Ministry tomorrow.' The crews' interest returned. 'I can't confirm or deny any rumour that I may be given the immense privilege to become a Minister; that is solely a matter for the PM. But I want it known that I would be greatly honoured and… humbled… to serve my country in any capacity bestowed upon me. I reiterate the promise I made to the people of this great country the day after I was elected; I will work diligently and to the best of my ability to enrich the lives of my countrymen and women. There is much that needs to be set right. I am fully committed to achieving just that.'

'Mr Bonney,' said Gail, 'you are practically admitting that you'll be elevated to the Ministry tomorrow. Why not confirm it? Otherwise, why have you come to talk to us.' The faces before him became expectant.

Thornton broke into a grin. 'You're getting way ahead of yourself, Ms Leslie. I say it again; the PM alone decides who will form the Ministry.' He gave a knowing smirk. 'But regardless of what takes place tomorrow, I will be at the forefront of initiating tough measures to address the declining ethical standards within our society. And be assured, members of parliament will not be exempt.' He gazed intently at the cameras facing him. 'My parents instilled in me the principles of honesty, integrity and the adherence to law and order. Those who flagrantly transgress those standards must be dealt with summarily and swiftly. With no leniency shown. That is all from me for tonight. I will have more to say after the PM's press conference tomorrow.'

G ail stared at him, mouth agape. Thornton had practically conceded that his elevation to the Ministry the next day, was a sure thing. As absurd as the notion was. Thornton's escapades and transgressions were no secret in media circles, though network heads seemed reluctant to allow them to go to air or print. The spiel he had delivered had been breathtaking in its hypocrisy and its reversion to populist drivel. Yet, the network may well run with a grab; it offered a speculative scoop on a night that had been a huge non-event. Ratings have a way of superseding credibility. Before the stunned TV reporter could conjure up a further question that did not incur the risk of slander, a self-satisfied Thornton turned and walked briskly inside the home of Geraldine Hughes, with a spring in his step and his head held aloof.

'Typical Bonney rant,' Mike mused, as he sat back against his seat. 'I hate listening to the man so bad. And he won't stop complaining about our treatment of him. But, unless someone senior torpedos him for stepping beyond the bounds of protocol with his appearance tonight, it pains me to think that we'll be dealing with that prick more often. Until that inevitable day comes when he falls flat on his arrogant face. I hope it happens soon.'

TRIUMPH

Thornton glided into the ornate living room of his opulent new home, with its liberal touches of stucco, expensive canvases, his framed election poster, solid oak doors, antique furniture, and plush orange carpet. He was resplendent in his deep crimson-and-black silk pyjamas, matching dressing gown and slippers. The dressing gown hung loose about his waist, partly concealing his expanding waistline. When he'd seen his image on TV he resolved to watch his diet and work out more in Audrey's home gym. Even more important; Audrey had to stay trim for the paparazzi. Not that she needed any prompting; she was in the gym most of the time whenever he was home.

But this evening was for celebrating. A log fire crackled softly as Tchaikovsky's *1812 Overture* blasted through the room, on a loop. It was fitting that Thornton swept into the room the instant Tchaikovsky's cannon fire shattered the air. He sipped from his expensive champagne.

A news bulletin on the large wall TV was about to start. He switched off his mobile phone, dialled up the volume of the TV and lowered the volume of the music.

To his displeasure, the first news report covered a protest held in the city centre where a few police officers were attacked and arrests made. 'Lock the bastards up and throw away the keys,' he snarled. He clapped when the TV station switched to cover the scandal. Thornton paced before the TV as the report dwelt on the tribulations of Prime Minister Simpson.

'Okay. Okay,' sneered Thornton. 'Enough of that loser.' He let out an exclamation of joy and rushed close to the TV as his own image filled the screen. Posture, smile, hair, all good. A couple of kilos less would have served him better.

The TV grab dwelt on his virtual admission on his elevation to the Ministry. His statement on ethics received only cursory coverage. He snorted in disappointment and paced the room. Well... tomorrow would be different, he assured himself. After Simpson's announcements, the media would dote on his every word. Roberts was in hiding. So, no distractions. Thornton would push hard with his message. He just need to keep his tummy tucked in.

The news moved on. 'That's all?' he fumed. 'Bugger.' Bristling, Thornton lowered the volume of the TV and raised the volume of Tchaikovsky's overture. He eased himself into his favourite, plush armchair, took a large sip of champagne, then embraced the armrests. He would need many strong coffees the next morning.

Audrey was curled up in the matching easy chair, close to the fire. She wore a grey woollen jumper over the top of her cotton pyjamas, When Thornton strode into the room, she placed the magazine she was reading on a coffee table and tucked herself up more, with her legs pressed beneath her chin, her arms wrapped around her legs. She had shown no interest in the TV broadcast; her gaze fixed on the fireplace.

Audrey. She had been, and remained, his ticket through some hard-to-access doors where his magic, black briefcase, with his name now emblazoned in silver across it, could do its vital work. When controversy had threatened to derail his plans, he'd presented beautiful Audrey to the world in a new, striking and expensive dress, standing resolutely beside him. It was Audrey who featured heavily in the subsequent news reports, defending her man. No reporter would dare challenge Audrey, dressed and groomed so immaculately, lest they'd be mauled mercilessly by the public. Pity that she wasn't as responsive in bed as Thornton had anticipated when she'd prowled across the stage at Rowan's. A young woman, who was curious about his large briefcase, gave him more satisfaction. Audrey was useful in many other ways. The media and the public adored her. She remembered trivial matters such as his parents' and siblings' birthdays and the birthdays of those who served his purpose. She sent them presents. Such a nice touch.

Noticing Thornton smiling, Audrey turned to him. 'You're finally sitting down. You've been on your phone so much tonight.'

Thornton admonished her with her eyes. She drew a breath, and sunk into her seat, clutching her legs tighter. 'Each phone call represents another jewel in my crown, Audrey,' he said. 'My future successes depend on the support I get from key players. Even the calls from colleagues who are critical of my actions tonight, are important. They let me know who I can rely on. And who need to be... err... convinced of my credentials.' He'd already compiled a mental list. Thornton sighed in satisfaction, in the way that a person appreciates their own ruse.

'It never ceases to amaze me how events keep working out to your benefit.'

Thornton shrugged. 'Very true, Audrey. I'll let you in to a secret; I will be appointed as Prime Minister sooner than even my backers will be expecting. When that happens, I will command a large team of dedicated PR people to deliver me the most favourable media exposure. My helpers do everything they can to further my cause. Willingly.'

'That's good of them.'

He smirked. 'In the meantime, my immediate priorities are to neutralise my enemies and increase my public profile. Roberts told me many times that I come across as arrogant. That criticism sealed his fate. But I can't ignore his advice entirely. I need to come across as humble. A man interested in the travails of the public. My team are working on it. As you are aware, humility doesn't come naturally to the impatient man that I am. The only drawback with my elevation is that I'll be under pressure to deal with policy matters. Sheer tedium.' He gave a mock swoon. 'I'm more comfortable repeating slogans that gel with the public. That way I enhance my reputation with minimal effort.' He broke into a chuckle. 'Now, I remind you, Audrey, don't breathe a word about my ambitions. Got that? The Party and the public must be kept in the dark.'

'I understand, Thornton.' Was she even listening?

'Look at me Audrey.' She turned her head. 'Make sure you select one of your finest dresses for my press conference in the morning. Preferably one you haven't worn in front of the media before. Not too flashy, of course. But definitely elegant. It will be my day, after all. Did you make that appointment with the hairdresser first thing in the morning?'

'Yes. Very early.' Audrey's head lowered to rest on an armrest as she placed her legs on the other armrest, still clutching them tightly about her. 'I have to say; I can't help but feel sorry for Mr Simpson. I find him to be more decent than many others I've met in politics.'

Thornton smirked. 'True. That irony isn't lost on me. He's the lamb set down amongst the pack of wolves that a re his fellow MPs. Not to mention the media, which feasts on the fallen. Lambs don't occupy the top echelon o f the food chain, Audrey.' He took the last sip of champagne and placed the glass on the carpet. 'But don't t hink of Simpson as a lamb, Audrey. He's a mighty t ough operator behind closed doors. I've learnt a great d eal from him. So, whether you like him or not, Simpson's time is nearly done. After all, he's the top man, a nd he has handled the scandal and the cover up very b adly. Even his closest supporters are baffled by his c lumsiness.'

'I still think it's sad what's happening to him.' Thornton broke into an impish grin. 'Yes, terribly sad. But blood has to be spilled, Audrey, to satisfy the baying of the wolves. His imminent departure will leave a void for the opportune to jostle their way into prominence. In the short-term, one of those people, will take over as PM. But only to warm my seat while I promote my image. When I'm ready, I will take over. I need to play my cards carefully. But my triumph, in due time, is assured.'

Audrey smiled nervously. 'You have an ability to make correct decisions that never ceases to amaze me.'

'I do, don't I?' He broke into a wide grin.

'You're so clever that way.'

Thornton shrugged. 'I must confess; I am. My sole concern is timing. I need to be PM some months before the next election. I need time in the limelight. Not enough for my liking. But some important strings will need to be tugged. In the Party room, for now, I'll lie low and get others to clear the path for me; I can't show my hand too early. I'll sow seeds of discontent amongst those who oppose me. You, Audrey, will play your part. Buy more eye-catching clothes for when we attend public events.' His thoughts drifted to the reporter, Gail Leslie. 'There is much for me to work out, but I'll get there. I don't have the slightest shred of doubt.'

Audrey looked at him quizzically. 'I'm sure you will, Thornton. People warm to you all the time. Even those who are critical of you at first, come around to your way of thinking.'

Thornton allowed himself a wry, smug smile. 'They do, don't they? Well... I'm just a nice, irresistible guy, aren't I? You know that better than anyone.'

'Yes. You must be.' Her face took on a quizzical expression.

Thornton let his head sink back, to gaze at the decorative silver-and-gold stucco flourishes in the ceiling, t he impressive crystal chandelier and his election poster, prominent on an otherwise featureless wall. He grinned as he closed his eyes to contemplate the unfolding of his glorious future. It would be delivered with the help of a growing number of rich, influential and powerful benefactors. It was all so easy. With no one the wiser.

He floated into the warm and pleasant daydream he'd imagined so many times over the years. As he had always known, that dream had been a premonition. He visualised himself in the plush back seat of a long, black limousine, driven by a chauffeur, as it cruised through cheering and adoring crowds. Their smiling faces pressed against the side windows.

Thornton was startled from his floating bliss. Audrey had shifted noisily in her easy chair, uttering an exclamation of surprise. Irritated, he glared at his wife. 'Bugger you! Don't disturb me when I'm relaxing,' he snapped.

Audrey drew herself deeper into her chair. 'Sorry, Thornton. I thought I heard something outside the window.'

'You're imagining things again,' he growled. 'It's probably next door's cat.' He closed his eyes and listened to the imperious notes of Tchaikovsky as he drifted off to his wonderful fantasy.

The next moment, Thornton's world went insane...

With an almighty crash, the living room door was flung open. A tall figure, dressed head-to-toe in black, his face concealed by a balaclava, stormed into the room. The man brandished a black pistol. Thornton leapt to his feet. He stared at the man in disbelief.

'Stay where you are. Both of you. Or you die right now.' The tall figure's booming voice tremored. The hand holding the gun shook; the man was very nervous. Then the gunman did something completely weird. He bowed deeply at Thornton.

Thornton recoiled. That bow was strangely familiar. But the unreality of what was taking place froze his mind. If the madman wasn't an apparition, why hadn't the house's security system been activated? How could an intruder slip by the security people?

'Who the hell are you?' Thornton blurted, seizing the initiative. 'What are you doing in my house? What do you want? How did you get past the security?'

His words seemed to embolden the tall man who adopted a dismissive stance. 'I don't answer to scum like you. I know who you are. You are the most scheming person in the entire world. How I figured this I don't know. But yes... Mr Thornton Bonney... I know who and what you are. You are evil. That realisation came to me, long ago, in the park. My mission is to stop you, otherwise you will grab ever more power, and render the public as ignorant, powerless slaves.'

Thornton blinked. 'What the hell are yabbering about?'

The hooded figure gave a haughty laugh. 'Oh yes, pretend to be unknowing. That is what your kind wants the likes of me to believe. All helped by the media. But I know the danger you pose.' The tall man sneered. 'It took a long time to track you down. Finding you became my destiny.'

'You're talking utter gibberish.' Thornton's anger rose. The idiot before him was insane. He glanced at the open door. Any second, the security people would come charging in and put an end to this annoying nightmare. How would the media report this story? He'd present a brave, defiant face to the reporters. The home invasion would reinforce his message that society needed fixing.

'Just what I'd expect you to say. It was so hard tracking you down. I didn't know your name. Or where you lived. You stopped coming to the park. Or to Rowan's. Then providence stepped in, as I knew it must. I watched TV tonight. Usually, I avoid the media because of the lies that you and your kind keep peddling. I wanted to hear the lies being told about those of us who marched this afternoon. And there you were. On the screen. I heard your name. My heart sang. I didn't need to write it down. Oh, you won't believe how discrete I had to be while I tried to find you. I couldn't risk suffering the same fate as Harry.'

Thornton was dumbfounded. 'Who the hell is Harry?'

'Don't lie to me!' The hooded man's body shook in anger; the gun wavered. 'You know who Harry is. Harry stumbled on your most evil plans. Just when he was about to wreck your scheme, you turned his mind into mush. Then you disappeared. Tell me; what did you do to Harry? Did you slip some pill into his drink? Or some drug?'

Thornton blinked, barely comprehending what was unfolding. 'Look you; I have no idea what you are ranting about.' When this unpleasant encounter was brought to its inevitable end, he would double his security measures. The negligent, incompetent security guards tonight would all be sacked. Where the hell were they? Surely, they must have worked out their surveillance had been breached. In case they hadn't, he would alert them. Thornton felt his mobile phone in his dressing gown pocket. He switched it on.

Thornton needed to play for time. 'How did you get inside?'

Smiling white teeth appeared from within the balaclava. 'You'll be amazed at the tricks I've picked up over the years, working in security. I disabled your alarm. Mind you, it's a very good system. You made a wise choice. Only the best experts are able to disable it. I took my time, working on it while I hid from the police. I could only act when the coast was clear, you realise. And dealing with your locked window was child's play. Also, a good locking system. All it needed was a bit of skill.' He smiled.

The man was rambling. That suited Thornton. 'You

do realise that the security people will rush in here any second now,' he said with confidence. 'They check in with me regularly. Save yourself and make a run for it while you can.'

When the man in black took a peek at the open door behind him, Thornton hastily tapped his mobile phone password.

'The police don't scare me, Mr Bonney. By the time they come, my task will be completed. You must understand,' he said, sneering, 'that I have pledged to bring the lost and frightened people of this world out of the fog of lies in which they have been cast by you and those who do your bidding. Today will be the most glorious day in my life. Today I will change the future. And I will avenge Harry.'

The tall, hooded man's eyes looked to the ceiling. Turning to one side, Thornton tapped out a hurried message to his minders, outside. *Help intruder.*

'My destiny is simple; you must die… Mr Bonney.'

Thornton gulped. The security guards would come bursting into the room, guns blazing, any moment. He only needed to delay this dark apparition. 'You said you saw me on TV. Didn't you listen to the speech I made? I was demanding that politicians—'

'Quiet! Yes, I saw you.'

'In that speech I pledged to rid politics of the very evils you talk about.' He forced a smile. Turning to the side, he switched his phone to call mode. 'You see, you are right. I'm on your side. I realise that the people of the world have been betrayed by the powerful. That is why—'

'Quiet!' screamed the man in black. 'Your lies slip from your lips as easily as the coiling of a serpent.'

Thornton was taken aback. Where were the security

people? 'Look,' he said, his arms open wide in supplication. 'What if I gave your organisation a very generous donation. You can use that money to spread your vital message to the world. How about I do that? Believe me, I truly want to. I have a great deal of money that I keep in a black briefcase. It's in my safe. I'll go fetch it.' He took a step.

'Stop! I don't want anything from your briefcase. You're not listening to me. I know who you are. I know that you are capable of doing so much evil. Now that I have unburdened myself from the feelings I've kept bottled up inside me, I will fulfil my destiny.'

It dawned on Thornton who the man was. He drew a breath. The man was dangerously deranged. Where were the guards? Incompetents! 'I fully understand your thinking. I beg you; teach me where I am failing. Lead me from this pathway of falsehoods that I have sunk into. I want so much to learn from you.'

'No!' snapped the man. 'Mr Bonney, if I showed you the correct path you would only foul it.'

To Thornton's relief, a hint of flashing blue penetrated through the bottom of the drapes. About time.

The tall man continued. 'The only path for you is death, Thornton Bonney.'

A bolt of pure electricity surged through Thornton's body as the hooded man aimed his gun. Die? No, no. Not him. It couldn't happen. Not with his great dream so tantalisingly within reach. Not after he'd been so meticulous with his planning. He deserved to reap his rewards.

There was a knock on the front door. 'Police here. Open up. Or we'll break down the door.'

Thornton swore and clenched his fists. Open up? 'Don't stand there doing nothing!' he bellowed. 'Imbeciles!' The tall man in black glanced over his shoulder and shuddered.

Thornton looked across at Audrey, his mind racing. Audrey had uncurled to stretch out in her easy chair, placing her hands on the chair's arm rests, her bare feet on the footrest. She was only a metre from the madman. She had to be poised to spring from her seat and tackle the man. Or maybe rush over to shield Thornton from the bullets. The police would do the rest. Thornton gasped; Audrey was unmoving. The expression on her face was one of curiosity. She just sat there. After everything he'd showered on her!

'We're coming in!' called a policeman. At last! They bashed at the front door. There was a crash as the door splintered.

The gun brandished by the man dressed in black jabbed at Thornton like an accusing finger. Thornton froze. 'Hey, wait! You can't…' Then the world of Thornton Bonney exploded in a conflagration of gunfire and pain. He grasped at his easy chair as the world about him lurched.

Tchaikovsky's cannons echoed throughout the room. They sounded oddly discordant. Bells tolled as the thronging crowd pressed against the black chauffeur-driven limousine transporting Thornton. From the back seat, Thornton gazed at his adoring admirers, lapping up their adulation. His swirling world was filled with gibbering, excited voices. Tchaikovsky's discordant cannons exploded again. Audrey was screaming. She had to be exuberant with joy after hearing that he had been appointed as Prime Minister. So soon? He stumbled towards her. This magnificent moment needed to be captured by a photo of the two of them, side by side. He'd make do with the camera on his mobile phone until he could organise the official Party photographer. The screaming and yelling persisted. It may even have been him screaming. His knees, his chin, smashed into the plush carpet. Thornton looked up, at a dark, billowing world. He was in great pain.

Straining his eyes, he discerned the ruddy, round face of Jilly Challen through the darkening fog. She screamed and waved her arms about furiously. She kept screaming. On and on.

'Shut up, you idiot,' Thornton snapped. The swirling fog darkened until it was no more.

THERE'S A LIGHT THAT SHINES

THERE'S A LIGHT THAT SHINES

Hey, it's me. Got back from the big city an hour ago. What a weird day! Before I start telling you what happened; go check out the museum at the Academy for Late Twentieth Century Music. Steal the money if you have to. Grandpa had told me about the place, but it took me winning the prize to audition there before I looked it up on the internet. The info and the photos on the website don't do it justice. It's incredible. From the main city train terminal, hop to the first subway station on the eastern line. The Academy is twelve blocks east from there. I had no money for a taxi. The sky was clear. So, I walked.

The road that passes the Academy is crawling with traffic. The footpath was packed with people rushing to or from the subway. I kept getting in everyone's way. Oh, you should have seen the looks I got! I'd hoped the walk would give me some peace of mind before my audition. No chance. Hell, I'd been dreaming about this day for weeks, so sure it would be the most wonderful day of my life. My mum kept telling me; 'you've picked a song that you love, and you know it back to front.

Don't fret; you'll be fine.' But walking to the Academy, I nearly pissed myself. I was so scared.

After passing cafés, shops and tall office and apartment buildings, I came across this big, wide-open park of lawn, flowers and trees. The grass was so lush and green, and cut perfectly straight-edged against the footpath. Totally different from the dry, stubby grass, and the dusty paddocks back home, with their scrawny trees and weary-looking cattle. Smack dab in the middle of all the greenery were three cube-shaped, off-white, three-storey buildings: the Academy. I stood, gaping like an idiot. Though, I've got to say that the buildings are not as new-looking as they look on the internet. Each building had three rows of small, square windows. Running from the top to the bottom of every corner were these three long, vertical wave patterns. Maybe they mean something; I have no idea.

People were walking through the park or spread out on the grass or sitting on benches, eating, reading, or drinking coffee. My stomach was in knots so I couldn't eat my sandwiches. There's a lily pond where two paths cross. I thought about wandering around to try and calm down. But that would have cut my time checking out the museum. I was especially excited to see the most famous hologram there. The one of my idols— and my inspiration—Lorna Kiss and Jason Tell, the one and only, fabulous Tainted Reputation.

I've worshipped the duo since I was maybe ten. Heck, I don't need to tell you, do I? I've bored you for years, raving about them. I'd cut out their pictures and articles from newspapers and magazines and stuck them on cardboard to put up on the walls of my room. I followed everything they did and put out on social media. When it came to picking a song to audition at the

Academy, the decision was easy; I would sing their biggest hit. *Persephone*. My favourite song. Always has been.

Anyway… the first building was the Ministry of Culture. The second one was the Academy of Jazz Concert Hall. Grandma liked Jazz. That left the last building. And, yep, there was this sign in big blue letters next to this picture of an African American: "The Rock and Blues Music Academy and Museum." Awesome.

Even remembering my mum's encouragement couldn't make me relax. Hell, the people I was going to perform for had turned many hopefuls into stars. Thinking that terrified and excited me at the same time. Ever since I won the singing competition at the local fair, I'd had lots of sleepless nights. I couldn't concentrate at school, annoying my teachers big time. Finally, it was my big day. But I had to muster the courage not to run away. I was scared that I wasn't ready, or I that I'd stuff up. Even after all the practicing.

Smaller writing said that the museum covered the period 1955 to 2009. Grandpa's era; not mine. I only knew the music from that era because Grandpa used to play it, like stuff from the Beatles, the Tumbling Stones and songs by African Americans. *Really* old stuff. I put up listening to it because I could see how much Grandpa loved it. Anyway… I stood in front of the tall double doors of the building for quite a while. Then I took a deep breath and went inside.

Part of my prize—along with the audition, train fare to the big city, and the subway ride—was free entry to the museum. That, on its own, would have been a fabulous reward. I had maybe an hour or so to check the place out before my audition.

The lobby was painted a light-yellow and was covered with lots of painted black images of singers and bands and blown-up copies of concert tickets from that era. Nice!

To my left was a souvenir shop with posters, e-posters and figurines. There were a tables out the front where a few kids, a couple of years older than me, drank from paper cups. The two posters of the Tainted Reputation... both stunning (what else would you expect?)... were to the side of the front door. If only I had the money. Nearly spat at the posters of Shawnaa and Pauuul next to them. I can't believe that those second-rate fakers are now all the rage. All they did was hitch a ride on the fame of the Tainted Reputation. Every time I hear their version of *Persephone* I want to vomit. I switch off the TV when their songs come on, or I run out of the building or mall I'm in. It's makes me sick just how many preteens have fallen for them. Morons! I'm sorry; I get worked up whenever I think of them. As you know.

Enough about them. Kids will wake up to them before long, I'm sure. Next to the souvenir shop were two grey lifts that would take me to the audition rooms. Apparently, they also hold tutorials and singing classes up there. Just thinking about getting in one of those lifts had me rushing to have a pee. Time was ticking so I joined the queue to get inside the museum. Had a short wait; there were only six adults and two teenagers in front of me. People tapped their devices on the turnstile and went inside.

When my turn came, I tapped on the ticket from my Jason device. A clean-cut man in a dark-blue suit on the other side of the turnstile, about my dad's age, stepped in front of me. 'You're quite tall for someone under sixteen, aren't you?' He looked at me, all suspicious.

'Want me to bring up my birth certificate?' I was all smiles.

He eyed me off like I was some hick from a struggling farm in the middle of nowhere. Well... he was right, but you know what I'm getting at. The guy soon guessed that I knew how to handle bastards like him who get a buzz from picking on people like me. The only way he could stop me going inside was to get me to lose my cool. If I did, it would be caught on CCTV, and I'd get chucked out. But I had him. And he knew it. Besides, the family behind me were making impatient noises, so he gave me a filthy look and stepped aside. I smiled (sort of) at him, and walked on, hurrying past a bored, grey-haired woman security guard standing beside a light-blue, transparent sliding door. The door opened up and I came into a narrow hallway with a tall, wide wall that was lit up by flashing lights; a bit like you see in nightclubs on TV.

Hanging from that wall was a display of real guitars, microphones, tambourines and drumsticks. Signs in large print at both sides read: "Anyone interfering with the holograms and other displays will be escorted out of the museum. Strictly no photos." I ducked around the wall. When I got to the other side, I swore. Well... I couldn't help it. People stared at me. The massive hall I walked into had me gob-smacked. I'd seen some pictures taken from inside the hall on the internet but standing right in front of the holograms, was something else. All of the glittering stacks of rubies and gems in Aladdin's cave could not have been more spectacular. Wow!

I just stared. Didn't know where to start. My tiny brain was being blown away. Everywhere there were

huge 3D statues, most in full colour. They were holograms, of course, but they looked solid.

Even the small ones were maybe three times taller
than me. A few floated in the air, mostly black-and-
white or brown-and-white 2D photos of people I didn't
know; most of them smiling. Many were African Americans. I didn't know the performers in most of the colour
3D holograms either. Some were massive! There were
performers on stage, at times baring it all, or caught in
the middle of a dance move. One was of a guy twirling
a microphone stand like it was a baton. Other photos
showed performers posing for the camera, usually smiling. Visitors of all ages drifted about; not too many of
them, though. It was easy to go pretty well wherever I
wanted. Couldn't help myself going wow, wow! People
smirked at me but I couldn't help myself.

Security guards in grey uniforms wandered around
the hall but didn't look like they wanted trouble. That
suited me just fine.

Some 3D performers had long hair; others had short
hair. Some were well dressed and groomed; others
looked more like the tramps who jangle around the subway. One display that I liked featured the Beatles—
Grandpa's favourite band. It had two really tall 3D
images of the group facing one another. On one side,
they were young and fresh and well dressed in suits, all
clean-cut and groomed. On the other side, they had long
hair and moustaches, and were dressed like carnival
people.

From what I read on the different captions, many of
the rock and blues stars came from poor families, like
me. That's probably why some of them misspelled the
name of their bands.

An entire wall had seven large screens in a row featuring videos of singers and bands. One showed a woman belting out a song into a microphone as she stomped her foot hard on the stage. Another showed this kid in a band running around the stage playing a guitar, dressed in his school clothes. Couldn't hear the songs; to listen you needed to get a pair of headphones from the booths in front of each screen. I didn't have time. I'd probably have to pay anyway. Pity. Would have been nice to listen for a while.

A sign beside a lift said that it could take me to a balcony where you could see the holograms from above and see instruments and other stuff from the era. I wondered how they were able to fit in the audition rooms inside the building.

It suddenly dawned on me that I still hadn't found the Tainted Reputation hologram. And time was ticking.

I only needed to follow the crowd to the far corner of the hall. And bang! There it was! Wow! what a hologram! I tell you; it was the biggest and most fantastic hologram in the entire building. As you'd expect, it drew the biggest crowd. Goes to show how worshipped the duo are still. Most people watching on were kids older than me. A few looked to be in their twenties.

For a while I was starstruck, and had to gather my breath. I wanted to take in every detail. Even though the hologram was huge, the image was so sharp you could make out beads of sweat on their faces. Thin Jason, with his jet-black hair and dressed in his usual tight, black pants and loose suit—this one with diamond-shaped spangles of purple, mauve and dark blue, and with the top buttons of his shirt undone—was leaping high into the air, one arm reaching straight up and the other pointing at the crowd. Athletic Lorna was frozen, doing one of her famous spins, balancing on the ball of her left foot, her arms outstretched, with her head leaning to the right. Her long blonde hair spun out like ropes on a maypole. She wore a sequined, low-cut blouse and a short, loose, light-blue dress. The spin caused her dress to press tight to the front of her thighs and flare out behind her. I followed a line of giggling teenagers to a spot near the chain barrier where you could crane your head and get a peek of her rounded buttock and a sliver of bright-red panties. Did the duo pick that image, or had their management team selected it? The same image was on one of their posters at the souvenir shop. They could easily have chosen photos with Lorna in leotards (maybe not—too much like that little show-off, Shaw-naa), tight shorts or a clingy, long dress with a slit up one side. Jason, of course, always wore much the same gear. Anyway, the hologram spun me out. But, then again, I was easy to please. Looking at that hologram made the whole trip to the big city worthwhile, even if I flunked the audition. Fingers crossed, though, I wouldn't.

I managed to tear my eyes away to mingle with the crowd staring at the large glass cases on the nearby wall. The display held some of the duo's costumes, tambourines and those things they shake about that sound like rattlesnakes. There were a few posters advertising past concerts and some rare, collectors' edition vinyl records. How much are they worth, eh!? A woman in a small booth sold souvenirs or took posed photos of the visitors. For a price.

As I waited to get a better look, an attendant came up beside me. He was a middle-aged black man with white hair, and a trimmed beard. I thought uh oh, maybe trouble. 'It's because of those two that this museum can afford to stay open,' he said. The guy grinned;

he was quite nice. 'They set up a trust fund because the entry fees can't cover our costs. Most of the attendants are volunteers. The fans of that era are dying out, so funding is a big problem. Most people these days come to see that hologram. Bet that's why you're here as well.'

'Oh, yeah,' I piped up. 'They're my idols. Always will be.' Nearly told him I was going to sing one of their songs for my audition, but I wanted to keep moving. 'More people should see this place. It's amazing.'

He smiled. 'I think so as well. It brings back so many memories. Of course, many old timers will tell you that the Tainted Reputation shouldn't have a display here. They were born after 2009. Their first hit was only six years ago, and their biggest hit came out about a year later.'

'*Persephone*,' I said. 'It's still my favourite. I'm sorry, but I think the hologram *does* belong here. After all, they helped revive the music from the sixties and seventies.'

The attendant's smile widened. 'Actually, even their publicity material admitted that they *reinterpreted* some, often obscure, songs from that era, changing them almost beyond recognition. But it worked for them, didn't it? They became famous and made their fortune. Others have tried to do the same, with limited success.'

'Oh, yeah. Definitely. The copycats are all… rubbish.' Nearly said crap. Might not have gone down well.

'You probably know that your idols have their own museum now, in their home city. We were lucky; they let us keep some of their stuff. Guess they had too much. They went through so many costume changes. Even in one night.'

'I'm glad they left some stuff.' I started to back off a bit. 'I'm sorry, but I need to go. I've got to be upstairs in twenty minutes. There's still more I want to see.'

'You're auditioning?' The attendant gave me a strange look that I only understood later. I was in a hurry, so I didn't ask him what he found strange. We smiled at each other, and I re-joined the crowd.

It's incredible to think that Lorna and Jason actually wore those costumes on display, or played those tambourines with their colourful ribbons. After taking one last, long look at easily the most fantastic hologram in the museum—maybe the whole world—I rushed to the museum's exit. I could have easily spent another half hour or more in there, but my life's dream was calling out to me. I vowed to come back some day. Hopefully, as a visiting celebrity.

As I walked to the lift to take me to the audition, I checked my breathing (important at these times) and kept reminding myself of my mother's encouragement. My e-letter—I'd learnt it by heart—instructed me to go to the third floor and report to the desk there. I got in the lift. I nearly fainted when the door opened. Everything was happening fast!

Sitting at the desk was a tall, tough-looking young guy in a dark-blue uniform. Behind him were misted, double sliding doors. I flashed my e-letter. For a few moments he just sat there and raised his eyebrow. I really think he was expecting me to apologise for disturbing him. Arsehole. He goes and casually taps something on his laptop, and he looked at the screen for a long time.

'I've come here for an audition,' I said, trying not to get angry.

He pulled a 'so what' expression on me. 'I can read. You'll be meeting with Helen Capuano.' He gave me a smug smile. 'Go through the doors and walk straight ahead. The waiting room is labelled. Check in with the woman walking around with a laptop. Then wait until you get called up. You're one of the last to arrive. You won't get a second chance if you miss your name being called out.' He looked down at his screen, done with me. Didn't wish me good luck. Bastard!

I braced myself and went through those misted sliding doors. I walked slowly along, wondering which famous stars must have walked down this very same corridor. And how many soon-to-be greats were destined to follow. Maybe me? Was that too much to hope for? But I had my fantasies. My friends back home kept chiding me about being on national TV real soon. Talk about pressure!

Along the corridor were doors with labels: recording studio, training rooms, offices... Between them were photos of the holograms, and a window on the opposite side that looked down into the museum. The view was interesting but nowhere near as good as seeing it all from the ground.

A sign next to the waiting room read: "All phones must remain switched off in the Waiting Room. E-devices can only be used with headphones. Singing in the Waiting Room is strictly prohibited".

I walked inside. If I'd been hit by a truck, I couldn't have been belted harder. I may have sworn. Actually, I'm sure I did. There were about fifteen people—five being adults—inside a fairly small room that was about two-thirds full. On one wall there was a big photo of a sunset (or was it a sunrise?), behind a hill, with a lake at the front reflecting the dark hill and the red sky. The brown, plastic rows of seats were like the ones at the train station. What shocked me were the kids in that room, all younger than me. They were short and so skinny. Their clothes looked really expensive; leotards, leggings, waistcoats, and short dresses—a riot of colour, sequins and spangles. Many kids looked like dolls with their plastered-on make-up, mascara and designer hair-cuts. Half of them were definitely Shawnaa and Pauuul clones. Sucked in!

I just stood there. Could these pampered copies of those fakes be what the Academy wanted to promote? Jesus! My eyes were popping out as those kids stretched or practiced dance moves, listening to music through their headphones. I'd heard rumours that some hopefuls get plastic surgery and facial implants to improve their looks. You know what? I reckon those rumours may be true. I got so worked up that I nearly walked straight out that door. I didn't belong in the same room... no, the same building... as these kids.

Everyone stopped to stare. There was me, standing in the doorway in my best (but faded) blue jeans and old Tainted Reputation T-shirt, looking much like some of the performers in the holograms. I pressed back against the door frame, accidently opening the automatic doors. As I worked out what to do, a short, neatly dressed and groomed woman in her thirties rushed over, carrying a small, thin laptop. She looked at me as if I were some sort of alien.

'Do you have an invitation?' she said, very stern-like. It was like being sent to the headmistress.

I showed her my appointment e-letter.

She pursed her lips. 'Name?' she snapped.

My name was there on the e-letter, but I told her anyway. She tapped her laptop, checked it and screwed up her face. 'What song are you doing? I presume you're here to sing?' She checked me out, not in a nice way.

'*Persephone*,' I whispered, trying to sound casual.

The woman broke into a patronising smile. She looked behind me. 'You're doing it solo?'

I nodded, embarrassed. 'Yup.'

She blinked. Some kids sniggered. I looked their way. Many of the kids and parents gave me mean looks. I felt like a complete idiot. Doing *Persephone* by myself. No wonder the woman thought me weird.

'Well, Helen won't need to search for that one on the playlist. Are you doing the Shawnaa and Pauuul or the Tainted Reputation version?'

'Tainted Reputation. The Shawnaa and Pauuul version is... way too commercial.' I probably should have kept my mouth shut, what with so many clones nearby. It was all I could manage do to hold back from telling her that I'd sooner stick my Jason device in a bucket of fresh cow dung than download the crap those two fakes churn out. But, if I started an argument, I'd cause trouble.

The woman looked at my device. 'You are aware that illegal downloads are punishable by law.'

Why ask me that? 'Yes. Of course.' (To the law enforcement people who might read this post; this is not me admitting I've illegally downloaded any material.)

She raised an eyebrow. 'Well... the Shawnaa and Pauuul version has been all the rage since they sang it on stage ten months ago. It was meant to be just a tribute, but it brought down the roof at the concert hall.'

I shrugged and gritted my teeth. Was she baiting me? 'The Tainted Reputation version is much, much better.'

She shrugged. 'Suit yourself.'

A boy and a girl, no older than thirteen, in swirly-coloured leotards... very much Shawnaa and Pauuul clones... came out of one of the three wooden doors that had large silver Roman numerals on it. The boy stopped and stared at me, like he'd seen a ghost. He was short and thin with a flashy smile. I could tell he was an arse-hole straight away. I looked away but the kid made a beeline for me, puffing out his skinny, pale cheeks. 'What's this? Are they letting people jangle here these days?' He glared at the woman who'd greeted me. She walked off. Left me. Just like that.

'I didn't come here to cause trouble.'

'Go back to where you came from,' the boy snarled. He shifted about like he wanted to take me on. I'm not a physical person... I run away if things look like getting violent... but doing farm work comes with a bit of mus-cle, so I figured I could easily take out a pathetic brat like him. He'd need a panel beater to fix his jaw before he could sing again. But I'd get the blame. Maybe get dragged away by the cops. That would end my day. The brat knew the others in the room were on his side. He got smiles and murmurs of approval from them. In-cluding by some parents.

'Go jangle in the subway,' someone called out. Others murmured agreement.

'Get the hell out of here,' the boy fumed, pointing at the door. 'Right now.' Everyone was looking on. Things threatened to get out of control.

'Make me.' I had to call his bluff, didn't I? If it came to push and shove, there was a CCTV camera nearby. If he threw the first punch... and I only damaged him a little bit, I'd go see my aunt. She knows a lot about the law.

The smart-arse gave me a dirty look. He took a peep over his shoulder, but the others in the room stayed where they were. He was on his own, so he huffed and puffed then he and his partner stormed off through the doorway, brushing hard against my shoulder. The others in the room glared at me. As if it was all my fault. I decided right there and then that I'd stay.

Just then a thin girl with long blonde hair, maybe a year younger than me, strode up. Her sequined clothes made her stand out as a fan of the Tainted Reputation. I took a defensive stance, but much to my surprise she actually smiled. 'Hi, I'm Chloe. I'll take a wild guess and assume that it's your first time here.' Like all the voices I'd heard since coming into the room, hers was angelic. I nodded, unsure.

Chloe smiled again. 'I bet they've assigned you to Helen, right?'

I nodded again. A couple of kids snickered. One whispered something that didn't sound complimentary.

Chloe shook her head. 'As we all say about Room 2 when she's in-house, it's "hell in there". But it's actually not a joke. A guy was supposed to come in with me. But once he was told it was Helen who he would audition for, that was it for him.'

A young girl in Shawnaa-style leotards who sat close by gave a cry of despair and was comforted by her mother. That girl had the weirdest haircut; short on the sides, long in other parts, even covering half of her face. It must have been her brother sitting beside her. His leotards had the same pattern as his sister's, but his hair was normal.

'So, she's tough?' I asked Chloe. I was feeling every bit as bad as the young girl.

'Oh yes, really tough. Helen usually does level three auditions. But sometimes, like today, she gets level one. That way the Academy gets through as many kids as quickly as possible. I hope I'm not upsetting you. But you need to know what you're in for.'

'Oh,' I managed to get out. I was thinking that maybe Chloe wasn't on my side after all.

She gave me a look of sympathy. 'Sorry to tell you. It's just that she hates doing level one. Her auditions are usually over in five minutes. And that's after giving feedback.'

'Shit!' I was choking up. Had I come all this way to be sent away in a few minutes?

'If you feel bad when you come out, see that door next to Room 3? It's the fire escape. Leave that way if you need to.'

I gulped as a woman's voice came through the intercom. 'Sheryl and Michael Tucker. Please go to Room 2.' The young girl who'd let out the cry of despair jumped to her feet. Her mother gave her a hug, and the girl, along with her silent brother, hurried through the door, heads bowed.

A smug-looking boy called out to me. 'You'll be out in one minute. Damn jangler. You shouldn't be here. My mother will complain about this.'

I went to the woman who'd greeted me. 'Can I go somewhere and have a quick practise please?' I felt so unprepared. My throat was dry. And it wasn't a dryness that could be set right with water. Every bit as important; I desperately wanted to get away from these nasty people.

The woman gave me an ugly look. 'When you come here, you are expected to be ready. If you're not, it's your fault. Anyway, there's a cost for using the rehearsal room. And you need to book it.'

I didn't know. I couldn't afford the fee, anyway. I glanced over at a couple of dancers who took up space in a corner to work on their routines. Some were so light and graceful on their feet they seemed to float.

I waited, staring at the photo that covered the side wall, for maybe seven minutes before the young girl who'd walked into Room 2 came out. She dashed past, leaving her brother behind, and out the sliding doors, looking as if a vampire was chasing her. Her concerned mother ran after her; her brother followed slowly. Chloe got called into Room 1. She gave me a short wave. I gave her a quick "good luck" before she went inside.

My name came over the intercom. Room 2. I started shaking. I wished I'd run off when I had the chance. I was about to be humiliated. How could I have possibly thought I could impress a tough assessor by doing my favourite song on my own, for Christ's sakes?

Get it over and done with and go home, I figured. That's how I think when I visit the dentist. At least I saw the museum. All eyes in the room followed me; some of the kids gave me mean looks. Some smiled. Nasty smiles. A few glanced at their phones; maybe to time how long I lasted. They'd most likely laugh when I came out.

I took a deep breath and went inside Room 2.

The theatre was real small. I was surprised. It only had six worn, padded mauve seats; in raised rows of three. There was a little wooden stage, covered by a brown rubber mat, with tiny speakers hanging off the wall at the sides. Two lights shone down on me. Two microphone stands stood at the front. The walls were off-white. A narrow set of steps beside one wall led to a small glass booth that was in semi-darkness. Inside, was a movie camera with a covering over it. Beside it was a short, unfriendly looking woman in a grey dress. She had tied-back, silver hair. That had to be Helen.

Helen didn't notice me at first; she was busy typing on a laptop. When she did notice me, I swear she took a step back and chuckled before covering her mouth. She said my name into her microphone. I had a knot in my throat and could only nod. I grabbed the water flask from my daypack and took a big sip.

She leaned forward. 'Let's get straight to it, eh? You've chosen… Tainted Reputation's version of *Persephone*.' She broke into a grin and stared at me so hard I started to cringe. 'Starting in five seconds.' Didn't even ask if I was ready. I wasn't.

She pressed a button. I barely had time to close my water bottle and toss it on my daypack before the familiar first chords of my favourite tune started.

I started singing. I was really nervous and made a complete hash of it. 'That'll do. Thank you,' comes her voice through the speakers. The music stopped. I was mid-sentence and had barely begun the second verse. She stared down at me from her booth, saying nothing. I wanted to cry. My audition was done.

'I can sing it better.' I sounded lame but, damn, that was nowhere near my best effort. What else could I say?

'I'm not so sure,' she answered, unsmiling. She paused for a while. 'Tell me; why do you sing?'

'Excuse me?'

'Why do you sing?' said this grey-haired woman looking down on me with a frown from her glass booth. 'To make money? Because you like to? Why?'

'I like singing.' I shrugged. What a stupid question.

'Right. I will be frank with you.' Helen leaned forward. 'You can take my advice or leave it. If you truly want to be a singer, never sing that song again. Never sing anything by Tainted Reputation, or any of their clones, again. Delete their songs from your device. You don't have the voice to sing their songs. You never will, because your voice is changing. You might have made a go of it, years ago. But no more, no matter how much you practice. Do you understand?'

I stood there, destroyed. The way she spoke was so casual, like a teacher telling me to chuck my chewing gum in the bin before going into class. Just like that, this bitch was telling me to rip up my dreams into tiny shreds and toss them all away. She didn't give a damn about my feelings. Never to listen to the favourite song of my idols? Crap! Those guys had lifted my spirits when I felt really down. 'Was I really that bad?' I choked up.

She stared hard at me. 'I'll put it this way. If you continue to sing their songs… even if you continue to listen to them, they will ruin you. Got that? If you try to make a living by jangling their songs, you'll die of starvation. Are you hearing me?'

I think I said something. I don't know. I'd gone numb.

'You won a singing competition in your hometown of…' She searched through her laptop, '…it doesn't matter.'

'Yes, I did.' I was starting to get angry. Heartless bitch!

'I'd be curious to find out why you won. One thing I'm certain of; it wasn't because of your rendition of that song.'

I turned to leave. I couldn't take anymore. She was enjoying humiliating me. There was no point telling her that I would never abandon the duo. She wouldn't understand. She didn't care. What sort of turncoat did she think I was?

'Look at me! Listen to what I'm telling you,' she went on. 'Your voice is very raw… very raw, but I can hear a strength within it. Even at your age, I can feel your passion. I believe that judge in your hometown must have recognised your potential. But not for singing the songs you prefer.'

'I live in…'

'I don't want your life's story,' she snapped. 'You told me you sing because you want to. What are you prepared to do to achieve that ambition?'

'I'm sorry?' Huh! She wasn't making any sense. She'd told me that she hated me. 'I won't stop singing. For anything.' Not for you, bitch! Screw you.

'Good. I want to offer you an opportunity to become a singer.' She half-smiled. 'But you need to sing songs that better match your evolving voice. Put your device in the slot under the speaker on your right. I want to upload some music for you.' She fiddled around in her booth, pressing buttons really quick. My head was spinning, but I did what she told me. She totally smashed my dreams… and then said she wanted to help. She had to be bullshitting!

'Done,' she said after I stood there, on the stage, stunned, for maybe a minute. 'I've uploaded some songs; a couple by the Beatles, and some songs by a couple of soloists and others from that era, or later. I haven't downloaded any recent songs that may suit you; the competition is too tough for you to break into that scene for the time being. I've chosen the songs I put on your device because they are fairly simple and straightforward. Pick one or two that appeal to you. Work on them. Will you do that?'

Jesus! Sing the old songs that Grandpa used to play? She had to be kidding. My friends would laugh at me.

'Fine.' She smiled when I didn't answer. 'I've also given you a video on how you can project the natural strength and emotion in your voice. That said, I don't want you to change how you sing. Your rawness and passion are why I'm offering you a chance to become a singer. Be aware that it will take time. And a lot of practice. I've arranged an appointment for you here in three months so I can assess how you are progressing. And, believe me, I'll need to see significant development and application. The date is on the calendar on your device. Change it if it's not suitable. Are you okay with that?' Helen spoke so fast I barely made out what she was saying.

All I could do was shrug.

'As for where you may stand in, say, a year or two's time, there's a limited but very loyal demand for singers who can genuinely sing the songs I downloaded. In their original style, with true passion. I think you are capable of doing that.' She stared at me for a while. 'But don't have any illusions about securing a recording contract. Or that you'll get hired to sing at some major venues. You don't have the image they're looking for. Sorry.'

'What are you saying?' I was so confused.

'If you get accepted by a band, or even if you become a solo artist, you won't make much money… sorry again… but, with application, there's a fair possibility you'll achieve your wish to be a singer. And get to perform before a live audience. The audiences will be small but enthusiastic. Don't get ahead of yourself, though. But don't get discouraged either. There will be times when you'll feel like giving up. Working on improving comes with times when you'll feel despondent. You'll have to push through those moods. Oh, don't neglect your schooling, either. That's very important.'

By that time, I'd had enough. She kept ranting on,

but I wasn't listening anymore. She hated me. That was all that mattered.

When Helen stopped crapping on, she looked down on me. 'Sounds good,' I said. Bullshit! I couldn't get the thought out of my head; forget the Tainted Reputation and sing songs that Grandpa listened to, instead? Jesus! I was edging towards the door. Never to come back.

'Fine. Thank you for coming.' Her expression hardened. 'But don't bother coming for your next appointment if you're not prepared to ditch songs like the one you performed just now. You need to convince me that you have the dedication to sing songs that will do justice to your developing voice. Okay?'

I started to leave. I was so pissed off.

'Don't forget your device,' she said.

'Right.' I snatched it from the download station.

'Oh, one last minor matter. I've included the original version of *Persephone* from the seventies. If you manage to sing it... properly... one day... but I'm not expecting you to try, because it's not straightforward. You won't make any extra money. What you'll see is the looks of amazement of those hearing that version for the first time. And the enthusiasm of people who despise the modern versions.'

It never dawned on me that there might be a version before the Tainted Reputation sang it. But... am I stupid or what? It made sense. The duo reinvented songs from Grandpa's era. I should have worked it out! 'I'll give it a try.' Ha!

'Good luck.' She smiled, nodded, and went back to her laptop.

Okay. After I left Room 2, I stopped outside the door to try and make sense of what had happened. Couldn't. Everything was a crazy blur. As I set off across the waiting room, I figured that I had two choices. Three really. Go and jangle and sing to my friends. Or try to sing the old songs she had downloaded for me. Could I bear that? The last choice was to give up. That was definitely an option. At least giving up would let me keep listening to the songs of my idols.

I wanted to give Helen the digit as I left Room 2. I very nearly did. But I managed a brief wave. There were fewer kids in the waiting room. When they saw me, they nudged each other, whispering, and grinning. They weren't nice grins.

I was thinking as I took the lift; at least listen to the music she had downloaded. Give it a try. What did I have to lose?

I found a seat in the park, with lush, green grass all around. I sat there, feeling alone, sad and angry in a big city where I didn't belong. And didn't want to. I put on my earphones. Okay, let's go, I thought to myself. I flicked to the songs Helen downloaded; eleven in all. Being curious, I selected the old version of *Persephone*.

The song was s-o-o slow. I was sure the recording had gotten distorted during the download. I got the familiar (much delayed) first line, but after that it was like listening to a completely different song. It was nothing like Tainted Reputation's version. And I'm positive Grandpa never played anything remotely like it. Three and a half minutes later and the version was still going! I didn't warm to it at all. Heck… you can dance to the Tainted Reputation version. This new song, or should I say the seventies' version, had to have an extra verse or two. It just kept going! On and on. Only when the band sang the line *'Now I know the years…'* did I realise that, yes, they were still actually singing *Persephone*. What a line! Lorna and Jason pounded out those words as they stood face to face, gazing lovingly into one another's eyes.

No way! Besides, Helen meant it to be a novelty. I tried another of her selections; one from the Beatles. I'm sure Grandpa played it a few times. It was... okay. Definitely easier to take in, and pleasingly short. It just sounded so... ancient!

I checked the time. And jumped. Damn! I dashed to the subway, bumping into people, but I missed my train home. I'd have had to wait an hour and a half for the next one. I was starving. Luckily, I still had the sandwich that I couldn't stomach earlier.

While I waited, I listened to more of Helen's music. She had to be seriously messing with me. I was about to give up. But I couldn't help thinking how gobsmacked those pampered poodles from the waiting room would be if I came in for another audition. I worked out that jangling wasn't an option. I mean; how long could I keep it up, particularly if I sang the same tune much of the time? And what if my voice did change a lot? Shit! I nearly burst out crying.

By the time the train was set to leave I was feeling really low. I'd come to the big city with my head filled with such wonderful dreams. But, like part of my sandwich, those dreams were rotting in a bin. I'd so much hoped that this would be the most wonderful day of my life. But it had been the worst. Maybe I deserved to be shot down in flames. How stupid of me to perform a song by a duet, by myself, competing against skinny doll-like kids with big egos and snotty parents? But they weren't the ones who'd wrecked everything. Helen had done that.

What would I tell everyone when I got home? They'd been so enthusiastic. And so sure that I was going places. I couldn't tell them the truth; that my audition had been crap. Maybe I'd string them along a little longer by showing them my invite to another audition. I'd use the free ticket to go to the city. Maybe only go visit the museum.

It was dark soon after the train pulled out of the station. To cheer myself up I brought up the Tainted Reputation version of *Persephone*. But I didn't press the start button. I couldn't shrug off the feeling that the music world preferred to hear those smug, skinny kids in the waiting room, with their colourful clothes and nasty looks.

Instead, I put on some music that Helen had downloaded for me. Could I ever do them? And for how long could I keep singing those old songs? Not for long. Helen was sending me on another dead end.

The world has moved on from that old stuff. It's only right it happens like that. But the music world seemed to be moving in the direction of those pampered dolls. Surely, there had to be something more. As I stared at the darkness outside the train window, I started recalling snatches of words that Helen had crapped on about when I'd stopped listening to her. Maybe what I managed to piece together, sitting there in my seat, was totally wrong but I think she admitted that singing the old songs would be just the beginning. So I can develop my voice. And get experience performing. Then... oh I am really guessing here, but maybe she said that the day would come to move on. I'd get to sing some original, modern, authentic... she definitely used the word authentic... songs. Don't ask me what it all means. And, hey, I could be completely wrong about what she said. But this new hope is all I have to cling to.

I spent much of the train trip mouthing one of the

Beatles' songs that was on my Jason device. Later, when the train was nearing my station, I listened to Helen's version of *Persephone* one more time. Oh yes, it was definitely only a novelty. If she truly thought I could sing it one day, she was a bigger fool than me.

The song ended as the bells rang on the level crossing, and the train eased slowly onto my platform. As the train was stopping, wheels screeching, with people moving towards the exits, my finger hovered over the delete button. I took a deep breath and pressed. In a blink of an eye, Lorna Kiss and Jason Tell were dispatched into oblivion.

A RETURN TO A PEACEFUL PLACE

A RETURN TO A PEACEFUL PLACE

W alter drove the car through an impressive, solid archway fashioned from blocks of smoothed fawn-coloured stone, and into the grounds of the nursing home. He whistled and nodded approvingly at the well-tended lawn, punctuated by beds of white, yellow and red flowers, green shrubs and impressive shade trees. The curved driveway was lined by a canopy of trees, ending at a visitors' car park set within parallel rows of flower beds that were partitioned by solid wooden planks of treated pine.

After parking his car, he strolled close to the edge of the driveway to take in the verdant surrounds basking in the early afternoon sun. Within the largest flower arrangement was a lily pond with a small but tasteful fountain. It appeared to be constructed of white porcelain. Varnished, ribbed wooden seats, mostly shaded, overlooked each of the flower beds. Sturdy wooden picnic tables with bench seats, were nearby. A neatly dressed family of three sat around one table; a group of six crowded on another; a white-haired person prominent in both groups. Two gardeners in blue overalls planted seedlings in a flower bed at the foot of the archway.

Walter smiled. His mother would be rapturous to be living in such a beautiful place. He imagined her sitting, curled up on a seat, as she had done in the town's main park, many years ago, while he played on the swings or the slide; her attention divided between her book and taking in the flowers and birds. Yes, the nursing home was well worth the expense. The staff would be aware that it was he who covered the substantial bills. Pleasing him more, the fees were paid with money that his estranged wife, Sally, couldn't get her hands on, pissing her off big time.

Walter strode towards the double-door entrance. He'd made the two-and-a-half-hour trip from the city in the car that he'd gifted his daughter when the company upgraded him to a shiny silver offering, a stylish Mercedes. His sister, Mary would chide him if he'd arrived in his new car. She'd see it as gloating. He wore clothes that were modest by his standards: brown trousers and plain white shirt. Also to ward off Mary's scoffing. She thought him to be a show-off. And she had a point. But Walter was adamant; he worked hard, diligently putting in long hours, working Saturdays, and many Sundays, often taking work home. He deserved the rewards he'd reaped.

Three shallow steps and a wide, angled ramp, led to double light-grey, sliding doors. Trimmed, waist-high dark-green shrubs flanked both sides of the entrance. If his memory served him correctly, the estate had been an upmarket guesthouse during his school days. It was a sprawling, mostly one-storey affair, apart from a wide loft with four windows that rose at its middle. The building was white with dark-green trimmings on its numerous large windows and wide awnings. A dark-grey slate roof set the building off nicely.

That morning, Walter had worked at home for an hour or so, before setting off. When he'd arrived in the town of his youth, he'd dropped into a café in the main street to check and send emails and SMSs. He demanded that his subordinates place progress reports on a couple of contracts on his desk by 9am the next day, a Monday. Those communications done, he'd sent Mary an SMS announcing his imminent arrival at the nursing home.

Mary was waiting for him inside, her back pressed against the off-white wall, beside the enquiries desk. She was dressed in navy-blue slacks and a light-blue T-shirt. Mary was fifty-eight; seven years his senior. She did not greet him with a smile. He hadn't expected her to. It had been years since they'd last hugged. Maybe fifteen months had passed since he'd seen her last. Their infrequent phone conversations, when she was able to reach him, were invariably terse.

'Glad you could make it, Walter.'

He paused, anticipating her to add "about time" to her unenthusiastic greeting. To his surprise, she held back. Mary had aged a great deal since he saw her last. She looked tired. Her face was more lined, and a hollow, dark greyness had formed beneath her eyes. Mary's hair was almost fully grey. She carried some extra kilos, especially on her hips.

Walter intended to break the ice by telling her she looked great. Better that he didn't; she'd admonish him for his blatant lie. If he asked her how she was, Mary would only shrug, as usual, and insist that she was fine. Her husband and three adult children would, no doubt, also be fine.

Mary had been a nurse for more than thirty years. She'd called it quits about three years earlier to care for their mother following the ageing lady's bad fall. These days, Mary volunteered at the nursing home. It was she who had organised to get their mother admitted to the home, attending appointments and assessments. She was the one who finally convinced their mother that she needed to go into care, and who had pressed the administrators to find the old lady a bed. Walter's contribution had been to sign the emailed documents and return them. He volunteered to pay the bills, of course. Mary and her husband, Ron, were battlers. Ron had done his back on a construction site years ago. Since then, he had done brief, intermittent stints as a basic handyman. But that was all. Mary and Ron lived in the modest house they'd bought, on mortgage, after they'd married.

'I know I should have come sooner,' Walter said. The topic was certain to come up some time; he may as well breach it. 'And I should come more often. You don't need to tell me.'

'She's your mother, Walter,' Mary said between gritted teeth. She huffed and led him along the hallway that sported photos of the nursing home and its gardens. 'She deserves better.'

Mary's superior tone grated him. It always did. Affronted, he stopped. He could not let the comment pass. He'd be wasting his breath, of course; Mary would not offer the slightest sympathy. Not for the tribulations he'd endured the last couple of years.

Walter puffed out his chest. 'Look, Mary. You have no idea how difficult it is for me to get any time off work. When I ask for a day off, the CEO stares at me like I'm a malingerer.' He waggled a finger at her. 'I can't just go and drop everything, you need to realise. I work long days, often seven days a week. My workplace is a viper's nest. If you show the remotest sign—any sign at all—of wilting under the pace, the back stabbers come slithering out from their holes. Then, at the end of each long day, I walk through my front door to be greeted by a cacophony of demanding cuckoos. I go from one family crisis to another. To top it all, there's Sally, who's hell-bent on making my divorce unnecessarily difficult.' His face contorted in anger. To his annoyance, Mary smirked. 'She's being a complete bitch over our settlement. She's turned it into a war. And there's me asking her to show some calm, rational thought. But no. She enjoys dragging the whole sordid thing out, sucking my energy. But conflict invigorates her. And, to top it all, I'm still easing my new partner into the house.'

Mary stared at her brother, hands on hips. 'Finished?'

Walter looked at her, sour-faced. 'Sure. But Mary, can't you realise, just a little, how stressed and overworked I am? Well…'

'You're right; I don't care,' Mary said matter-of-factly. 'It's the welfare of our mother that matters to me. Get it into your skull; she won't be with us for much longer. You and I… we need to make her final days as comfortable as humanly possible. She needs to depart this world knowing that she is loved. And that we will remember her with fondness.'

Walter pulled a face. 'Oh, I see. It's emotional blackmail now, is it?'

Mary snorted and walked on to a T-junction in the nursing home. Fuming, Walter's joined her. His gaze shifted to his left, at the wide, white double doors with Perspex windows at their top. Through the windows, he saw residents in dressing gowns, visitors, nurses and orderlies strolling up and down the corridor, ducking in and out of rooms. No one was inclined to come and greet his sister and him.

It had been a mistake to mention his new love, Jan. Sally had surely told Mary all the sordid details, undoubtedly richly embellished, despite the two women having never been on friendly terms. Sally had cottoned on to his affair with his secretary far earlier than he'd thought. Even when the affair became evident, Sally hadn't complained overly. And why should she? She lavished in the fruits of his labours, didn't she? But Sally had been biding her time. When her vitriol erupted, Walter discovered just how thorough her vengeance had been planned. She sought to extract maximum material embellishment from him, sure. But Sally was far more focused on inflicting as much suffering upon him as she could. Desperate, Walter had offered her the peace offering of the house. She turned it down, with a smile that would freeze a fire in its grate; the house reminded her too much of him. Yet, she kept delaying the sale of the house. Her intransigence was hurting them both. It made no sense.

Jan, his new love, badly wanted to offload the house that bore Sally's unmistakable stamp throughout. Miffed, Jan kept demanding that major renovations had to be made. For Christ's sake! Why on Earth renovate a house they both longed to be rid of? Making matters worse, Sally pushed back hard on releasing any money to cover any renovation. But Jan would not be appeased. She kept at him; 'If you truly love me...'

'How are your kids?' Mary asked, twisting the knife deeper into his gut.

Walter sighed. 'Still at home with me. Chloe keeps having regular counselling. She's practically a hermit, living in her part of the house.' When she did emerge, it inevitably spelt trouble. Walter was certain that Chloe had let Sally know how much Jan hated the house. 'Tom is behaving himself. He'll be off his community order in two months' time.' Hopefully, Tom would grow out of his drunken vandalism phase.

At work, Walter gave as good as he got. And then some. It was eat or be eaten. At nights, with his work set aside, a relieved Walter sought relaxation on a comfortable easy chair in his "quiet room". This room was his sanctuary… a place where he demanded not to be disturbed. Too many times, his simple request was ignored. Even late at night. Hell… he was the principal income earner (by far), wasn't he? He deserved more respect. But he got precious little. His sister was no different. She reinforced his long-held, firm belief that people are selfish. Yes, even Mary. Caring for her mother could well be a ploy to grab an increased share of the inheritance.

'Okay. Enough talk. Let's go and see her.' Mary jerked her head to the side. She led Walter not through the windowed doors, as he'd expected. Instead, she set off in the opposite direction, along a cream-coloured corridor with wide, off-white doors. The place disturbed him. It seemed depressing, soulless. Some doors they passed were open, revealing residents, many bed-ridden, and a few visitors, sitting on chairs. Nurses and orderlies moved about in their blue or olive-coloured clothing, pushing trays or medical equipment on carts. One frail-looking female resident in a dressing gown tottered about in the corridor; a wrinkled old man was being pushed along in a wheelchair.

'It's been over a year since you last saw her,' Mary said with *that* voice. 'The last time was when I was hanging on a precipice of a physical and mental breakdown, and had to get away for a while. Even then, it was weeks before you turned up.' She glared at him. 'I was a wreck.'

He spread his arms in a plea. 'I couldn't get off work. I kept telling you.'

The timing had been awkward. Budgets were being pieced together and he needed to strongly push his case. He had to deal with some emotionally charged phone calls from Mary before agreeing to care for his mother. But he was adamant that he'd stay at the old lady's home for only one week. He'd employed a full-time maid to help out. There was an upside, though; it was time away from Sally.

As events panned out, Walter stayed at his mother's house for just five nights. He turned up at night on the first day, prompting Mary to leave the house keys in the letter box before she and her husband headed off. His shortened stay compelled Mary to end her holiday early. The day he broke the news to her, his CEO had rung him to discuss progress on a major contract. Walter, already anxious at not being able to directly oversee how the contract was progressing, volunteered to return to work. His work had occupied much of his time at his mother's home, anyway. He spent hours each day on the back porch, making and receiving calls, emails, reports and SMSs from colleagues. With each passing day, he became increasingly convinced that his colleagues were being deliberately slow in responding to his requests. More frustrating were the wasted hours on the phone trying to placate Sally. Jan was better behaved but needed solemn promises of quality time together on his return. When he'd informed Mary that he had to leave, he'd bluntly refused to negotiate. Mary had let loose with a burst of invective. But he'd held firm.

In truth, Walter had despised being back in his boring hometown. Each day was sheer tedium. Also, he wasn't cut out to care for an old person. Never mind that it had been the maid who had tirelessly done the bulk of the drudgery. On his last day, he sacked the maid, and left the key in the letter box for Mary. With his imminent divorce, he needed cash to deny Sally's demands.

Mary and Walter wandered a short way down the corridor before she halted beside an open door. She grasped her brother by the arm. 'I need to tell you before we go in. Mum's gone downhill a lot over the last few months. She hardly eats most days. She's now completely blind. I told you that the other day, didn't I?'

Walter hesitated. 'Yes.'

'On a good day she can hear if I yell. But she hasn't responded to anyone's voice for a few days now. You also know, don't you, that she is totally reliant on a wheelchair to get around? For going to the toilet and those sorts of things.'

Walter nodded. 'Yes. You told me.' He winced. 'Has she really gone downhill as much as that? She was quite active that time I looked after her. She was always busy, as usual. She got along fine with her walking cane.'

Mary folded her arms. 'She made a special effort for you. But whatever energy reserves she drew on back then, they're gone now.' The two stood silent for a time. 'I'm preparing you; don't expect much when you see her.' She looked at him intently.

'Right. Let's go inside.'

Mary hesitated. 'She knows you've been planning to come. I told her a few weeks ago when she was better. She's been asking for you every day since.' Mary pursed her lips. 'Oh, one more thing; she's probably going to rant on about some lookout. She's been on about it since I said you were coming. What do you know about a lookout the two of you went to?'

Walter shook his head. 'A lookout? No, I don't know anything about any lookout. Are you talking about around here?'

'I think so. She said that you used to play there when you were twelve or so. It used to be your favourite place for years, according to her. She used to drive you there. The Barkley boy came with you sometimes.'

'Oh, that place.' Walter smiled at the recollection. 'It's more of a ridge. You pass over it on the road to The Heights. Yes, Mum used to drive me and Johnny there. She'd read a book under some trees, next to this stream. It's a nice spot. Very peaceful. There were usually a few ducks hanging about, and other birds. Johnny and I used to run around, climb trees, and jump over the stream to clamber on this small hillock of crumbling sandstone.' In the early years, the boys played pirates. They went on to listening to cricket or music on a transistor radio and, finally, to flicking through a worn copy of *Playboy* that Johnny insisted he'd found hidden in the hollow of a tree. Johnny Barkley was a skinny live wire, a barrel of laughs; a constant source of entertainment. His favourite word was wowll. He snuck the word into the conversation whenever he could, getting the word from listening to Jimi Hendrix; *Wowll around the watchtower…*

'Ah yes. I think I know where it is. Anyway, she wants you to take her there.'

Walter recoiled. 'Just me?'

'Yes, you. I might not know the right spot. She never took me there. Besides, her memories of that place are all of you.'

Walter pursed his lips. 'But... is it okay to take her outside the nursing home? If she's as frail as you say she is? And what's the point if she's blind?'

'The doctor advised strongly against it. But Mum's heart has been set on going for weeks now. Walter, she will never be any healthier than she is right now. I'm hoping she'll get a boost by going and start eating more. She's been a bit depressed lately. To my way of thinking, it's worth the risk. And she'll get to spend some time with you. After all, it's been a while. She'd really like that. So, take her, Walter.'

Walter drew a breath. 'But ask the doctors first. They're the experts. What if she has a turn? Or needs to go to a toilet.'

Mary looked hard at him. 'She'll have an incontinence bag, Walter. Look: she really... really... wants to go. Take her. Just for a short time. Don't let her spend the rest of her days rotting away in this place. She's still sharp; she knows her end is near. Pretend you're taking her if you must. She most likely won't know if you stop somewhere in the open air. But her mind is still intact, so you'll need to be clever about how you go about it.' She tapped her head. 'No, what am I saying? Just take her to the lookout, Walter. You won't need to stay there long.'

Walter sighed, then nodded reluctantly. 'Okay then. I'll do it. But I refuse to be held responsible if she has a bad turn.'

'That's understood, Walter. By everyone.'

Walter cupped his chin with his fingers, recalling the past. 'Gee, I haven't been to that place since I was, maybe, sixteen.'

'Was that when you started dating Becky... whatever her surname was?'

Walter shrugged. 'Yeah. I started dating her about a year later.' Becky was a girl who had a perennial smile. Not long after they began dating, she took to delightfully dropping her undies for him. To think that, to begin with, she seemed to prefer Johnny.

Mary looked at him sourly. 'Whatever happened to her?'

'Not sure.' Walter glanced along the corridor. 'We grew apart soon after I went to uni. Studying took up more and more of my time. And I studied really hard, Mary. Someone told me a couple of years later that Becky had moved to another town. That's as much as I know.' She had started talking about wanting a baby. Hell... he was nineteen and was being feted by his lecturers. His grandmother greeted him as her "handsome and clever young man". Becky was seventeen.

'You didn't ask her family or friends for her new address?'

Walter shrugged. 'Oh, I intended to. But my studies left me no spare time.'

'Becky was a... simple lass. I liked her a lot. She had a lovely nature.'

'Yes, she was nice.' Walter looked, grim-faced, at his sister. Mary had never warmed to Sally, who became his wife. Walter met Sally during the last month of his second year at university. Sally was statuesque; she dressed and groomed smartly. He spent most of his scholarship cash on her (along with the cash he earned from making 'deals,' and getting 'loans' from his parents), going hungry at times. It was money well spent; his mates couldn't disguise their envy.

'Well... let's go inside.' Mary ushered Walter into the room. 'Do the disinfectant at the door first.'

Four bed-ridden women lay sleeping or propped up on pillows in a square room with bland, cream-coloured walls. Each wrinkled face had dark, sunken eyes. One of the women slept slack-jawed and dribbling. The four beds were separated by medical equipment, empty visitors' chairs and small cabinets that sported vases of flowers, a few get-well cards and some keepsakes. Metal railings circled above the beds; heavy light-blue drapes were gathered beside the walls.

It was the wrong room. None of these skeletal women, with their grey, shrivelled faces, was his mother. He turned to leave.

Glancing back from the doorway, he was stunned to see Mary walking purposely across to the far corner of the room. She hovered over a woman whose withered head peered above the bedsheets. Her hair, white like the pillows, stuck out in clumps, like duck down. The sheets hid a body that barely made an imprint.

Walter gasped as he shuffled to the bed. 'Oh my God!' He shook his head. 'I had no idea...'

'I kept telling you,' came the sneering reply. 'For obvious reasons I chose not to send you any photos.' She gently lifted their mother's head to adjust a pillow. The old lady mumbled something.

'But... when I last saw her...' He paused to wince. 'People get old, yes. But... I never thought that Mum would ever look like this.' He slowly approached the skeletal figure, his hands folded in reverence. 'Hello,

Mum. It's nice to... be with you again. I'm so sorry. I should have come earlier.'

She did not react.

Mary snorted. 'She can't hear you, Walter. Touch her arm. That's what I do. The staff do it as well. It lets her know someone is with her.'

He lifted the bedsheet a little. The arm that extended flat from a floral nightgown was nothing more than a dark twig. Even when he saw her last, her hands and arms had been strong and sinewy, able to sew quilts using large needles and thick threads. He placed his hand gently on the thin arm. She moved her head a little to face him with dark, empty eyes. Her other arm reached across to touch the back of his hand, dwelling near his thumb. 'Is that you, Walter?' She had no teeth. Her lips and tongue were purple.

'Yes, it's me. Mum, I'm sorry I didn't come any—'

'Other hand,' the old lady whispered. 'Other hand.'

He touched her wrist with his other hand. She reached from under the bedsheet to caress the back of that hand, finding the scar there.

'Hello, Walter.' She burst into a wrinkled smile. Her ugly, purple tongue licked her thin, dark lips as she swallowed some spittle. She looked towards his chest with unseeing eyes. 'I knew you would come.' Her voice was unsteady, broken by her rasping breathing. 'I know it's hard for you. Being so busy.' He looked towards his sister on the opposite side of the bed. Mary crossed her arms and averted her face. 'You got that scar when that Berkley boy pushed you out of a tree. Your hand got ripped on a branch.' She paused to regather her breath.

His sister snorted. Walter drew a breath. 'I slipped, Mum. He didn't push me.'

'I had to rush you to Doctor Mann to have stitches. Remember.' She grimaced.

Walter's shoulders slumped. 'He didn't push me. I was skylarking. Showing off. I fell. At the doctor's, I blamed him. I couldn't admit that I'd been stupid.'

His mother's eyes searched for his face. 'Your father wanted to go around to the boy's home and have it out with his parents.' She took a few deep breaths. 'But you pleaded with him not to go.' She shifted a little in the bed.

'If he'd gone there, I would have been sprung.'

'That boy did that to you, yet you didn't want him to get into trouble.'

'It would have been me who got into trouble,' Walter said.

'He deserved a good telling off, that boy. He could have killed you.' She cleared her throat, struggling for breath.

Walter flinched at her laboured breathing. Her sunken chest rose and fell. Talking seemed to be sucking the life from her. He patted her arm. 'It doesn't matter.'

'He pushed you, Walter!' Agitated, she swallowed, her body stiffening.

Walter sighed; his eyes drawn to the open door. Once more, Mary looked the other way. 'It's been so long since I've seen you, Mum. There always seemed to be a major problem keeping me from coming. But I should have—' He stared at her withered arm. 'And here you are. You can't see me; you can't hear me. I'm worried that you'll break if I give you even the smallest hug.'

Her face brightened, extenuating the wrinkles around her mouth. 'Go tell the nurse to bring my wheelchair, Walter. Take me to the lookout. Let's go right away. I want to go.' Her tongue licked at her dark lips, and she drew breath. 'Mary doesn't know about the lookout. She said it was okay. Take me there.'

His sister began walking towards the open door.

'Mum. You're going to get better.' He glanced at Mary, who stopped to glare at him.

'I remember sitting by the brook, listening to the birds. You boys playing. They were wonderful days.'

'Yes. They were.' He also remembered those days with fondness.

'You'll take me there, Walter, won't you?'

Walter took a deep breath. 'Yes, Mum. I will.'

'I'll get the wheelchair,' said Mary. 'You stay with her. Keep tapping her arm.' She left the room.

'Fetch a wheelchair, Walter.' His mother's voice faltered. A look of worry etched across her face. Perhaps she thought she wasn't going.

'They're getting a wheelchair.' He patted her arm. She grinned, seemingly re-assured.

'Get them to fetch a wheelchair. Let's go now.' With an effort, she lifted herself onto her elbows. But, after a few seconds, she dropped back onto the pillow.

'Mary is fetching it.' He patted her arm again.

Mary returned, followed by a young nurse who pushed a portable wheelchair.

'You're going to take her?' the nurse asked, stern-faced. Walter nodded, worried at the prospect. His mother was so incredibly fragile. The nurse looked at Mary, who nodded.

'Do everything very slowly. Very slowly,' pressed the nurse. 'Okay? Taking her involves a risk. The doctors have discussed this outing with Mary a few times. We expected it to happen a few weeks ago.' The nurse looked sternly at Mary, who shrugged. 'Your mother has been raving about this day for weeks. So, although we have major reservations, we have decided to allow it to take place, at Mary's insistence. But please; exercise a great deal of care. Be especially patient getting her in and out of the car. Take your time. She's frail and blind. To get the wheelchair inside the car you fold it like so. And like so.' She demonstrated the workings to him. 'Can you manage that?'

'Are they getting my wheelchair, Walter?' Mary wandered over and tapped the back of her mother's hand twice. The old lady smiled with those ugly lips; her sunken cheeks wrinkled.

Walter straightened the wheelchair and then folded it as he'd been shown. The procedure was quite straightforward. He nodded. 'Easy.' But he shifted in his stance, anxious. His mother was so brittle.

'Make sure she's well strapped in,' the nurse said. 'Not overly tight. But enough so she can't slip through. Try to stop her from slumping over too much. Easier said than done, I know. Maybe lean the wheelchair back a little. Do the best you can.'

'Have you fetched the wheelchair, Walter?' His mother's shaking arm protruded from the bed. The nurse raised the wheelchair and placed the old lady's hand on the wheel. That got her smiling again, revealing those purple lips and toothless mouth. Her face so horribly shrunken.

'Let's get her out of her bed,' the nurse said. 'We'll do it very slowly. Stand there. Copy my actions. Be very, very gentle.'

With the nurse on one side and Walter on the other, the two of them slowly lifted the old lady into a sitting position. The nurse then placing her arm around her waist. Walter did likewise. Jointly, they lowered her onto the wheelchair; the old lady's feet reaching for the footrest. 'I'll help you get her into the car. But you'll be on your own after. Are you okay with that? Be sure to apply the brake on the chair after each time you move her.' He nodded. She showed him how to apply the brake. 'If you need my help…'

'He can ring me,' Mary said. 'Don't take any chances, Walter. I know what to do.'

The nurse butted in. She smiled faintly. 'Now we'll get this madam all dressed up for her outing. Please take a seat so we can draw the curtains. You've come on a lovely, sunny day. They're predicting rain tomorrow.'

Walter stepped aside as the long drapes swished his mother out of sight. Dressing her took some time. Walter heard her grunt in discomfort a few times. He did not look forward to the outing, which seemed overly fraught. If she had a bad turn, he'd be caught well out of his depth. When the drapes were drawn back, his mother was clothed in thick black slacks and a floral jumper. They seemed oversized for her painfully thin body. A thick blanket was wrapped around her lap.

The nurse strapped in the skeletal figure and looked up, perhaps to make sure Walter took it all in. Mary nodded, then Walter wheeled his mother carefully out of the room, with Mary and the nurse trailing.

'Be sure to take your time,' the nurse said. 'Remember that the doctor's advice was for her not to go. But we couldn't bear to leave her nursing a broken heart.'

'For sure,' Mary said. 'Don't keep her out for too long, Walter. She gets cold easily. Even on a warm day like this.'

'I'll be careful. Promise.'

Walter's mother grinned toothlessly all the way to

the car. Child-like, she rocked a little from side to side in the wheelchair. The nurse grinned. 'Now you're being very naughty, madam,' she said to the old lady, who was oblivious to her words.

Walking beside the wheelchair, Mary was lost in thought. She looked at Walter, concerned. Walter was nervous but remained circumspect, hoping he gave the impression of being confident. He and the nurse slowly and gently lifted his mother, with Mary looking on. They placed her carefully in the front seat of the car. Walter found his mother to be so light... incredibly so. She was no longer a woman; merely a shadow. Mary reached in and adjusted her jumper. As they strapped on the seat belt, the old lady's hand dwelt on the scar on Walter's hand. 'Look what that boy did to you,' she said between breaths. 'I never liked him. Oh, I still took the two of you there a couple more times.'

'Don't talk, Mum,' Walter said, patting her arm.

'If he'd hurt you again, I would have been banging on the boy's front door. I tell you.' Her wrinkled face contorted in anger.

Mary patted her mother's arm a few times. 'Don't get worked up over something that happened a long time ago.'

Walter took a nervous glance, fingers crossed, at Mary, as he jumped into the car.

He set off along the driveway with its canopy of trees, passing the colourful beds of flowers, the pond of water lilies with its pretty white fountain, then he headed out through the solid archway of fawn-coloured stone. His mother sat, quiet and smiling, with her arms folded across her lap as she stared, unseeing through the windscreen. Walter cleared his throat. 'Johnny didn't push me, Mum. I lied to you back then.' Of all the memories of their times together, why had she dwelt on one that made him cringe?

As he drove, he pondered some urgent decisions that needed to be made. Most importantly, he needed to quiz the doctors (definitely not Mary) about his mother's treatment and prognosis. The news would almost undoubtedly be bleak. Just how bleak would determine whether he would stay until maybe noon the next day or return the following Sunday. There was little point staying longer when all he was able to do was pat his mother's arm and let her touch his scar. If it rained the next day, he couldn't take her outside. There was also another uncomfortable matter to consider, at a more appropriate occasion. He'd need to breach with Mary the topic of selling their mother's home. It was obvious that she would never return to it. But this wasn't the time.

His mother rocked back and forward in her seat. 'I remember the day you ran over, all excited.' She gasped. Walter feared that each breath would be her last. 'You told me you and that Berkley boy found some hieroglyphs.' Her voice became a panting whisper. 'Across the other side of the stream.'

Walter brightened, recalling the moment of discovery. 'They weren't hieroglyphs. We just called them that. We had no idea what they were. They were some sort of strange symbols. You could only see them—'

'What were they, Walter? Did you find out?'

'No, we didn't. You could only see them when you shone a torch down a gap between the rocks. We figured they must have been carved on some wall, but the structure must have collapsed. The symbols looked very old. They were worn... some were almost gone completely... and covered with moss. I'm sure no one else knew they were there.'

His mother was smiling again, perhaps lost in her memories.

Walter arrived at the place where his mother used to park her car, on a gravelly area next to the 'lookout'. A footpath had since been built in its place and the road had been widened. He was compelled to drive on, make a U-turn, and park on a sliver of grass on the opposite side of the road.

'Are we there?' His mother seemed disorientated.

'Yes, Mum. The lookout is right across the road.'

'Where are we?' Her sunken eyes darted about.

'We're there. At the lookout.' He patted her arm.

His mother looked about anxiously as if to peer at her surrounds. Walter moved quickly, lifting the wheelchair from the back of the car. He unfolded it and wheeled it to the passenger's door.

'Are we there?' His mother reached across to the empty driver's seat.

'Yes, Mum.' Walter opened the passenger's door, tapped his mother twice on the arm, then gently and awkwardly manoeuvred her until he could set her down carefully onto the wheelchair. As before, her feet searched for the footrest. She was so light. So thin.

'Yes! We are there! I can tell.' She burst into a wrinkled smile. 'I can hear the birds singing.'

Walter cocked his head. The only sound he heard came from a line of cars gliding past. The road was far busier than it had been all those years ago. Walter also made out a dull rumble drifting towards them from the freeway, built twelve years before, through the narrow valley below. If his guess was right, an entrance to the freeway must be nearby, on the opposite side of the stream.

'Wheel me close to where the birds are, Walter.'

Walter stood, perplexed. She repeated her request. He paused for a break in the traffic before wheeling his mother across the road and onto the footpath. He gazed towards the spot where his mother would read beneath a tree beside the stream while he played nearby or on the small sandstone hillock.

'It's so wonderful to be here again! Thank you, Walter for bringing me. You're so generous with your time.' Wincing, Walter tapped her arm. 'I've always loved the birds and the beautiful stream.' She paused for breath, grinning. 'It's been so long. So many memories.' She gasped and gripped Walter's arm. Her hand trembled. 'But don't take me down that slippery path. Remember the time I slipped?' She chuckled; more like a cackle. She had walked with a limp for days afterwards. 'It's okay. I can hear everything from here. And, in my mind, I know what is in front of me.'

He wanted her to stop speaking. The effort had to be sapping her strength. 'Yes. We'll stay here for a while.'

'I can smell flowers,' she said, beaming. 'What kind are they? I can't tell. It is spring, isn't it? Or early summer.' Her face hardened. She pointed towards the valley. 'Down there is where that Berkley boy pushed you off the tree.'

Walter tapped her arm. 'Don't talk, Mum.'

'He always greeted me with a hello, he did. But I never forgave him. He never apologised, did he?' She snorted; her face scrunched up in anger.

Walter sighed. 'I was skylarking. I damaged my hand trying to grab a branch to stop from falling.'

'That hillock is to my left, isn't it?' He tapped her arm. 'You remember when you found those hieroglyphs? Did you ever find out what they were?'

'No. It was our secret.'

'You showed them to me once. What were they, Walter?'

'I have no idea.'

'It's such a lovely day. Just like those times years ago.' The old lady paused. 'Is that the sound of the stream I can just make out?' She strained her unseeing eyes and cocked her head. 'I wish I could see it all just one more time.' She took a deep breath. 'Quiet now. Let me listen. And let me remember.'

She reached out a hand. Walter took it.

They stayed, unmoving, for perhaps fifteen minutes. Walter kept his hand on his mother's arm. When she began shivering, he drew the blanket over her. He stepped away and pulled out his phone. He sent SMSs to Jan and to his boss. Walter let his boss know that he would be arriving late the following day. He was convinced that his mother was dying. He sent a SMS to Jan announcing that he would arrive home some time tomorrow night. He switched off the phone to avoid any, possibly tedious, conversation.

'I'm getting cold, Walter,' his mother complained soon after, even with the blanket wrapped tightly around her. Though the afternoon was pleasantly warm, she was shivering. The near-translucent skin on her hands were blue. 'We need to go. Bring me back tomorrow.'

'If you want.' Tomorrow's visit would need to be brief. And in the morning. It would not happen at all if the forecast of rain proved correct.

Walter wheeled his mother across the road, gently placed her in the car and drove back to the nursing home. She didn't stop grinning, though her face was lined by tiredness. For his part, Walter struggled not to sob.

'Thank you for taking me to the lookout, Walter. It was wonderful. And being with you.' She leaned back in her seat and shut her eyes.

A tear ran down Walter's cheek.

There were no birds. Either they'd been scared away, or their chirping was drowned out, by the traffic. The trees he'd climbed and played beneath were gone. An estate of five near-identical, small, nondescript houses with small patches of lawn and car ports, stood in their place, erected on blocks of land partly built up by land-fill, reachable by sloping driveways.

The sandstone hillock was gone. Walter figured it must have been bulldozed to make way for the freeway entrance. All that remained was a low pile of fawn-coloured rocks barely visible in the overgrown grass, beside a metal road barrier. Whatever the 'hieroglyphs' had been, they were no more. No one would ever examine them, let alone decipher them. Nor would anyone discover who had carved them. Or why.

Where the stream had been was a deep, concreted, straight drain that ended at a wide metal grate, to disappear from sight.

Many years ago, an ex-school mate rang Walter to let him know that Johnny Berkley had been killed in a road accident in the mining town where he had moved to. Johnny was twenty-three.

ABOUT THE AUTHOR

Ian Aisch was born in Tremadog, North Wales. His early childhood was spent in nearby Penrhyndeudraeth where his backyard looked over the village and across to Tremadog Bay. At a back corner of the yard, he watched heritage steam trains chug by. His father worked in the local powder works.

Shortly after turning seven, his family took up the £10 offer to migrate to Australia, and settle in Echuca, Victoria, where Ian attended school. He studied Sociology and Politics at Monash University in Melbourne before working in the public service, first in Canberra and then Melbourne. Ian later became an editor at Lonely Planet in Melbourne, on the back of his other deep interest, travel.

In 2021 he self-published his acclaimed first science fiction novel, *Lost and Plooglitless*. This book of five stories has taken ten years, off and on, to complete.

He lives in Victoria's Macedon Ranges.

Thanks need to go to the owners of cafés in Woodend, and the Top of the Range Café on Mt Macedon, where many of these words were written. An especially huge thanks goes to the Woodend Library and, to a lesser extent, Kyneton Library, where most of the writing took place. The many stimulating holiday destinations Ian has visited also played a huge part, including feeding Ian's long-standing interest in environmental issues. Another deep thank you goes to Holgate's Brewhouse, though very little writing was done there.

ALSO RELEASED BY ZYGOL BOOKS

Lost and Plooglitless
By Ian Aisch

R oss Blakey, an Earthman, is forced, by the point of a sword, to journey with an imposing Zygol female warrior and her grumpy male cook. He is given no explanation why.

Constant peril follows Blakey and his two companions during their trek. He is pounded by the relentless and agonising, dust-filled wind of a harsh desert. But things get even worse. He is captured by warriors and attacked by a massive swarm of vulture-like flying beasts. Throughout his ordeals, Blakey's stumbling ignorance of Zygols customs and principles soon causes his captors, and everyone else he encounters, to want him dead. Each promise of death will be increasingly excruciating. Rescue is impossible.

. . .

Here is an excerpt from *Lost and Plooglitless*
Crouched in the shallow lake, with his back to the Safi, Blakey craned his head to look at her. 'Are you going to sit there and watch the whole time?'

She smiled. 'Of course, I have been ordered to not let you out of my sight. Ignore me. Wash yourself… thoroughly. There are soap leaves in the pouch before you.'

Ross Blakey began rinsing his hair.

The Safi chuckled. 'Are you uncomfortable with me watching you?'

Blakey glared at her. 'Well, yes… I am.'

'Would you be more relaxed if I bathed with you?'

Blakey nearly choked on the water running down his face. 'If you want…'

The Safi undid her belt. She removed her tunic and undergarment and waded casually into the wooden enclosure.

Ross Blakey's eyes dwelt on the lithe young body before him. Maybe she was a little thin, but she was easy on the eye. 'Look, I'm grateful for what you've done for me. I really am.'

The Safi curled up on the opposite side of the enclosure to Blakey. 'Now bathe. No touching.'

'Don't be concerned. I'm not going to risk getting myself into more trouble than I'm in already.'

The Safi grinned. 'You will most certainly try nothing. Know that I don't shiver for you. Ha! What a terrifying thought.'

Blakey badly needed this wash. Not as much as several double whiskies, sure. A rescue helicopter and pilot would be better still. He fetched some silky soap leaves and, by rubbing them together, generated a thin lather, which he applied to his arms.

'You are not doing it properly,' the Safi scoffed. 'Let

me show you.' She fetched two handfuls of soap leaves and approached him. Her youthful, smiling face and her clear, bright eyes and lithe body, made Blakey sigh.

'You scrunch up the leaves like this. See the extra lather I'm getting?' Then, with unhurried and sweeping movements, she applied the lather to his shoulders and chest. Blakey basked in the Safi's touch. With her being so pleasingly close, he couldn't help but be mesmerised by her beautiful, laughing and alive green eyes. Well, if this was to be his last hour alive, this was how he wanted to spend it.

Laughing, the Safi fetched some more leaves. Blakey now had a good idea of how to scrunch them up but figured he'd leave the task to the Safi. She brushed his arms aside and applied more lather. All over his body. 'Now stand close to the sluice and rinse.'

Blakey sighed in disappointment but did as he was told, washing the lather away as the Safi lifted the sluice.

After his wash, Blakey rested on his side, letting the gentle current of the stream pass across his body. He was in no hurry to leave. Why should he?

'Tbatra,' she whispered in his ear—wait here. The Safi stood and strode up the bank of the lake. She reached down, then returned, smiling, with something hidden behind her back. She sat beside Blakey and leaned towards him.

From behind her, the Safi produced a kraxl. Blakey tried to yell, but the sight of the glinting metal froze his throat. He tried weakly to ward her off, but his muscles were paralysed in panic. 'Ooooh shit!' he blurted as the naked Safi knelt against him and brought the kraxl to his throat. 'Oh my God!' So this was how his life would end. Executed by a beautiful naked young woman who be believed was the only Zygol who cared —perhaps just a little—for him. Was this her secret plan? How had he offended her so badly?

The Safi scowled. Then, to Blakey's surprise, she smiled. The smile of a sadistic psychopath. 'Are all Earthmen such cowards as you?' she asked. 'I have done this before. It is easy.'

Blakey swallowed. He closed his eyes and waited to die.

'Stay still,' she commanded. 'I promise you will feel no pain.' She took Blakey's chin. He felt the kraxl's cold blade against his throat.

TO BE RELEASED IN 2024

A Stormy Day in June
By Ian Aisch

Throughout his school years, Bill Thomas was a short, skinny nonentity of a nerd. Eleni Karagiannis had been relentlessly bullied at school. Some nine years later, Eleni and Bill happen to bump into one another on Melbourne's Degraves Street during a winter storm.

Here is an excerpt from *A Stormy Day in June*
At last, Bill managed to fight his way through the crowd to reach the plain, grey-concreted subway entrance. He folded his umbrella and tapped it beside the top step, grimacing at the sight of the sopping, cold wetness of his trousers below his knees.

'Bill?' It was a woman's voice. He spun around but did not recognise anyone. Through the throng of people disgorging from the entrance, he noticed a stunning, shapely young woman, about his age, standing on the third-most upper step, leaning against the wall opposite. She had long, black hair that tumbled in soft waves across her shoulders. A waist-long cream, woollen cardigan covered a yellow dress. Draped across her shoulder was a canvas carry-bag. The woman hadn't dressed for the inclement weather. But neither had he. Occasional drops of rain bounced from raised umbrellas onto her hair and shoulders, glinting like pearls under the subway lights. As pleasing to the eye as this woman was, Bill figured she wasn't anyone he knew.

Must have been some other Bill. *Move on.* 'Bill Thomas?' Stunned, Bill halted stock-still. The woman took a stride up a step, perhaps preparing to leave. *Who...?* Curious, Bill pushed his way through the human slipstream, ignoring shoves and terse words, until he was pressed up against the subway wall beside her. She gazed quizzically at him. For a while, nothing registered, then a couple of cogs turned. Yes, he knew her somehow...

'Don't you recognise me?' The young woman smiled, uncertain. That made her more familiar. Her voice even more-so. Looking closer... 'Eleni?' Her surname escaped him; it was something Greek. But, yes, her name was Eleni. An image surfaced in his mind of a chubby, grim-faced and rebellious schoolgirl, a year beneath his, back in the small town of Stone Ridge. He recalled her wicked and disarming sense of humour and sharp tongue. She was a girl a clique of cool kids treated with derision. Many boys didn't talk to her out of fear of being ostracised by these cool kids. Eleni had copped relentless taunts. She was 'the fat bitch', 'that fat chick', 'wog'. And many more. Rumours were spread about her. She had anger issues. Particularly with thin, pretty girls.

As for the rumours, Bill had worked out back then that spiteful people think nothing of lying to put others down. Heck, at school, he had been short and weedy; he knew what it was like to be scorned, even by a snide, sideways glance. Even so, he had kept his distance from Eleni, though she'd given him hints of a smile at times. Had she known he was on her side? To his shame, he'd been too much of a coward to show it.

The woman who stood beside him was somehow the same, yet remarkably and pleasingly different to the girl he remembered, what, nine years previous? Her eyes, which could have countenanced resentment towards him for what she had endured at school, were clear and bright. Could dark eyes, in the gloom, possibly sparkle? They seemed to. He cringed, ashamed by her friendly welcome; he hadn't deserved it, having lamely cold-shouldered her all those years ago.

Eleni's smile broadened when Bill spoke her name. It was a delightful smile. Bill recalled that the few times she did smile back at school, it had been bright and pleasant.

'Yes, it's me. Fancy bumping into you here.'

'Yeah. I work in the city centre.' He pointed vaguely in the direction of his workplace as he struggled to ignore the wet coldness consuming his lower legs and feet.

'Coincidently, I was talking to Rowan Dalton—you remember Rowan—in Stone Ridge a few weeks ago. He runs a café on the main drag. Your name came up. He said your job is about siphoning off other people's money to make yourself filthy rich. Very clever, Bill. Then, I suppose, after you've extracted every single drop of vitality from them, you leave their corpses dangling like dead flies in a spider's web. Is that true? Is that what you do? Suck people's life juices? Eleni frowned as she eyed Bill's suit and tie, then she raised an eyebrow.

For a second or two Bill was taken aback. He broke into a grin. 'And you, Eleni? You are obviously still the same stirring pain in the backside you always were. Yes, that's exactly what I do. And I love the job I do.'

They both chuckled. Eleni's eyes danced like the raindrops falling on her hair. Passing commuters, sullen and impatient, glared at the two stationary obstacles as they jostled to burst into the grey, sodden air.

Maybe ask Eleni to wait for a couple of minutes while he hoped to retrieve his mobile phone. If she couldn't wait, get her to write her phone number. It was super-urgent that he track down his phone. Problem was; should she dash off instead, it would surely be goodbye forever. *Bugger the phone.* So, with rain bouncing off raised umbrellas, he steeled himself to ask Eleni to have a coffee with him. This new Eleni, standing pleasantly beside him.

ZYGOL BOOKS

To order a book from Zygol Books in Australia, your primary contact should be:

Zygol Books
21 Barbara Street, Woodend
Victoria
Australia 3442
(03) 5427 2182

You may be able to secure copies from:
Top of the Range Café
Mt Macedon
(03) 5427 3466

Also check out:
www.zygolbooks.com.au, **(or Zygol Books on Facebook) or Amazon.com.au.**

ACKNOWLEDGMENTS

Regardless of how you view this book, it would have been much poorer if not for the help of the following people:

AJ Collins, Ebony McKenna. The front and back cover were designed by Olive Reekie.

www.ingramcontent.com/pod-product-compliance
Lightning Source LLC
Chambersburg PA
CBHW070545120726
47909CB00007B/2244

* 9 7 8 0 6 4 8 7 0 0 8 5 2 *